The Woman of Mystery

The Woman of Mystery

Maurice Leblanc

MINT EDITIONS

The Woman of Mystery was first published in 1916.

This edition published by Mint Editions 2021.

ISBN 9781513292441 | E-ISBN 9781513295299

Published by Mint Editions®

 MINT
EDITIONS

minteditionbooks.com

Publishing Director: Jennifer Newens
Design & Production: Rachel Lopez Metzger
Project Manager: Micaela Clark
Typesetting: Westchester Publishing Services

Contents

I

THE MURDER

S uppose I were to tell you," said Paul Delroze, "that I once stood face
to face with him on French. . ."

Élisabeth looked up at him with the fond expression of a bride to
whom the least word of the man she loves is a subject of wonder:

"You have seen William II in France?"

"Saw him with my own eyes; and I have never forgotten a single one of
the details that marked the meeting. And yet it happened very long ago."

He was speaking with a sudden seriousness, as though the revival
of that memory had awakened the most painful thoughts in his mind.

"Tell me about it, won't you, Paul?" asked Élisabeth.

"Yes, I will," he said. "In any case, though I was only a child at the
time, the incident played so tragic a part in my life that I am bound to
tell you the whole story."

The train stopped and they got out at Corvigny, the last station
on the local branch line which, starting from the chief town in the
department, runs through the Liseron Valley and ends, fifteen miles
from the frontier, at the foot of the little Lorraine city which Vauban,
as he tells us in his "Memoirs," surrounded "with the most perfect
demilunes imaginable."

The railway-station presented an appearance of unusual animation.
There were numbers of soldiers, including many officers. A crowd of
passengers—tradespeople, peasants, workmen and visitors to the
neighboring health-resorts served by Corvigny—stood amid piles of
luggage on the platform, awaiting the departure of the next train for
the junction.

It was the last Thursday in July, the Thursday before the mobilization
of the French army.

Élisabeth pressed up against her husband:

"Oh, Paul," she said, shivering with anxiety, "if only we don't have
war!"

"War! What an idea!"

"But look at all these people leaving, all these families running away
from the frontier!"

"That proves nothing."

"No, but you saw it in the paper just now. The news is very bad. Germany is preparing for war. She has planned the whole thing. . . Oh, Paul, if we were to be separated! . . . I should know nothing about you. . . and you might be wounded. . . and. . ."

He squeezed her hand:

"Don't be afraid, Élisabeth. Nothing of the kind will happen. There can't be war unless somebody declares it. And who would be fool enough, criminal enough, to do anything so abominable?"

"I am not afraid," she said, "and I am sure that I should be very brave if you had to go. Only. . . only it would be worse for us than for anybody else. Just think, darling: we were only married this morning!"

At this reference to their wedding of a few hours ago, containing so great a promise of deep and lasting joy, her charming face lit up, under its halo of golden curls, with a smile of utter trustfulness; and she whispered:

"Married this morning, Paul! . . . So you can understand that my load of happiness is not yet very heavy."

There was a movement among the crowd. Everybody gathered around the exit. A general officer, accompanied by two aides-de-camp, stepped out into the station-yard, where a motor-car stood waiting for him. The strains were heard of a military band; a battalion of light infantry marched down the road. Next came a team of sixteen horses, driven by artillery-men and dragging an enormous siege-piece which, in spite of the weight of its carriage, looked light, because of the extreme length of the gun. A herd of bullocks followed.

Paul, who was unable to find a porter, was standing on the pavement, carrying the two traveling-bags, when a man in leather gaiters, green velveteen breeches and a shooting-jacket with horn buttons, came up to him and raised his cap:

"M. Paul Delroze?" he said. "I am the keeper at the château."

He had a powerful, open face, a skin hardened by exposure to the sun and the cold, hair that was already turning gray and that rather uncouth manner often displayed by old servants whose place allows them a certain degree of independence. For seventeen years he had lived on the great estate of Ornequin, above Corvigny, and managed it for Élisabeth's father, the Comte d'Andeville.

"Ah, so you're Jérôme?" cried Paul. "Good! I see you had the Comte d'Andeville's letter. Have our servants come?"

"They arrived this morning, sir, the three of them; and they have been helping my wife and me to tidy up the house and make it ready to receive the master and the mistress."

He took off his cap again to Élisabeth, who said:

"Then you remember me, Jérôme? It is so long since I was here!"

"Mlle. Élisabeth was four years old then. It was a real sorrow for my wife and me when we heard that you would not come back to the house. . . nor Monsieur le Comte either, because of his poor dead wife. So Monsieur le Comte does not mean to pay us a little visit this year?"

"No, Jérôme, I don't think so. Though it is so many years ago, my father is still very unhappy."

Jérôme took the bags and placed them in a fly which he had ordered at Corvigny. The heavy luggage was to follow in the farm-cart.

It was a fine day and Paul told them to lower the hood. Then he and his wife took their seats.

"It's not a very long drive," said the keeper. "Under ten miles. But it's up-hill all the way."

"Is the house more or less fit to live in?" asked Paul.

"Well, it's not like a house that has been lived in; but you'll see for yourself, sir. We've done the best we could. My wife is so pleased that you and the mistress are coming! You'll find her waiting for her at the foot of the steps. I told her that you would be there between half-past six and seven. . ."

The fly drove off.

"He seems a decent sort of man," said Paul to Élisabeth, "but he can't have much opportunity for talking. He's making up for lost time."

The street climbed the steep slope of the Corvigny hills and constituted, between two rows of shops, hotels and public buildings, the main artery of the town, blocked on this day with unaccustomed traffic. Then it dipped and skirted Vauban's ancient bastions. Next came a switchback road across a plain commanded on the right and left by the two forts known as the Petit and the Grand Jonas.

As they drove along this winding road, which meandered through fields of oats and wheat beneath the leafy vault formed overhead by the close-ranked poplars, Paul Delroze came back to the episode of his childhood which he had promised to tell to Élisabeth:

"As I said, Élisabeth, the incident is connected with a terrible tragedy, so closely connected that the two form only one episode in my memory. The tragedy was much talked about at the time; and your father, who was a friend of my father's, as you know, heard of it through the newspapers. The reason why he did not mention it to you was that I asked him not to, because I wanted to be the first to tell you of events. . . so painful to myself."

Their hands met and clasped. He knew that every one of his words would find a ready listener; and, after a brief pause, he continued:

"My father was one of those men who compel the sympathy and even the affection of all who know them. He had a generous, enthusiastic, attractive nature and an unfailing good-humor, took a passionate interest in any fine cause and any fine spectacle, loved life and enjoyed it with a sort of precipitate haste. He enlisted in 1870 as a volunteer, earned his lieutenant's commission on the battlefield and found the soldier's heroic existence so well suited to his tastes that he volunteered a second time for Tonkin, and a third to take part in the conquest of Madagascar. . . On his return from this campaign, in which he was promoted to captain and received the Legion of Honor, he married. Six years later he was a widower."

"You were like me, Paul," said Élisabeth. "You hardly enjoyed the happiness of knowing your mother."

"No, for I was only four years old. But my father, who felt my mother's death most cruelly, bestowed all his affection upon me. He made a point of personally giving me my early education. He left nothing undone to perfect my physical training and to make a strong and plucky lad of me. I loved him with all my heart. To this day I cannot think of him without genuine emotion. . . When I was eleven years old, I accompanied him on a journey through France, which he had put off for years because he wanted me to take it with him at an age when I could understand its full meaning. It was a pilgrimage to the identical places and along the roads where he had fought during the terrible year."

"Did your father believe in the possibility of another war?"

"Yes; and he wanted to prepare me for it. 'Paul,' he said, 'I have no doubt that one day you will be facing the same enemy whom I fought against. From this moment pay no attention to any fine words of peace that you may hear, but hate that enemy with all the hatred of which you are capable. Whatever people may say, he is a barbarian, a vainglorious, bloodthirsty brute, a beast of prey. He crushed us once and he will not rest content until he has crushed us again and, this time, for good. When that day comes, Paul, remember all the journeys which we have made together. Those which you will take will mark so many triumphant stages, I am sure of it. But never forget the names of these places, Paul; never let your joy in victory wipe out their names of sorrow and humiliation: Froeschwiller, Mars-la-Tour, Saint-Privat and the rest. Mind, Paul, and remember!' And he then smiled. 'But why should I trouble? He himself, the enemy, will make it his business to arouse hatred in the hearts of those who have forgotten and those who have not seen. Can he change? Not he! You'll see, Paul, you'll see. Nothing that I can say to you will equal the terrible reality. They are monsters.'"

Paul Delroze ceased. His wife asked him a little timidly:

"Do you think your father was absolutely right?"

"He may have been influenced by cruel recollections that were too recent in his memory. I have traveled a good deal in Germany, I have even lived there, and I believe that the state of men's minds has altered. I confess, therefore, that I sometimes find a difficulty in understanding my father's words. And yet. . . and yet they very often disturb me. And then what happened afterwards is so inexplicable."

The carriage had slackened its pace. The road was rising slowly towards the hills that overhang the Liseron Valley. The sun was setting in the direction of Corvigny. They passed a diligence, laden with trunks, and two motor cars crowded with passengers and luggage. A picket of cavalry galloped across the fields.

"Let's get out and walk," said Paul Delroze.

They followed the carriage on foot; and Paul continued:

"The rest of what I have to tell you, Élisabeth, stands out in my memory in very precise details, that seem to emerge as though from a thick fog in which I cannot see a thing. For instance, I just know that, after this part of our journey, we were to go from Strasburg to the Black Forest. Why our plans were changed I cannot tell. . . I can see myself one morning in the station at Strasburg, stepping into the train for the Vosges. . . yes, for the Vosges. . . My father kept on reading a letter which he had just received and which seemed to gratify him. The letter may have affected his arrangements; I don't know. We lunched in the train. There was a storm brewing, it was very hot and I fell asleep, so that all I can remember is a little German town where we hired two bicycles and left our bags in the cloak-room. It's all very vague in my mind. We rode across the country."

"But don't you remember what the country was like?"

"No, all I know is that suddenly my father said: 'There, Paul, we're crossing the frontier; we're in France now.' Later on—I can't say how long after—he stopped to ask his road of a peasant, who showed him a short-cut through the woods. But the road and the short-cut are nothing more in my mind than an impenetrable darkness in which my thoughts are buried. . . Then, all of a sudden, the darkness is rent and I see, with astonishing plainness, a glade in the wood, tall trees, velvety moss and an old chapel. And the rain falls in great, thick drops, and my father says, 'Let's take shelter, Paul.' Oh, how I remember the sound of his voice and how exactly I picture the little chapel, with its walls green with damp! We went and put our bicycles under shelter at the back, where the roof projected a little way beyond the choir. Just then the sound of a conversation reached us from the inside and we heard the grating of a door that opened round the corner. Some one came out and said, in German, 'There's no one here. Let us make haste.' At that moment we were coming round the chapel, intending to go in by this side door; and it so happened that my father, who was leading the way, suddenly found himself in the presence of the man who had spoken in German. Both of them stepped back, the stranger apparently very much annoyed and my father astounded at the unexpected meeting. For a second or two, perhaps, they stood looking at each other without moving. I heard my father say, under his breath, 'Is it possible? The Emperor?' And I myself, surprised as I was at the words, had not a doubt of it, for I had often seen the Kaiser's portrait; the man in front of us was the German Emperor."

"The German Emperor?" echoed Élisabeth. "You can't mean that!"

"Yes, the Emperor in France! He quickly lowered his head and turned the velvet collar of his great, flowing cape right up to the brim of his hat, which was pulled down over his eyes. He looked towards the chapel. A lady came out, followed by a man whom I hardly saw, a sort of servant. The lady was tall, a young woman still, dark and rather good-looking. . . The Emperor seized her arm with absolute violence and dragged her away, uttering angry words which we were unable to hear. They took the road by which we had come, the road leading to the frontier. The servant had hurried into the woods and was walking on ahead. 'This really is a queer adventure,' said my father, laughing. 'What on earth is William doing here? Taking the risk in broad daylight, too! I wonder if the chapel possesses some artistic interest. Come and see, Paul.' . . . We went in. A dim light made its way through a window black with dust and cobwebs. But this dim light was enough to show us some stunted pillars and bare walls and not a thing that seemed to deserve the honor of an imperial visit, as my father put it, adding, 'It's quite clear that William came here as a tripper, at hazard, and that he is very cross at having his escapade discovered. I expect the lady who was with him told him that he was running no danger. That would account for his irritation and his reproaches.'"

Paul broke off again. Élisabeth nestled up against him timidly. Presently he continued:

"It's curious, isn't it, Élisabeth, that all these little details, which really were comparatively unimportant for a boy of my age, should have been recorded faithfully in my mind, whereas so many other and much more essential facts have left no trace at all. However, I am telling you all this just as if I still had it before my eyes and as if the words were still sounding in my ears. And at this very moment I can see, as plainly as I saw her at the moment when we left the chapel, the Emperor's companion coming back and crossing the glade with a hurried step; and I can hear her say to my father, 'May I ask a favor of you, monsieur?' She had been running and was out of breath, but did not wait for him to answer and at once added, 'The gentleman you saw would like to speak to you.' This was said in perfect French without the least accent. . . My father hesitated. But his hesitation seemed to shock her as though it were an unspeakable offense against the person who had sent her; and she said, in a harsher tone, 'Surely you do not mean to refuse!' 'Why not?' said my father, with obvious impatience. 'I am not here to receive orders.' She restrained herself and said, 'It is not an order, it is a wish.' 'Very well,' said my father, 'I will agree to the interview. I will wait for your friend here.' She seemed shocked. 'No, no,' she said, 'you must. . .' 'I must put myself out, must I?' cried my father, in a loud voice. 'You expect me to cross the frontier to where somebody is condescending to expect me? I am sorry, madam, but I will not consent to that. Tell your friend that if he fears an indiscretion on my part he can set his mind at rest. Come along, Paul.' He took off his hat to the lady and bowed. But she barred his way: 'No, no,' she said, 'you must do what I ask. What is a promise of discretion worth? The thing must be settled one way or the other; and you yourself will admit. . .' Those were the last words I heard. She was standing opposite my father in a violent and hostile attitude. Her face was distorted with an expression of fierceness that terrified me. Oh, why did I not foresee what was going to happen? . . . But I was so young! And it all came so quickly! . . . She walked up to my father and, so to speak, forced him back to the foot of a large tree, on the right of the chapel. They raised their voices. She made a threatening gesture. He began to laugh. And suddenly, immediately, she whipped out a knife—I can see the blade now, flashing through the darkness—and stabbed him in the chest, twice. . . twice, there, full in the chest. My father fell to the ground."

Paul Delroze stopped, pale with the memory of the crime.

"Oh," faltered Élisabeth, "your father was murdered? . . . My poor Paul, my poor darling!" And in a voice of anguish she asked, "What happened next, Paul? Did you cry out?"

"I shouted, I rushed towards him, but a hand caught me in an irresistible grip. It was the man, the servant, who had darted out of the woods and seized me. I saw his knife raised above my head. I felt a terrible blow on my shoulder. Then I also fell."

II

The Locked Room

The carriage stood waiting for them a little way ahead. They had sat down by the roadside on reaching the upland at the top of the ascent. The green, undulating valley of the Liseron opened up before them, with its little winding river escorted by two white roads which followed its every turn. Behind them, under the setting sun, some three hundred feet below, lay the clustering mass of Corvigny. Two miles in front of them rose the turrets of Ornequin and the ruins of the old castle.

Terrified by Paul's story, Élisabeth was silent for a time. Then she said:

"Oh, Paul, how terrible it all is! Were you very badly hurt?"

"I can remember nothing until the day when I woke up in a room which I did not know and saw a nun and an old lady, a cousin of my father's, who were nursing me. It was the best room of an inn somewhere between Belfort and the frontier. Twelve days before, at a very early hour in the morning, the innkeeper had found two bodies, all covered with blood, which had been laid there during the night. One of the bodies was quite cold. It was my poor father's. I was still breathing, but very slightly. . . I had a long convalescence, interrupted by relapses and fits of delirium, in which I tried to make my escape. My old cousin, the only relation I had left, showed me the most wonderful and devoted kindness. Two months later she took me home with her. I was very nearly cured of my wound, but so greatly affected by my father's death and by the frightful circumstances surrounding it that it was several years before I recovered my health completely. As to the tragedy itself. . ."

"Well?" asked Élisabeth, throwing her arm round her husband's neck, with an eager movement of protection.

"Well, they never succeeded in fathoming the mystery. And yet the police conducted their investigations zealously and scrupulously, trying to verify the only information which they were able to employ, that which I gave them. All their efforts failed. You know, my information was very vague. Apart from what had happened in the glade and in front of the chapel, I knew nothing. I could not tell them where to find the chapel, nor where to look for it, nor in what part of the country the tragedy had occurred."

"But still you had taken a journey, you and your father, to reach that part of the country; and it seems to me that, by tracing your road back to your departure from Strasburg. . ."

"Well, of course they did their best to follow up that track; and the French police, not content with calling in the aid of the German police, sent their shrewdest detectives to the spot. But this is exactly what afterwards, when I was of an age to think out things, struck me as so strange: not a single trace was found of our stay at Strasburg. You quite understand? Not a trace of any kind. Now, if there was one thing of which I was absolutely certain, it was that we had spent at least two days and nights at Strasburg. The magistrate who had the case in hand, looking upon me as a child and one who had been badly knocked about and upset, came to the conclusion that my memory must be at fault. But I knew that this was not so; I knew it then and I know it still."

"What then, Paul?"

"Well, I cannot help seeing a connection between the total elimination of undeniable facts—facts easily checked or reconstructed, such as the visit of a Frenchman and his son to Strasburg, their railway journey, the leaving of their luggage in the cloak-room of a town in Alsace, the hiring of a couple of bicycles—and this main fact, that the Emperor was directly, yes, directly mixed up in the business."

"But this connection must have been as obvious to the magistrate's mind as to yours, Paul."

"No doubt; but neither the examining magistrate nor any of his colleagues and the other officials who took my evidence was willing to admit the Emperor's presence in Alsace on that day."

"Why not?"

"Because the German newspapers stated that he was in Frankfort at that very hour."

"In Frankfort?"

"Of course, he is stated to be wherever he commands and never at a place where he does not wish his presence known. At any rate, on this point also I was accused of being in error and the inquiry was thwarted by an assemblage of obstacles, impossibilities, lies and alibis which, to my mind, revealed the continuous and all-powerful action of an unlimited authority. There is no other explanation. Just think: how can two French subjects put up at a Strasburg hotel without having their names entered in the visitors' book? Well, whether because the book was destroyed or a page torn out, no record whatever of the names was found. So there was one proof, one clue gone. As for the hotel proprietor and waiters, the railway booking clerks and porters, the man who owned the bicycles: these were so many subordinates, so many accomplices, all of whom received orders to be silent; and not one of them disobeyed."

"But afterwards, Paul, you must have made your own search?"

"I should think I did! Four times since I came of age I have been over the whole frontier from Switzerland to Luxemburg, from Belfort to Longwy, questioning the inhabitants, studying the country. I have spent hours and hours in cudgeling my brains in the vain hope of extracting the slightest recollection that would have given me a gleam of light. But all without result. There was not one fresh glimmer amid all that darkness. Only three pictures showed through the dense fog of the past, pictures of the place and the things which witnessed the crime: the trees in the glade, the old chapel and the path leading through the woods. And then there was the figure of the Emperor and. . . the figure of the woman who killed my father."

Paul had lowered his voice. His face was distorted with grief and loathing.

"As for her," he went on, "if I live to be a hundred, I shall see her before my eyes as something standing out in all its details under the full light of day. The shape of her lips, the expression of her eyes, the color of her hair, the special character of her walk, the rhythm of her movements, the outline of her body: all this is recorded within myself, not as a vision which I summon up at will, but as something that forms part of my very being. It is as though, during my delirium, all the mysterious powers of my brain had collaborated to assimilate entirely those hateful memories. There was a time when all this was a morbid obsession: nowadays, I suffer only at certain hours, when the night is coming in and I am alone. My father was murdered; and the woman who murdered him is alive, unpunished, happy, rich, honored, pursuing her work of hatred and destruction."

"Would you know her again if you saw her, Paul?"

"Would I know her again! I should know her among a thousand. Even if she were disfigured by age, I should discover in the wrinkles of the old woman that she had become the face of the younger woman who stabbed my father to death on that September evening. Know her again! Why, I noticed the very shade of the dress she wore! It seems incredible, but there it is. A gray dress, with a black lace scarf over the shoulders; and here, in the bodice, by way of a brooch, a heavy cameo, set in a gold snake with ruby eyes. You see, Élisabeth, I have not forgotten and I never shall forget."

He ceased. Élisabeth was crying. The past which her husband had revealed to her was filling her with the same sense of horror and bitterness. He drew her to him and kissed her on the forehead.

"You are right not to forget," she said. "The murder will be punished because it has to be punished. But you must not let your life be subject to these memories of hatred. There are two of us now and we love each other. Let us look towards the future."

THE CHÂTEAU D'ORNEQUIN IS A handsome sixteenth century building of simple design, with four peaked turrets, tall windows with denticulated pinnacles and a light balustrade projecting above the first story. The esplanade is formed by well-kept lawns which surround the courtyard and lead on the right and left to gardens, woods and orchards. One side of these lawns ends in a broad terrace overlooking the valley of the Liseron. On this terrace, in a line with the house, stand the majestic ruins of a four-square castle-keep.

The whole wears a very stately air. The estate, surrounded by farms and fields, demands active and careful working for its maintenance. It is one of the largest in the department.

Seventeen years before, at the sale held upon the death of the last Baron d'Ornequin, Élisabeth's father, the Comte d'Andeville, bought it at his wife's desire. He had been married for five years and had resigned his commission in the cavalry in order to devote himself entirely to the woman he loved. A chance journey brought them to Ornequin just as the sale, which had hardly been advertised in the local press, was about to be held. Hermine d'Andeville fell in love with the house and the domain; and the Count, who was looking for an estate whose management would occupy his spare time effected the purchase through his lawyer by private treaty.

During the winter that followed, he directed from Paris the work of restoration which was necessitated by the state of disrepair in which the former owner had left the house. M. d'Andeville wished it to be not only comfortable but also elegant; and, little by little, he sent down all the tapestries, pictures, objects of art and knicknacks that adorned his house in Paris.

They were not able to take up their residence until August. They then spent a few delightful weeks with their dear Élisabeth, at this time four years old, and their son, Bernard, a lusty boy to whom the Countess had given birth that same year. Hermine d'Andeville was devoted to her children and never went beyond the confines of the park. The Count looked after his farms and shot over his coverts, accompanied by Jérôme, his gamekeeper, a worthy Alsatian, who had been in the late owner's service and who knew every yard of the estate.

At the end of October, the Countess took cold; the illness that followed was pretty serious; and the Comte d'Andeville decided to take her and the children to the south. A fortnight later she had a relapse; and in three days she was dead.

The Count experienced the despair which makes a man feel that life is over and that, whatever happens, he will never again know the sense of joy nor even an alleviation of any sort. He lived not so much for the sake of his children as to cherish within himself the cult of her whom he had lost and to perpetuate a memory which now became the sole reason of his existence.

He was unable to return to the Château d'Ornequin, where he had known too perfect a happiness; on the other hand, he would not have strangers live there; and he ordered Jérôme to keep the doors and shutters closed and to lock up the Countess' boudoir and bedroom in such a way that no one could ever enter. Jérôme was also to let the farms and to collect the tenants' rents.

This break with the past was not enough to satisfy the Count. It seems strange in a man who existed only for the sake of his wife's memory, but everything that reminded him of her—familiar objects, domestic surroundings, places and landscapes—became a torture to him; and his very children filled him with a sense of discomfort which he was unable to overcome. He had an elder sister, a widow, living in the country, at Chaumont. He placed his daughter Élisabeth and his son Bernard in her charge and went abroad.

Aunt Aline was the most devoted and unselfish of women; and under her care Élisabeth enjoyed a grave, studious and affectionate childhood in which her heart developed together with her mind and her character. She received the education almost of a boy, together with a strong moral discipline. At the age of twenty, she had grown into a tall, capable, fearless girl, whose face, inclined by nature to be melancholy, sometimes lit up with the fondest and most innocent of smiles. It was one of those faces which reveal beforehand the pangs and raptures held in store by fate. The tears were never far from her eyes, which seemed as though troubled by the spectacle of life. Her hair, with its bright curls, lent a certain gaiety to her appearance.

At each visit that the Comte d'Andeville paid his daughter between his wanderings he fell more and more under her charm. He took her one winter to Spain and the next to Italy. It was in this way that she became acquainted with Paul Delroze at Rome and met him again at Naples and Syracuse, from which town Paul accompanied the d'Andevilles on a long excursion through Sicily. The intimacy thus formed attached the two young people by a bond of which they did not realize the full strength till the time came for parting.

Like Élisabeth, Paul had been brought up in the country and, again like her, by a fond kinswoman who strove, by dint of loving care, to make him forget the tragedy of his childhood. Though oblivion failed to come, at any rate she succeeded in continuing his father's work and in making of Paul a manly and industrious lad, interested in books, life and the doings of mankind. He went to school and, after performing his military service, spent two years in Germany, studying some of his favorite industrial and mechanical subjects on the spot.

Tall and well set up, with his black hair flung back from his rather thin face, with its determined chin, he made an impression of strength and energy.

His meeting with Élisabeth revealed to him a world of ideas and emotions which he had hitherto disdained. For him as for her it was a sort of intoxication mingled with amazement. Love created in them two new souls, light and free as air, whose ready enthusiasm and expansiveness formed a sharp contrast with the habits enforced upon them by the strict tendency of their lives. On his return to France he asked for Élisabeth's hand in marriage and obtained her consent.

On the day of the marriage contract, three days before the wedding, the Comte d'Andeville announced that he would add the Château d'Ornequin to Élisabeth's dowry. The young couple decided that they would live there and that Paul should look about in the valleys of the neighboring manufacturing district for some works which he could buy and manage.

They were married on Thursday, the 30th of July, at Chaumont. It was a quiet wedding, because of the rumors of war, though the Comte d'Andeville, on the strength of information to which he attached great credit, declared that no war would take place. At the breakfast in which the two families took part, Paul made the acquaintance of Bernard d'Andeville, Élisabeth's brother, a schoolboy of barely seventeen, whose holidays had just begun. Paul took to him, because of his frank bearing and high spirits; and it was arranged that Bernard should join them in a few days at Ornequin. At one o'clock Élisabeth and Paul left Chaumont by train. They were going hand-in-hand to the château where the first years of their marriage were to be spent and perhaps all that happy and peaceful future which opens up before the dazzling eyes of lovers.

It was half-past six o'clock when they saw Jérôme's wife standing at the foot of the steps. Rosalie was a stout, motherly body with ruddy, mottled cheeks and a cheerful face.

Before dining, they took a hurried turn in the garden and went over the house. Élisabeth could not contain her emotion. Though there were no memories to excite her, she seemed, nevertheless, to rediscover something of the mother whom she had known for such a little while, whose features she could not remember and who had here spent the last happy days of her life. For her, the shade of the dead woman still trod those garden paths. The great, green lawns exhaled a special fragrance. The leaves on the trees rustled in the wind with a whisper which she seemed already to have heard in that same spot and at the same hour of the day, with her mother listening beside her.

"You seem depressed, Élisabeth," said Paul.

"Not depressed, but unsettled. I feel as though my mother were welcoming us to this place where she thought she was to live and where we have come with the same intention. And I somehow feel anxious. It is as though I were a stranger, an intruder, disturbing the rest and peace of the house. Only think! My mother has been here all alone for such a time! My father would never come here; and I was telling myself that we have no right to come here either, with our indifference for everything that is not ourselves."

Paul smiled:

"Élisabeth, my darling, you are simply feeling that impression of uneasiness which one always feels on arriving at a new place in the evening."

"I don't know," she said. "I daresay you are right. . . But I can't shake off the uneasiness; and that is so unlike me. Do you believe in presentiments, Paul?"

"No, do you?"

"No, I don't either," she said, laughing and giving him her lips.

They were surprised to find that the rooms of the house looked as if they had been constantly inhabited. By the Count's orders, everything had remained as it was in the far-off days of Hermine d'Andeville. The knickknacks were there, in the same places, and every piece of embroidery, every square of lace, every miniature, all the handsome eighteenth century chairs, all the Flemish tapestry, all the furniture which the Count had collected in the old days to add to the beauty of his house. They were thus entering from the first into a charming and home-like setting.

After dinner they returned to the gardens, where they strolled to and fro in silence, with their arms entwined round each other's waists. From the terrace they looked down upon the dark valley, with a few lights gleaming here and there. The old castle-keep raised its massive ruins against a pale sky, in which a remnant of vague light still lingered.

"Paul," said Élisabeth, in a low voice, "did you notice, as we went over the house, a door closed with a great padlock?"

"In the middle of the chief corridor, near your bedroom, you mean?"

"Yes. That was my poor mother's boudoir. My father insisted that it should be locked, as well as the bedroom leading out of it; and Jérôme put a padlock on the door and sent him the key. No one has set foot in it since. It is just as my mother left it. All her own things—her unfinished work, her books—are there. And on the wall facing the door, between the two windows that have always been kept shut, is her portrait, which my father had ordered a year before of a great painter of his acquaintance, a full-length portrait which, I understand, is the very image of her. Her *prie-Dieu* is beside it. This morning my father gave me the key of the boudoir and I promised him that I would kneel down on the *prie-Dieu* and say a prayer before the portrait of the mother whom I hardly knew and whose features I cannot imagine, for I never even had a photograph of her."

"Really? How was that?"

"You see, my father loved my mother so much that, in obedience to a feeling which he himself was unable to explain, he wished to be alone in his recollection of her. He wanted his memories to be hidden deep down in himself, so that nothing would remind him of her except his own will and his grief. He almost begged my pardon for it this morning, said that perhaps he had done me a wrong; and that is why he wants us to go together, Paul, on this first evening, and pray before the picture of my poor dead mother."

"Let us go now, Élisabeth."

Her hand trembled in her husband's hand as they climbed the stairs to the first floor. Lamps had been lighted all along the passage. They stopped in front of a tall, wide door surmounted with gilded carvings.

"Unfasten the lock, Paul," said Élisabeth.

Her voice shook as she spoke. She handed him the key. He removed the padlock and seized the door-handle. But Élisabeth suddenly gripped her husband's arm:

"One moment, Paul, one moment! I feel so upset. This is the first time that I shall look on my mother's face. . . and you, my dearest, are beside me. . . I feel as if I were becoming a little girl again."

"Yes," he said, pressing her hand passionately, "a little girl and a grown woman in one."

Comforted by the clasp of his hand, she released hers and whispered:

"We will go in now, Paul darling."

He opened the door and returned to the passage to take a lamp from a bracket on the wall and place it on the table. Meanwhile, Élisabeth had walked across the room and was standing in front of the picture. Her mother's face was in the shadow and she altered the position of the lamp so as to throw the full light upon it.

"How beautiful she is, Paul!"

He went up to the picture and raised his head. Élisabeth sank to her knees on the *prie-Dieu*. But presently, hearing Paul turn round, she looked up at him and was stupefied by what she saw. He was standing motionless, livid in the face, his eyes wide open, as though gazing at the most frightful vision.

"Paul," she cried, "what's the matter?"

He began to make for the door, stepping backwards, unable to take his eyes from the portrait of Hermine d'Andeville. He was staggering like a drunken man; and his arms beat the air around him.

"That. . . that. . ." he stammered, hoarsely.

"Paul," Élisabeth entreated, "what is it? What are you trying to say?"

"That. . . that is the woman who killed my father!"

III

The Call to Arms

The hideous accusation was followed by an awful silence. Élisabeth was now standing in front of her husband, striving to understand his words, which had not yet acquired their real meaning for her, but which hurt her as though she had been stabbed to the heart.

She moved towards him and, with her eyes in his, spoke in a voice so low that he could hardly hear:

"You surely can't mean what you said, Paul? The thing is too monstrous!"

He replied in the same tone:

"Yes, it is a monstrous thing. I don't believe it myself yet. I refuse to believe it."

"Then—it's a mistake, isn't it?—Confess it, you've made a mistake."

She implored him with all the distress that filled her being, as though she were hoping to make him yield. He fixed his eyes again on the accursed portrait, over his wife's shoulder, and shivered from head to foot:

"Oh, it is she!" he declared, clenching his fists. "It is she—I recognize her—it is the woman who killed my—"

A shock of protest ran through her body; and, beating her breast, she cried:

"My mother! My mother a murderess! My mother, whom my father used to worship and went on worshiping! My mother, who used to hold me on her knee and kiss me!—I have forgotten everything about her except that, her kisses and her caresses! And you tell me that she is a murderess!"

"It is true."

"Oh, Paul, you must not say anything so horrible! How can you be positive, such a long time after? You were only a child; and you saw so little of the woman. . . hardly a few minutes. . ."

"I saw more of her than it seems humanly possible to see," exclaimed Paul, loudly. "From the moment of the murder her image never left my sight. I have tried to shake it off at times, as one tries to shake off a nightmare; but I could not. And the image is there, hanging on the wall. As sure as I live, it is there; I know it as I should know your image after twenty years. It is she. . . why, look, on her breast, that brooch set in a gold snake! . . . a cameo, as I told you, and the snake's eyes. . . two rubies! . . . and the black lace scarf around the shoulders! It's she, I tell you, it's the woman I saw!"

A growing rage excited him to frenzy; and he shook his fist at the portrait of Hermine d'Andeville.

"Hush!" cried Élisabeth, under the torment of his words. "Hold your tongue! I won't allow you to. . ."

She tried to put her hand on his mouth to compel him to silence. But Paul made a movement of repulsion, as though he were shrinking from his wife's touch; and the movement was so abrupt and so instinctive that she fell to the ground sobbing while he, incensed, exasperated by his sorrow and hatred, impelled by a sort of terrified hallucination that drove him back to the door, shouted:

"Look at her! Look at her wicked mouth, her pitiless eyes! She is thinking of the murder! . . . I see her, I see her! . . . She goes up to my father. . . she leads him away. . . she raises her arm. . . and she kills him! . . . Oh, the wretched, monstrous woman! . . ."

He rushed from the room.

PAUL SPENT THE NIGHT IN the park, running like a madman wherever the dark paths led him, or flinging himself, when tired out, on the grass and weeping, weeping endlessly.

Paul Delroze had known no suffering save from his memory of the murder, a chastened suffering which, nevertheless, at certain periods became acute until it smarted like a fresh wound. This time the pain was so great and so unexpected that, notwithstanding his usual self-mastery and his well-balanced mind, he utterly lost his head. His thoughts, his actions, his attitudes, the words which he yelled into the darkness were those of a man who has parted with his self-control.

One thought and one alone kept returning to his seething brain, in which his ideas and impressions whirled like leaves in the wind; one terrible thought:

"I know the woman who killed my father; and that woman's daughter is the woman whom I love."

Did he still love her? No doubt, he was desperately mourning a happiness which he knew to be shattered; but did he still love Élisabeth? Could he love Hermine d'Andeville's daughter?

When he went indoors at daybreak and passed Élisabeth's room, his heart beat no faster than before. His hatred of the murderess destroyed all else that might stir within him: love, affection, longing, or even the merest human pity.

The torpor into which he sank for a few hours relaxed his nerves a little, but did not change his mental attitude. Perhaps, on the contrary, and without even thinking about it, he was still more unwilling than before to meet Élisabeth. And yet he wanted to know, to ascertain, to gather all the essential particulars and to make quite certain before taking the resolve that would decide the great tragedy of his life in one way or another.

Above all, he must question Jérôme and his wife, whose evidence was of no small value, owing to the fact that they had known the Comtesse d'Andeville. Certain matters concerning the dates, for instance, might be cleared up forthwith.

He found them in their lodge, both of them greatly excited, Jérôme with a newspaper in his hand and Rosalie making gestures of dismay.

"It's settled, sir," cried Jérôme. "You can be sure of it: it's coming!"

"What?" asked Paul.

"Mobilization, sir, the call to arms. You'll see it does. I saw some gendarmes, friends of mine, and they told me. The posters are ready."

Paul remarked, absent-mindedly:

"The posters are always ready."

"Yes, but they're going to stick them up at once, you'll see, sir. Just look at the paper. Those swine—you'll forgive me, sir, but it's the only word for them—those swine want war. Austria would be willing to negotiate, but in the meantime the others have been mobilizing for several days. Proof is, they won't let you cross into their country any more. And worse: yesterday they destroyed a French railway station, not far from here, and pulled up the rails. Read it for yourself, sir!"

Paul skimmed through the stop-press telegrams, but, though he saw that they were serious, war seemed to him such an unlikely thing that he did not pay much attention to them.

"It'll be settled all right," he said. "That's just their way of talking, with their hand on the sword-hilt; but I can't believe. . ."

"You're wrong, sir," Rosalie muttered.

He no longer listened, thinking only of the tragedy of his fate and casting about for the best means of obtaining the necessary replies from Jérôme. But he was not able to contain himself any longer and he broached the subject frankly:

"I daresay you know, Jérôme, that madame and I have been to the Comtesse d'Andeville's room."

The statement produced an extraordinary effect upon the keeper and his wife, as though it had been a sacrilege to enter that room so long kept locked, the mistress' room, as they called it among themselves.

"You don't mean that, sir!" Rosalie blurted out.

And Jérôme added:

"No, of course not, for I sent the only key of the padlock, a safety-key it was, to Monsieur le Comte."

"He gave it us yesterday morning," said Paul.

And, without troubling further about their amazement, he proceeded straightaway to put his questions:

"There is a portrait of the Comtesse d'Andeville between the two windows. When was it hung there?"

Jérôme did not reply at once. He thought for a moment, looked at his wife, and then said:

"Why, that's easily answered. It was when Monsieur le Comte sent all his furniture to the house. . . before they moved in."

"When was that?"

Paul's agony was unendurable during the three or four seconds before the reply.

"Well?" he asked.

When the reply came at last it was decisive:

"Well, it was in the spring of 1898."

"Eighteen hundred and ninety-eight!"

Paul repeated the words in a dull voice: 1898 was the year of his father's murder!

Without stopping to reflect, with the coolness of an examining magistrate who does not swerve from the line which he has laid out, he asked:

"So the Comte and Comtesse d'Andeville arrived. . ."

"Monsieur le Comte and Madame le Comtesse arrived at the castle on the 28th of August, 1898, and left for the south on the 24th of October."

Paul now knew the truth, for his father was murdered on the 19th of September. And all the circumstances which depended on that truth, which explained it in its main details or which proceeded from it at once appeared to him. He remembered that his father was on friendly terms with the Comte d'Andeville. He said to himself that his father, in the course of his journey in Alsace, must have learnt that his friend d'Andeville was living in Lorraine and must have contemplated paying him a surprise visit. He reckoned up the distance between Ornequin and Strasburg, a distance which corresponded with the time spent in the train. And he asked:

"How far is this from the frontier?"

"Three miles and three-quarters, sir."

"On the other side, at no great distance, there's a little German town, is there not?"

"Yes, sir, Èbrecourt."

"Is there a short-cut to the frontier?"

"Yes, sir, for about half-way: a path at the other end of the park."

"Through the woods?"

"Through Monsieur le Comte's woods."

"And in those woods. . ."

To acquire total, absolute certainty, that certainty which comes not from an interpretation of the facts but from the facts themselves, which would stand out visible and palpable, all that he had to do was to put the last question: in those woods was not there a little chapel in the middle of a glade? Paul Delroze did not put the question. Perhaps he thought it too precise, perhaps he feared lest it should induce the gamekeeper to entertain thoughts and comparisons which the nature of the conversation was already sufficient to warrant. He merely asked:

"Was the Comtesse d'Andeville away at all during the six weeks which she spent at Ornequin? For two or three days, I mean?"

"No, sir, Madame le Comtesse never left the grounds."

"She kept to the park?"

"Yes, sir. Monsieur le Comte used to drive almost every afternoon to Corvigny or in the valley, but Madame la Comtesse never went beyond the park and the woods."

Paul knew what he wanted to know. Not caring what Jérôme and his wife might think, he did not trouble to find an excuse for his strange series of apparently disconnected questions. He left the lodge and walked away.

Eager though he was to complete his inquiry, he postponed the investigations which he intended to pursue outside the park. It was as though he dreaded to face the final proof, which had really become superfluous after those with which chance had supplied him. He therefore went back to the château and, at lunch-time, resolved to accept this inevitable meeting with Élisabeth. But his wife's maid came to him in the drawing-room and said that her mistress sent her excuses. Madame was not feeling very well and asked did monsieur mind if she took her lunch in her own room. He understood that she wished to leave him entirely free, refusing, on her side, to appeal to him on behalf of a mother whom she respected and, if necessary, submitting beforehand to whatever eventual decision her husband might make.

Lunching by himself under the eyes of the butler and footman waiting at table, he felt in the utmost depths of his heart that his happiness was gone and that Élisabeth and he, thanks to circumstances for which neither of them was responsible, had on the very day of their marriage become enemies whom no power on earth could bring together. Certainly, he bore her no hatred and did not reproach her with her mother's crime; but unconsciously he was angry with her, as for a fault, inasmuch as she was her mother's daughter.

For two hours after lunch he remained closeted with the portrait in the boudoir: a tragic interview which he wished to have with the murderess, so as to fill his eyes with her accursed image and give fresh strength to his memories. He examined every slightest detail. He studied the cameo, the swan with unfurled wings which it represented, the chasing of the gold snake that formed the setting, the position of the rubies and also the draping of the lace around the shoulders, not to speak of the shape of the mouth and the color of the hair and the outline of the face.

It was undoubtedly the woman whom he had seen that September evening. A corner of the picture bore the painter's signature; and underneath, on the frame, was a scroll with the inscription:

Portrait of the Comtesse H.

No doubt the portrait had been exhibited with that discreet reference to the Comtesse Hermine.

"Now, then," said Paul. "A few minutes more, and the whole past will come to life again. I have found the criminal; I have now only to find the place of the crime. If the chapel is there, in the woods, the truth will be complete."

He went for the truth resolutely. He feared it less now, because it could no longer escape his grasp. And yet how his heart beat, with great, painful throbs, and how he loathed the idea of taking the road leading to that other road along which his father had passed sixteen years before!

A vague movement of Jérôme's hand had told him which way to go. He crossed the park in the direction of the frontier, bearing to his left and passing a lodge. At the entrance to the woods was a long avenue of fir-trees down which he went. Four hundred yards farther it branched into three narrow avenues. Two of these proved to end in impenetrable thickets. The third led to the top of a mound, from which he descended, still keeping to his left, by another avenue of fir-trees.

In selecting this road, Paul realized that it was just this avenue of firs the appearance of which aroused in him, through some untold resemblance of shape and arrangement, memories clear enough to guide his steps. It ran straight ahead for some time and then took a sudden turn into a cluster of tall beeches whose leafy tops met overhead. Then the road sloped upwards; and, at the end of the dark tunnel through which he was walking, Paul perceived the glare of light that points to an open space.

The anguish of it all made his knees give way beneath him; and he had to make an effort to proceed. Was it the glade in which his father had received his death-blow? The more that luminous space became revealed to his eyes, the more did he feel penetrated with a profound conviction. As in the room with the portrait, the past was recovering the very aspect of the truth in and before him.

It was the same glade, surrounded by a ring of trees that presented the same picture and covered with a carpet of grass and moss which the same paths divided as of old. The same glimpse of sky was above him, outlined by the capricious masses of foliage. And there, on his left, guarded by two yew-trees which Paul recognized, was the chapel.

The chapel! The little old massive chapel, whose lines had etched themselves like furrows into his brain! Trees grow, become taller, alter their form. The appearance of a glade is liable to change. Its paths will sometimes interlock in a different fashion. A man's memory can play him a trick. But a building of granite and cement is immutable. It takes centuries to give it the green-gray color that is the mark which time sets upon the stone; and this bloom of age never alters. The chapel that stood there, displaying a grimy-paned rose-window in its east front, was undoubtedly that from which the German Emperor had stepped, followed by the woman who, ten minutes later, committed the murder.

Paul walked to the door. He wanted to revisit the place in which his father had spoken to him for the last time. It was a moment of tense emotion. The same little roof which had sheltered their bicycles projected at the back; and the door was the same, with its great rusty clamps and bars.

He stood on the single step that led to it, raised the latch and pushed the door. But as he was about to enter, two men, hidden in the shadow on either side, sprang at him.

One of them aimed a revolver full in his face. By some miracle, Paul noticed the gleaming barrel of the weapon just in time to stoop before the bullet could strike him. A second shot rang out, but he had hustled the man and now snatched the revolver from his hand, while his other aggressor threatened him with a dagger. He stepped backwards out of the chapel, with outstretched arm, and twice pulled the trigger. Each time there was a click but no shot. The mere fact, however, of his firing at the two scoundrels terrified them, and they turned tail and made off as fast as they could.

Bewildered by the suddenness of the attack, Paul stood for a second irresolute. Then he fired at the fugitives again, but to no purpose. The revolver, which was obviously loaded in only two chambers, clicked but did not go off.

He then started running after his assailants; and he remembered that long ago the Emperor and his companion, on leaving the chapel, had taken the same direction, which was evidently that of the frontier.

Almost at the same moment the men, seeing themselves pursued, plunged into the wood and slipped in among the trees; but Paul, who was swifter of foot, rapidly gained ground on them, all the more so as he had gone round a hollow filled with bracken and brambles into which the others had ventured.

Suddenly one of them gave a shrill whistle, probably a warning to some accomplice. Soon after they disappeared behind a line of extremely dense bushes. When he had passed through these, Paul saw at a distance of sixty yards before him a high wall which seemed to shut in the woods on every side. The men were half-way to it; and he perceived that they were making straight for a part of the wall containing a small door.

Paul put on a spurt so as to reach the door before they had time to open it. The bare ground enabled him to increase his speed, whereas the men, who were obviously tired, had reduced theirs.

"I've got them, the ruffians!" he murmured. "I shall at last know. . ."

A second whistle sounded, followed by a guttural shout. He was now within twenty yards of them and could hear them speak.

"I've got them, I've got them!" he repeated, with fierce delight.

And he made up his mind to strike one of them in the face with the barrel of his revolver and to spring at the other's throat.

But, before they even reached the wall, the door was pushed open from the outside and a third man appeared and let them through.

Paul flung away the revolver; and his impetus was such and the effort which he made so great that he managed to seize the door and draw it to him.

The door gave way. And what he then saw scared him to such a degree that he started backwards and did not even dream of defending himself against this fresh attack. The third man—Oh, hideous nightmare! Could it moreover be anything but a nightmare?—the third ruffian was raising a knife against him; and Paul knew his face. . . it was a face resembling the one which he had seen before, a man's face and not a woman's, but the same sort of face, undoubtedly the same sort: a face marked by fifteen additional years and by an even harder and more wicked expression, but the same sort of face, the same sort!

And the man stabbed Paul, even as the woman of fifteen years ago, even as she who was since dead had stabbed Paul's father.

Paul Delroze staggered, but rather as the result of the nervous shock caused by the sudden appearance of this ghost of the past; for the blade of the dagger, striking the button on the shoulder-strap of his shooting-jacket, broke into splinters. Dazed and misty-eyed, he heard the sound of the door closing, the grating of the key in the lock and lastly the hum of a motor car starting on the other side of the wall. When Paul recovered from his torpor there was nothing left for him to do. The man and his two confederates were out of reach.

Besides, for the moment he was utterly absorbed in the mystery of the likeness between the figure from the past and that which he had just seen. He could think of but one thing:

"The Comtesse d'Andeville is dead; and here she is revived under the aspect of a man whose face is the very face which she would have to-day. Is it the face of some relation, of a brother of whom I never heard, a twin perhaps?"

And he reflected:

"After all, am I not mistaken? Am I not the victim of an hallucination, which would be only natural in the crisis through which I am passing? How do I know for certain that there is any connection between the present and the past? I must have a proof."

The proof was ready to his hand; and it was so strong that Paul was not able to doubt for much longer. He caught sight of the remains of the dagger in the grass and picked up the handle. On it four letters were engraved as with a red-hot iron: an H, an E, an R and an M.

H, E, R, M; the first four letters of Hermine! . . . At this moment, while he was staring at the letters which were to him so full of meaning, at this moment, a moment which Paul was never to forget, the bell of a church nearby began to ring in the most unusual manner: a regular, monotonous, uninterrupted ringing, which sounded at once brisk and unspeakably sinister.

"The tocsin," he muttered to himself, without attaching the full sense to the word. And he added: "A fire somewhere, I expect."

A few minutes later Paul had succeeded in climbing over the wall by means of the projecting branches of a tree. He found a further stretch of woods, crossed by a forest road. He followed the tracks of a motor car along this road and reached the frontier within an hour.

A squad of German constabulary were sitting round the foot of the frontier post; and he saw a white road with Uhlans trotting along it. At the end of it was a cluster of red roofs and gardens. Was this the little town where his father and he had hired their bicycles that day, the little town of Èbrecourt?

The melancholy bell never ceased. He noticed that the sound came from France; also that another bell was ringing somewhere, likewise in France, and a third from the direction of the Liseron; and all three on the same hurried note, as though sending forth a wild appeal around them.

He repeated, anxiously:

"The tocsin! . . . The alarm! . . . And it's being passed on from church to church. . . Can it mean that. . ."

But he drove away the terrifying thought. No, his ears were misleading him; or else it was the echo of a single bell thrown back in the hollow valleys and ringing over the plains.

Meanwhile he was gazing at the white road which issued from the little German town, and he observed that a constant stream of horsemen was arriving there and spreading across-country. Also a detachment of French dragoons appeared on the ridge of a hill. The officer in command scanned the horizon through his field-glasses and then trotted off with his men.

Thereupon, unable to go any farther, Paul walked back to the wall which he had climbed and found that the wall was prolonged around the whole of the estate, including the woods and the park. He learnt besides from an old peasant that it was built some twelve years ago, which explained why Paul had never found the chapel in the course of his explorations along the frontier. Once only, he now remembered, some one had told him of a chapel; but it was one situated inside a private estate; and his suspicions had not been aroused.

While thus following the road that skirted the property, he came nearer to the village of Ornequin, whose church suddenly rose at the end of a clearing in the wood. The bell, which he had not heard for the last moment or two, now rang out again with great distinctness. It was the bell of Ornequin. It was frail, shrill, poignant as a lament and more solemn than a passing-bell, for all its hurry and lightness.

Paul walked towards the sound. A charming village, all aflower with geraniums and Marguerites, stood gathered about its church. Silent groups were studying a white notice posted on the Mayor's office. Paul stepped forward and read the heading:

"Mobilization Order."

At any other period of his life these words would have struck him with all their gloomy and terrific meaning. But the crisis through which he was passing was too powerful to allow room for any great emotion within him. He scarcely even contemplated the unavoidable consequences of the proclamation. Very well, the country was mobilizing: the mobilization would begin at midnight... Very well, every one must go; he would go... And this assumed in his mind the form of so imperative an act, the proportions of a duty which so completely exceeded every minor obligation and every petty individual need that he felt, on the contrary, a sort of relief at thus receiving from the outside the order that dictated his conduct. There was no hesitation possible. His duty lay before him: he must go.

Go? In that case why not go at once? What was the use of returning to the house, seeing Élisabeth again, seeking a painful and futile explanation, granting or refusing a forgiveness which his wife did not ask of him, but which the daughter of Hermine d'Andeville did not deserve?

In front of the principal inn a diligence stood waiting, marked, "Corvigny-Ornequin Railway Service." A few passengers were getting in. Without giving a further thought to a position which events were developing in their own way, he climbed into the diligence.

At the Corvigny railway station he was told that his train would not leave for half an hour and that it was the last, as the evening train, which connected with the night express on the main line, was not running. Paul took his ticket and then asked his way to the jobmaster of the village. He found that the man owned two motor cars and arranged with him to have the larger of the two sent at once to the Château d'Ornequin and placed at Mme. Paul Delroze's disposal.

And he wrote a short note to his wife:

Élisabeth

"Circumstances are so serious that I must ask you to leave Ornequin. The trains have become very uncertain; and I am sending you a motor car which will take you to-night to your aunt at Chaumont. I suppose that the servants will go with you and that, if there should be war (which seems to me very unlikely, in spite of everything), Jérôme and Rosalie will shut up the house and go to Corvigny.

"As for me, I am joining my regiment. Whatever the future may hold in store for us, Élisabeth, I shall never forget the woman who was my bride and who bears my name.

PAUL DELROZE

IV

A Letter from Élisabeth

It was nine o'clock; there was no holding the position; and the colonel was furious.

He had brought his regiment in the middle of the night—it was in the first month of the war, on the 22nd of August, 1914—to the junction of those three roads one of which ran from Belgian Luxemburg. The Germans had taken possession of the lines of the frontier, seven or eight miles away, on the day before. The general commanding the division had expressly ordered that they were to hold the enemy in check until mid-day, that is to say, until the whole division was able to come up with them. The regiment was supported by a battery of seventy-fives.

The colonel had drawn up his men in a dip in the ground. The battery was likewise hidden. And yet, at the first gleams of dawn, both regiment and battery were located by the enemy and lustily shelled.

They moved a mile or more to the right. Five minutes later the shells fell and killed half a dozen men and two officers.

A fresh move was effected, followed in ten minutes by a fresh attack. The colonel pursued his tactics. In an hour there were thirty men killed or wounded. One of the guns was destroyed. And it was only nine o'clock.

"Damn it all!" cried the colonel. "How can they spot us like this? There's witchcraft in it."

He was hiding, with his majors, the captain of artillery and a few dispatch-riders, behind a bank from above which the eye took in a rather large stretch of undulating upland. At no great distance, on the left, was an abandoned village, with some scattered farms in front of it, and there was not an enemy to be seen in all that deserted extent of country. There was nothing to show where the hail of shells was coming from. The seventy-fives had "searched" one or two points with no result. The firing continued.

"Three more hours to hold out," growled the colonel. "We shall do it; but we shall lose a quarter of the regiment."

At that moment a shell whistled between the officers and the dispatch-riders and plumped down into the ground. All sprang back, awaiting the explosion. But one man, a corporal, ran forward, lifted the shell and examined it.

"You're mad, corporal!" roared the colonel. "Drop that shell and be quick about it."

The corporal replaced the projectile quietly in the hole which it had made; and then without hurrying, went up to the colonel, brought his heels together and saluted:

"Excuse me, sir, but I wanted to see by the fuse how far off the enemy's guns are. It's two miles and fifty yards. That may be worth knowing."

"By Jove! And suppose it had gone off?"

"Ah, well, sir, nothing venture, nothing have!"

"True, but, all the same, it was a bit thick! What's your name?"

"Paul Delroze, sir, corporal in the third company."

"Well, Corporal Delroze, I congratulate you on your pluck and I dare say you'll soon have your sergeant's stripes. Meanwhile, take my advice and don't do it again. . ."

He was interrupted by the sudden bursting of a shrapnel-shell. One of the dispatch-riders standing near him fell, hit in the chest, and an officer staggered under the weight of the earth that spattered against him.

"Come," said the colonel, when things had restored themselves, "there's nothing to do but bow before the storm. Take the best shelter you can find; and let's wait."

Paul Delroze stepped forward once more.

"Forgive me, sir, for interfering in what's not my business; but we might, I think, avoid. . ."

"Avoid the peppering? Of course, I have only to change our position again. But, as we should be located again at once. . . There, my lad, go back to your place."

Paul insisted:

"It might be a question, sir, not of changing our position, but of changing the enemy's fire."

"Really!" said the colonel, a little sarcastically, but nevertheless impressed by Paul's coolness. "And do you know a way of doing it?"

"Yes, sir."

"What do you mean?"

"Give me twenty minutes, sir, and by that time the shells will be falling in another direction."

The colonel could not help smiling:

"Capital! You'll make them drop where you please, I suppose?"

"Yes, sir."

"On that beet-field over there, fifteen hundred yards to the right?"

"Yes, sir."

The artillery-captain, who had been listening to the conversation, made a jest in his turn:

"While you are about it, corporal, as you have already given me the distance and I know the direction more or less, couldn't you give it to me exactly, so that I may lay my guns right and smash the German batteries?"

"That will be a longer job, sir, and much more difficult," said Paul. "Still, I'll try. If you don't mind examining the horizon, at eleven o'clock precisely, towards the frontier, I'll let off a signal."

"What sort of signal?"

"I don't know, sir. Three rockets, I expect."

"But your signal will be no use unless you send it off immediately above the enemy's position."

"Just so, sir."

"And, to do that, you'll have to know it."

"I shall, sir."

"And to get there."

"I shall get there, sir."

Paul saluted, turned on his heel and, before the officers had time either to approve or to object, he slipped along the foot of the slope at a run, plunged on the left down a sort of hollow way, with bristling edges of brambles, and disappeared from sight.

"That's a queer fellow," said the colonel. "I wonder what he really means to do."

The young soldier's pluck and decision disposed the colonel in his favor; and, though he felt only a limited confidence in the result of the enterprise, he could not help looking at his watch, time after time, during the minutes which he spent with his officers, behind the feeble rampart of a hay-stack. They were terrible minutes, in which the commanding officer did not think for a moment of the danger that threatened himself, but only of the danger of the men in his charge, whom he looked upon as children.

He saw them around him, lying at full length on the stubble, with their knapsacks over their heads, or snugly ensconced in the copses, or squatting in the hollows in the ground. The iron hurricane increased in violence. It came rushing down like a furious hail bent upon hastily completing its work of destruction. Men suddenly leapt to their feet, spun on their heels and fell motionless, amid the yells of the wounded, the shouts of the soldiers exchanging remarks and even jokes and, over everything, the incessant thunder of the bursting bomb-shells.

And then, suddenly, silence! Total, definite silence, an infinite lull in the air and on the ground, giving a sort of ineffable relief!

The colonel expressed his delight by bursting into a laugh:

"By Jupiter, Corporal Delroze knows his way about! The crowning achievement would be for the beet-field to be shelled, as he promised."

He had not finished speaking when a shell exploded fifteen hundred yards to the right, not in the beet-field, but a little in front of it. The second went too far. The third found the spot. And the bombardment began with a will.

There was something about the performance of the task which the corporal had set himself that was at once so astounding and so mathematically accurate that the colonel and his officers had hardly a doubt that he would carry it out to the end and that, notwithstanding the insurmountable obstacles, he would succeed in giving the signal agreed upon.

They never ceased sweeping the horizon with their field-glasses, while the enemy redoubled his efforts against the beet-field.

At five minutes past eleven, a red rocket went up. It appeared a good deal farther to the right than they would have suspected. And it was followed by two others.

Through his telescope the artillery-captain soon discovered a church-steeple that just showed above a valley which was itself invisible among the rise and fall of the plateau; and the spire of the steeple protruded so very little that it might well have been taken for a tree standing by itself. A rapid glance at the map showed that it was the village of Brumoy.

Knowing, from the shell examined by the corporal, the exact distance of the German batteries, the captain telephoned his instructions to his lieutenant. Half an hour later the German batteries were silenced; and as a fourth rocket had gone up the seventy-fives continued to bombard the church as well as the village and its immediate neighborhood.

At a little before twelve, the regiment was joined by a cyclists company riding ahead of the division. The order was given to advance at all costs.

The regiment advanced, encountering no resistance, as it approached Brumoy, except a few rifle shots. The enemy's rearguard was falling back.

The village was in ruins, with some of its houses still burning, and displayed a most incredible disorder of corpses, of wounded men, of dead horses, demolished guns and battered caissons and baggage-wagons. A whole brigade had been surprised at the moment, when, feeling certain that it had cleared the ground, it was about to march to the attack.

But a shout came from the top of the church, the front and nave of which had fallen in and presented an appearance of indescribable chaos. Only the tower, perforated by gun-fire and blackened by the smoke from some burning joists, still remained standing, bearing by some miracle of equilibrium, the slender stone spire with which it was crowned. With his body leaning out of this spire was a peasant, waving his arms and shouting to attract attention.

The officers recognized Paul Delroze.

Picking their way through the rubbish, our men climbed the staircase that led to the platform of the tower. Here, heaped up against the little door admitting to the spire, were the bodies of eight Germans; and the door, which was demolished and had dropped crosswise, barred the entrance in such a way that it had to be chopped to pieces before Paul could be released.

Toward the end of the afternoon, when it was manifest that the obstacles to the pursuit of the enemy were too serious to be overcome, the colonel embraced Corporal Delroze in front of the regiment mustered in the square.

"Let's speak of your reward first," he said. "I shall recommend you for the military medal; and you will be sure to get it. And now, my lad, tell your story."

And Paul stood answering questions in the middle of the circle formed around him by the officers and the non-commissioned officers of each company.

"Why, it's very simple, sir," he said. "We were being spied upon."

"Obviously; but who was the spy and where was he?"

"I learnt that by accident. Beside the position which we occupied this morning, there was a village, was there not, with a church?"

"Yes, but I had the village evacuated when I arrived; and there was no one in the church."

"If there was no one in the church, sir, why did the weather-vane point the wind coming from the east, when it was blowing from the west? And why, when we changed our position, was the vane pointed in our direction?"

"Are you sure of that?"

"Yes, sir. And that was why, after obtaining your leave, I did not hesitate to slip into the church and to enter the steeple as stealthily as I could. I was not mistaken. There was a man there whom I managed to overmaster, not without difficulty."

"The scoundrel! A Frenchman?"

"No, sir, a German dressed up as a peasant."

"He shall be shot."

"No, sir, please. I promised him his life."

"Never!"

"Well, you see, sir, I had to find out how he was keeping the enemy informed."

"Well?"

"Oh, it was simple enough! The church has a clock, facing the north, of which we could not see the dial, where we were. From the inside, our friend worked the hands so that the big hand, resting by turns on three or four figures, announced the exact distance at which we were from the church, in the direction pointed by the vane. This is what I next did myself; and the enemy at once, redirecting his fire by my indications, began conscientiously to shell the beet-field."

"He did," said the colonel, laughing.

"All that remained for me to do was to move on to the other observation-post, where the spy's messages were received. There I would learn the essential details which the spy himself did not know; I mean, where the enemy's batteries were hidden. I therefore ran to this place; and it was only on arriving here that I saw those batteries and a whole German brigade posted at the very foot of the church which did the duty of signaling-station."

"But that was a mad piece of recklessness! Didn't they fire on you?"

"I had put on the spy's clothes, sir, *their* spy's. I can speak German, I knew the pass-word and only one of them knew the spy and that was the officer on observation-duty. Without the least suspicion, the general commanding the brigade sent me to him as soon as I told him that the French had discovered me and that I had managed to escape them."

"And you had the cheek. . . ?"

"I had to, sir; and besides I held all the trump cards. The officer suspected nothing; and, when I reached the platform from which he was sending his signals, I had no difficulty in attacking him and reducing him to silence. My business was done and I had only to give you the signals agreed upon."

"Only that! In the midst of six or seven thousand men!"

"I had promised you, sir, and it was eleven o'clock. The platform had on it all the apparatus required for sending day or night signals. Why shouldn't I use it? I lit a rocket, followed by a second and a third and then a fourth; and the battle commenced."

"But those rockets were indications to draw our fire upon the very steeple where you were! It was you we were firing on!"

"Oh, I assure you, sir, one doesn't think of those things at such moments! I welcomed the first shell that struck the church. And then the enemy left me hardly any time for reflection. Half-a-dozen fellows at once came climbing the tower. I accounted for some of them with my revolver; but a second assault came and, later on, still another. I had to take refuge behind the door that closes the spire. When they had broken it down, it served me as a barricade; and, as I had the arms and ammunition which I had taken from my first assailants and was inaccessible and very nearly invisible, I found it easy to sustain a regular siege."

"While our seventy-fives were blazing away at you."

"While our seventy-fives were releasing me, sir; for you can understand that, once the church was destroyed and the nave in flames, no one dared to venture up the tower. I had nothing to do, therefore, but wait patiently for your arrival."

Paul Delroze had told his story in the simplest way and as though it concerned perfectly natural things. The colonel, after congratulating him again, confirmed his promotion to the rank of sergeant and said:

"Have you nothing to ask me?"

"Yes, sir, I should like to put a few more questions to the German spy whom I left behind me and, at the same time, to get back my uniform, which I hid."

"Very well, you shall dine here and we'll give you a bicycle afterwards."

Paul was back at the first church by seven o'clock in the evening. A great disappointment awaited him. The spy had broken his bonds and fled.

All Paul's searching, in the church and village, was useless. Nevertheless, on one of the steps of the staircase, near the place where he had flung himself upon the spy, he picked up the dagger with which his adversary had tried to strike him. It was exactly similar to the dagger which he had picked up in the grass, three weeks before, outside the little gate in the Ornequin woods. It had the same three-cornered blade, the same brown horn handle and, on the handle, the same four letters: H, E, R, M.

The spy and the woman who bore so strange a resemblance to Hermine d'Andeville, his father's murderess, both made use of an identical weapon.

NEXT DAY, THE DIVISION TO which Paul's regiment belonged continued the offensive and entered Belgium after repulsing the enemy. But in the evening the general received orders to fall back.

The retreat began. Painful as it was to one and all, it was doubly so perhaps to those of our troops which had been victorious at the start. Paul and his comrades in the third company could not contain themselves for rage and disappointment. During the half a day which they spent in Belgium, they saw the ruins of a little town that had been destroyed by the Germans, the bodies of eighty women who had been shot, old men hung up by their feet, stacks of murdered children. And they had to retire before those monsters!

Some of the Belgian soldiers had attached themselves to the regiment; and, with faces that still bore traces of horror at the infernal visions which they had beheld, these men told of things beyond the conception of the most vivid imagination. And our fellows had to retire. They had to retire with hatred in their hearts and a mad desire for vengeance that made their hands close fiercely on their rifles.

And why retire? It was not a question of being defeated, because they were falling back in good order, making sudden halts and delivering violent counter-attacks upon the disconcerted enemy. But his numbers overpowered all resistance. The wave of barbarians reformed itself. The place of each thousand dead was taken by two thousand of the living. And our men retired.

One evening, Paul learnt one of the reasons for this retreat from a week-old newspaper; and he was painfully affected by the news. On the 20th of August, Corvigny had been taken by assault, after some hours of bombardment effected under the most inexplicable conditions, whereas the stronghold was believed to be capable of holding out for at least some days, which would have strengthened our operations against the left flank of the Germans.

So Corvigny had fallen; and the Château d'Ornequin, doubtless abandoned, as Paul himself hoped, by Jérôme and Rosalie, was now destroyed, pillaged and sacked with the methodical thoroughness which the Huns applied to their work of devastation. On this side, too, the furious horde were crowding precipitately.

Those were sinister days, at the end of August, the most tragic days perhaps that France has ever passed through. Paris was threatened, a dozen departments were invaded. Death's icy breath hung over our gallant nation.

It was on the morning of one of these days that Paul heard a cheerful voice calling to him from a group of young soldiers behind him:

"Paul, Paul! I've got my way at last! Isn't it a stroke of luck?"

Those young soldiers were lads who had enlisted voluntarily and been drafted into the regiment; and Paul at once recognized Élisabeth's brother, Bernard d'Andeville. He had no time to think of the attitude which he had best take up. His first impulse would have been to turn away; but Bernard had seized his two hands and was pressing them with an affectionate kindness which showed that the boy knew nothing as yet of the breach between Paul and his wife.

"Yes, it's myself, old chap," he declared gaily. "I may call you old chap, mayn't I? It's myself and it takes your breath away, what? You're thinking of a providential meeting, the sort of coincidence one never sees: two brothers-in-law dropping into the same regiment. Well, it's not that: it happened at my express request. I said to the authorities, 'I'm enlisting by way of a duty and pleasure combined,' or words to that effect. 'But, as a crack athlete and a prize-winner in every gymnastic and drill-club I ever joined, I want to be sent to the front straight away and into the same regiment as my brother-in-law, Corporal Paul Delroze.' And, as they couldn't do without my services, they packed me off here. . . Well? You don't look particularly delighted. . . ?"

Paul was hardly listening. He said to himself:

"This is the son of Hermine d'Andeville. The boy who is now touching me is the son of the woman who killed. . ."

But Bernard's face expressed such candor and such open-hearted pleasure at seeing him that he said:

"Yes, I am. Only you're so young!"

MAURICE LEBLANC

"I? I'm quite ancient. Seventeen the day I enlisted."

"But what did your father say?"

"Dad gave me leave. But for that, of course, I shouldn't have given him leave."

"What do you mean?"

"Why, he's enlisted, too."

"At his age?"

"Nonsense, he's quite juvenile. Fifty the day he enlisted! They found him a job as interpreter with the British staff. All the family under arms, you see. . . Oh, I was forgetting, I've a letter for you from Élisabeth!"

Paul started. He had deliberately refrained from asking after his wife. He now said, as he took the letter:

"So she gave you this. . . ?"

"No, she sent it to us from Ornequin."

"From Ornequin? How can she have done that? Élisabeth left Ornequin on the day of mobilization, in the evening. She was going to Chaumont, to her aunt's."

"Not at all. I went and said good-bye to our aunt: she hadn't heard from Élisabeth since the beginning of the war. Besides, look at the envelope: 'M. Paul Delroze, care of M. d'Andeville, Paris, etc.' And it's post-marked Ornequin and Corvigny."

Paul looked and stammered:

"Yes, you're right; and I can read the date on the post-mark: 18 August. The 18th of August. . . and Corvigny fell into the hands of the Germans two days later, on the 20th. So Élisabeth was still there."

"No, no," cried Bernard, "Élisabeth isn't a child! You surely don't think she would have waited for the Huns, so close to the frontier! She would have left the château at the first sound of firing. And that's what she's telling you, I expect. Why don't you read her letter, Paul?"

Paul, on his side, had no idea of what he was about to learn on reading the letter; and he opened the envelope with a shudder.

What Élisabeth wrote was:

Paul,

"I cannot make up my mind to leave Ornequin. A duty keeps me here in which I shall not fail, the duty of clearing my mother's memory. Do understand me, Paul. My mother remains the purest of creatures in my eyes. The woman who nursed me in her arms, for whom my father retains all his love, must not be even suspected. But you yourself accuse her; and it is against you that I wish to defend her. To compel you to believe me, I shall find the proofs that are not necessary to convince me. And it seems to me that those proofs can only be found here. So I shall stay.

"Jérôme and Rosalie are also staying on, though the enemy is said to be approaching. They have brave hearts, both of them, and you have nothing to fear, as I shall not be alone.

Élisabeth Delroze

Paul folded up the letter. He was very pale.

Bernard asked:

"She's gone, hasn't she?"

"No, she's there."

"But this is madness! What, with those beasts about! A lonely country-house! . . . But look here, Paul, she must surely know the terrible dangers that threaten her! . . . What can be keeping her there? Oh, it's too dreadful to think of. . ."

Paul stood silent, with a drawn face and clenched fists. . .

V

The Peasant-Woman at Corvigny

Three weeks before, on hearing that war was declared, Paul had felt rising within him the immediate resolution to get killed at all costs. The tragedy of his life, the horror of his marriage with a woman whom he still loved in his heart, the certainty which he had acquired at the Château d'Ornequin: all this had affected him to such a degree that he came to look upon death as a boon. To him, war represented, from the first and without the least demur, death. However much he might admire the solemnly impressive and magnificently consoling events of those first few weeks—the perfect order of the mobilization, the enthusiasm of the soldiers, the wonderful unity that prevailed in France, the awakening of the souls of the nation—none of these great spectacles attracted his attention. Deep down within himself he had determined that he would perform acts of such kind that not even the most improbable hazard could succeed in saving him.

Thus he thought that he had found the desired occasion on the first day. To overmaster the spy whose presence he suspected in the church steeple and then to penetrate to the very heart of the enemy's lines, in order to signal the position, meant going to certain death. He went bravely. And, as he had a very clear sense of his mission, he fulfilled it with as much prudence as courage. He was ready to die, but to die after succeeding. And he found a strange unexpected joy in the act itself as well as in the success that attended it.

The discovery of the dagger employed by the spy made a great impression on him. What connection did it establish between this man and the one who had tried to stab him? What was the connection between these two and the Comtesse d'Andeville, who had died sixteen years ago? And how, by what invisible links, were they all three related to that same work of treachery and spying of which Paul had surprised so many instances?

But Élisabeth's letter, above all, came upon him as a very violent blow. She was over there, amidst the bullets and the shells, the hot fighting around the château, the madness and the fury of the victors, the burning, the shooting, the torturing and atrocities! She was there, she so young and beautiful, almost alone, with no one to defend her! And she was there because he, Paul, had not had the grit to go back to her and see her once more and take her away with him!

These thoughts produced in Paul fits of depression from which he would suddenly awaken to thrust himself in the path of some danger, pursuing his mad enterprises to the end, come what might, with a quiet courage and a fierce obstinacy that filled his comrades with both surprise and admiration. And from that time onward he seemed to be seeking not so much death as the unspeakable ecstasy which a man feels in defying it.

Then came the 6th of September, the day of the unheard-of miracle when our great general-in-chief, addressing his armies in words that will never perish, at last ordered them to fling themselves upon the enemy. The gallantly-borne but cruel retreat came to an end. Exhausted, breathless, fighting against odds for days, with no time for sleep, with no time to eat, marching only by force of prodigious efforts of which they were not even conscious, unable to say why they did not lie down in the road-side ditches to await death, such were the men who received the word of command:

"Halt! About face! And now have at the enemy!"

And they faced about. Those dying men recovered their strength. From the humblest to the most illustrious, each summoned up his will and fought as though the safety of France depended upon him alone. There were as many glorious heroes as there were soldiers. They were asked to conquer or die. They conquered.

Paul shone in the front rank of the fearless. He himself knew that what he did and what he endured, what he tried to do and what he succeeded in doing surpassed the limits of reality. On the 6th and the 7th and the 8th and again from the 11th to the 13th, despite his excessive fatigue, despite the deprivations of sleep and food which it seemed impossible for the human frame to resist, he had no other sensation than that of advancing and again advancing—and always advancing. Whether in sunshine or in shade, whether on the banks of the Marne or on the woody slopes of the Argonne, whether north or east, when his division was sent to reinforce the troops on the frontier, whether lying flat and creeping along in the plowed fields or on his feet and charging with the bayonet, he was always going forward and each step was a delivery and each step was a conquest.

Each step also increased the hatred in his heart. Oh, how right his father had been to loathe those people! Paul now saw them at work.

On every side were stupid devastation and unreasoning destruction, on every side arson, pillage and death, hostages shot, women murdered, bestially, for the love of the thing. Churches, country-houses, mansions of the rich and cabins of the poor: nothing remained. The very ruins had been razed to the ground, the very corpses tortured.

O the delight of defeating such an enemy! Though reduced to half its full strength, Paul's regiment, released like a pack of hounds, never ceased biting at the wild beast which it was hunting. The quarry seemed more vicious and formidable the nearer it approached to the frontier; and our men kept rushing at it in the mad hope of giving it the death-stroke.

One day Paul read on a sign-post at a cross-roads:

> Corvigny, 14 Kil.
> Ornequin, 31 Kil. 400.
> The Frontier, 33 Kil. 200.

Corvigny! Ornequin! A thrill passed through his frame when he saw those unexpected words. As a rule, absorbed as he was by the heat of the conflict and by his private cares, he paid little attention to the names of the places which he passed; and he learnt them only by chance. And now suddenly he was within so short a distance of the Château d'Ornequin! "Corvigny, 14 kilometers:" less than nine miles! . . . Were the French troops making for Corvigny, for the little fortified place which the Germans had taken by assault and taken under such strange conditions?

That day, they had been fighting since daylight against an enemy whose resistance seemed to grow slacker and slacker. Paul, at the head of a squad of men, was sent to the village of Bléville with orders to enter it if the enemy had retired, but go no farther. And it was just beyond the last houses of the village that he saw the sign-post.

At the time, he was not quite easy in his mind. A Taube had flown over the country a few minutes before. There was the possibility of an ambush.

"Let's go back to the village," he said. "We'll barricade ourselves while we wait."

But there was a sudden noise behind a wooded hill that interrupted the road in the Corvigny direction, a noise that became more and more definite, until Paul recognized the powerful throb of a motor, doubtless a motor carrying a quick-firing gun.

"Crouch down in the ditch," he cried to his men. "Hide yourselves in the haystacks. Fix bayonets. And don't move any of you!"

He had realized the danger of that motor's passing through the village, plunging in the midst of his company, scattering panic and then making off by some other way.

He quickly climbed the split trunk of an old oak and took up his position in the branches a few feet above the road.

The motor soon came in sight. It was, as he expected, an armored car, but one of the old pattern, which allowed the helmets and heads of the men to show above the steel plating.

It came along at a smart pace, ready to dart forward in case of alarm. The men were stooping with bent backs. Paul counted half-a-dozen of them. The barrels of two Maxim guns projected beyond the car.

He put his rifle to his shoulder and took aim at the driver, a fat Teuton with a scarlet face that seemed dyed with blood. Then, when the moment came, he calmly fired.

"Charge, lads!" he cried, as he scrambled down from his tree.

But it was not even necessary to take the car by storm. The driver, struck in the chest, had had the presence of mind to apply the brakes and pull up. Seeing themselves surrounded, the Germans threw up their hands:

"*Kamerad! Kamerad!*"

And one of them, flinging down his arms, leapt from the motor and came running up to Paul:

"An Alsatian, sergeant, an Alsatian from Strasburg! Ah, sergeant, many's the day that I've been waiting for this moment!"

While his men were taking the prisoners to the village, Paul hurriedly questioned the Alsatian:

"Where has the car come from?"

"Corvigny."

"Any of your people there?"

"Very few. A rearguard of two hundred and fifty Badeners at the most."

"And in the forts?"

"About the same number. They didn't think it necessary to mend the turrets and now they've been taken unprepared. They're hesitating whether to try and make a stand or to fall back on the frontier; and that's why we were sent to reconnoiter."

"So we can go ahead?"

"Yes, but at once, else they will receive powerful reinforcements, two divisions."

"When?"

"To-morrow. They're to cross the frontier, to-morrow, about the middle of the day."

"By Jove! There's no time to be lost!" said Paul.

While examining the guns and having the prisoners disarmed and searched, Paul was considering the best measures to take, when one of his men, who had stayed behind in the village, came and told him of the arrival of a French detachment, with a lieutenant in command.

Paul hastened to tell the officer what had happened. Events called for immediate action. He offered to go on a scouting expedition in the captured motor.

"Very well," said the officer. "I'll occupy the village and arrange to have the division informed as soon as possible."

The car made off in the direction of Corvigny, with eight men packed inside. Two of them, placed in charge of the quick-firing guns, studied the mechanism. The Alsatian stood up, so as to show his helmet and uniform clearly, and scanned the horizon on every side.

All this was decided upon and done in the space of a few minutes, without discussion and without delaying over the details of the undertaking.

"We must trust to luck," said Paul, taking his seat at the wheel. "Are you ready to see the job through, boys?"

"Yes; and further," said a voice which he recognized, just behind him.

It was Bernard d'Andeville, Élisabeth's brother. Bernard belonged to the 9th company; and Paul had succeeded in avoiding him, since their first meeting, or at least in not speaking to him. But he knew that the youngster was fighting well.

"Ah, so you're there?" he said.

"In the flesh," said Bernard. "I came along with my lieutenant; and, when I saw you getting into the motor and taking any one who turned up, you can imagine how I jumped at the chance!" And he added, in a more embarrassed tone, "The chance of doing a good stroke of work, under your orders, and the chance of talking to you, Paul. . . for I've been unlucky so far. . . I even thought that. . . that you were not as well-disposed to me as I hoped. . ."

"Nonsense," said Paul. "Only I was bothered. . ."

"You mean, about Élisabeth?"

"Yes."

"I see. All the same, that doesn't explain why there was something between us, a sort of constraint. . ."

At that moment, the Alsatian exclaimed:

"Lie low there! . . . Uhlans ahead! . . ."

A patrol came trotting down a cross-road, turning the corner of a wood. He shouted to them, as the car passed:

"Clear out, Kameraden! Fast as you can! The French are coming!"

Paul took advantage of the incident not to answer his brother-in-law. He had forced the pace; and the motor was now thundering along, scaling the hills and shooting down them like a meteor.

The enemy detachments became more numerous. The Alsatian called out to them or else by means of signs incited them to beat an immediate retreat.

"It's the funniest thing to see," he said, laughing. "They're all galloping behind us like mad." And he added, "I warn you, sergeant, that at this rate we shall dash right into Corvigny. Is that what you want to do?"

"No," replied Paul, "we'll stop when the town's in sight."

"And, if we're surrounded?"

"By whom? In any case, these bands of fugitives won't be able to oppose our return."

Bernard d'Andeville spoke:

"Paul," he said, "I don't believe you're thinking of returning."

"You're quite right. Are you afraid?"

"Oh, what an ugly word!"

But presently Paul went on, in a gentler voice:

"I'm sorry you came, Bernard."

"Is the danger greater for me than for you and the others?"

"No."

"Then do me the honor not to be sorry."

Still standing up and leaning over the sergeant, the Alsatian pointed with his hand:

"That spire straight ahead, behind the trees, is Corvigny. I calculate that, by slanting up the hills on the left, we ought to be able to see what's happening in the town."

"We shall see much better by going inside," Paul remarked. "Only it's a big risk. . . especially for you, Alsatian. If they take you prisoner, they'll shoot you. Shall I put you down this side of Corvigny?"

"You haven't studied my face, sergeant."

The road was now running parallel with the railway. Soon, the first houses of the outskirts came in sight. A few soldiers appeared.

"Not a word to these," Paul ordered. "It won't do to startle them. . . or they'll take us from behind at the critical moment."

He recognized the station and saw that it was strongly held. Spiked helmets were coming and going along the avenues that led to the town.

"Forward!" cried Paul. "If there's any large body of troops, it can only be in the square. Are the guns ready? And the rifles? See to mine for me, Bernard. And, at the first signal, independent fire!"

The motor rushed at full speed into the square. As he expected, there were about a hundred men there, all massed in front of the church-steps, near their stacked rifles. The church was a mere heap of ruins; and almost all the houses in the square had been leveled to the ground by the bombardment.

The officers, standing on one side, cheered and waved their hands on seeing the motor which they had sent out to reconnoiter and whose return they seemed to be expecting before making their decision about the defense of the town. There were a good many of them, their number no doubt including some communication officers. A general stood a head and shoulders above the rest. A number of cars were waiting some little distance away.

The street was paved with cobble-stones and there was no raised pavement between it and the square. Paul followed it; but, when he was within twenty yards of the officers, he gave a violent turn of the wheel and the terrible machine made straight for the group, knocking them down and running over them, slanted off slightly, so as to take the stacks of rifles, and then plunged like an irresistible mass right into the middle of the detachment, spreading death as it went, amid a mad, hustling flight and yells of pain and terror.

"Independent fire!" cried Paul, stopping the car.

And the firing began from this impregnable blockhouse, which had suddenly sprung up in the center of the square, accompanied by the sinister crackle of the two Maxim guns.

In five minutes, the square was strewn with killed and wounded men. The general and several officers lay dead. The survivors took to their heels.

Paul gave the order to cease fire and took the car to the top of the avenue that led to the station. The troops from the station were hastening up, attracted by the shooting. A few volleys from the guns dispersed them.

Paul drove three times quickly round the square, to examine the approaches. On every side the enemy was fleeing along the roads and paths to the frontier. And on every hand the inhabitants of Corvigny came out of their houses and gave vent to their delight.

"Pick up and see to the wounded," Paul ordered. "And send for the bell-ringer, or some one who understands about the bells. It's urgent!"

An aged sacristan appeared.

"The tocsin, old man, the tocsin for all you're worth! And, when you're tired, have some one to take your place! The tocsin, without stopping for a second!"

This was the signal which Paul had agreed upon with the French lieutenant, to announce to the division that the enterprise had succeeded and that the troops were to advance.

It was two o'clock. At five, the staff and a brigade had taken possession of Corvigny and our seventy-fives were firing a few shells. By ten o'clock in the evening, the rest of the division having come up meantime, the Germans had been driven out of the Grand Jonas and the Petit Jonas and were concentrating before the frontier. It was decided to dislodge them at daybreak.

"Paul," said Bernard to his brother-in-law, at the evening roll-call, "I have something to tell you, something that puzzles me, a very queer thing: you'll judge for yourself. Just now, I was walking down one of the streets near the church when a woman spoke to me. I couldn't make out her face or her dress at first, because it was almost dark, but she seemed to be a peasant-woman from the sound of her wooden shoes on the cobbles. 'Young man,' she said—and her way of expressing herself surprised me a little in a peasant-woman—'Young man, you may be able to tell me something I want to know.' I said I was at her service and she began, 'It's like this: I live in a little village close by. I heard just now that your army corps was here. So I came, because I wanted to see a soldier who belonged to it, only I don't know the number of his regiment. I believe he has been transferred, because I never get a letter from him; and I dare say he has not had mine. Oh, if you only happened to know him! He's such a good lad, such a gallant fellow.' I asked her to tell me his name; and she answered, 'Delroze, Corporal Paul Delroze.'"

"What!" cried Paul. "Did she want me?"

"Yes, Paul, and the coincidence struck me as so curious that I just gave her the number of your regiment and your company, without telling her that we were related. 'Good,' she said. 'And is the regiment at Corvigny?' I said it had just arrived. 'And do you know Paul Delroze?' 'Only by name,' I answered. I can't tell you why I answered like that, or why I continued the conversation so as not to let her guess my surprise: 'He has been promoted to sergeant,' I said, 'and mentioned in dispatches. That's how I come to have heard his name. Shall I find out where he is and take you to him?' 'Not yet,' she said, 'not yet. I should be too much upset.'"

"What on earth did she mean?"

"I can't imagine. It struck me as more and more suspicious. Here was a woman looking for you eagerly and yet putting off the chance of seeing you. I asked her if she was very much interested in you and she said yes, that you were her son."

"Her son!"

"Up to then I am certain that she did not suspect for a second that I was cross-examining her. But my astonishment was so great that she drew back into the shadow, as though to put herself on the defensive. I slipped my hand into my pocket, pulled out my little electric lamp, went up to her, pressed the spring and flung the light full in her face. She seemed disconcerted and stood for a moment without moving. Then she quickly lowered a scarf which she wore over her head and, with a strength which I should never have believed, struck me on the arm and made me drop my lamp. Then came a second of absolute silence. I couldn't make out where she was: whether in front of me, or on the right or the left. There was no sound to tell me if she was there still or not. But I understood presently, when, after picking up my lamp and switching on the light again, I saw her two wooden shoes on the ground. She had stepped out of them and run away on her stocking-feet. I hunted for her, but couldn't find her. She had disappeared."

Paul had listened to his brother-in-law's story with increasing attention.

"Then you saw her face?" he asked.

"Oh, quite distinctly! A strong face, with black hair and eyebrows and a look of great wickedness. . . Her clothes were those of a peasant-woman, but too clean and too carefully put on: I felt somehow that they were a disguise."

"About what age was she?"

"Forty."

"Would you know her again?"

"Without a moment's hesitation."

"What was the color of the scarf you mentioned?"

"Black."

"How was it fastened? In a knot?"

"No, with a brooch."

"A cameo?"

"Yes, a large cameo set in gold. How did you know that?"

Paul was silent for some time and then said:

"I will show you to-morrow, in one of the rooms at Ornequin, a portrait which should bear a striking resemblance to the woman who spoke to you, the sort of resemblance that exists between two sisters perhaps. . . or. . . or. . ." He took his brother-in-law by the arm and, leading him along, continued, "Listen to me, Bernard. There are terrible things around us, in the present and the past, things that affect my life and Élisabeth's. . . and yours as well. Therefore, I am struggling in the midst of a hideous obscurity in which enemies whom I do not know have for twenty years been pursuing a scheme which I am quite unable to understand. In the beginning of the struggle, my father died, the victim of a murder. To-day it is I that am being threatened. My marriage with your sister is shattered and nothing can bring us together again, just as nothing will ever again allow you and me to be on those terms of friendship and confidence which we had the right to hope for. Don't ask me any questions, Bernard, and don't try to find out any more. One day, perhaps—and I do not wish that day ever to arrive—you will know why I begged for your silence."

VI

What Paul Saw at Ornequin

P aul Delroze was awakened at dawn by the bugle-call. And, in the artillery duel that now began, he at once recognized the sharp, dry voice of the seventy-fives and the hoarse bark of the German seventy-sevens.

"Are you coming, Paul?" Bernard called from his room. "Coffee is served downstairs."

The brothers-in-law had found two little bedrooms over a publican's shop. While they both did credit to a substantial breakfast, Paul told Bernard the particulars of the occupation of Corvigny and Ornequin which he had gathered on the evening before:

"On Wednesday, the nineteenth of August, Corvigny, to the great satisfaction of the inhabitants, still thought that it would be spared the horrors of war. There was fighting in Alsace and outside Nancy, there was fighting in Belgium; but it looked as if the German thrust were neglecting the route of invasion offered by the valley of the Liseron. The fact is that this road is a narrow one and apparently of secondary importance. At Corvigny, a French brigade was busily pushing forward the defense-works. The Grand Jonas and the Petit Jonas were ready under their concrete cupolas. Our fellows were waiting."

"And at Ornequin?" asked Bernard.

"At Ornequin, we had a company of light infantry. The officers put up at the house. This company, supported by a detachment of dragoons, patrolled the frontier day and night. In case of alarm, the orders were to inform the forts at once and to retreat fighting. The evening of Wednesday was absolutely quiet. A dozen dragoons had galloped over the frontier till they were in sight of the little German town of Èbrecourt. There was not a movement of troops to be seen on that side, nor on the railway-line that ends at Èbrecourt. The night also was peaceful. Not a shot was fired. It is fully proved that at two o'clock in the morning not a single German soldier had crossed the frontier. Well, at two o'clock exactly, a violent explosion was heard, followed by four others at close intervals. These explosions were due to the bursting of five four-twenty shells which demolished straightway the three cupolas of the Grand Jonas and the two cupolas of the Petit Jonas."

"What do you mean? Corvigny is fifteen miles from the frontier; and the four-twenties don't carry as far as that!"

"That didn't prevent six more shells falling at Corvigny, all on the church or in the square. And these six shells fell twenty minutes later, that is to say, at the time when it was to be presumed that the alarm would have been given and that the Corvigny garrison would have assembled in the square. This was just what had happened; and you can imagine the carnage that resulted."

"I agree; but, once more, the frontier was fifteen miles away. That distance must have given our troops time to form up again and to prepare for the attacks foretold by the bombardment. They had at least three or four hours before them."

"They hadn't fifteen minutes. The bombardment was not over before the assault began. Assault isn't the word: our troops, those at Corvigny as well as those which hastened up from the two forts, were decimated and routed, surrounded by the enemy, shot down or obliged to surrender, before it was possible to organize any sort of resistance. It all happened suddenly under the blinding glare of flash-lights erected no one knew where or how. And the catastrophe was immediate. You may take it that Corvigny was invested, attacked, captured and occupied by the enemy, all in ten minutes."

"But where did he come from? Where did he spring from?"

"Nobody knows."

"But the night-patrols on the frontier? The sentries? The company on duty at Ornequin?"

"Never heard of again. No one knows anything, not a word, not a rumor, about those three hundred men whose business it was to keep watch and to warn the others. You can reckon up the Corvigny garrison, with the soldiers who escaped and the dead whom the inhabitants identified and buried. But the three hundred light infantry of Ornequin disappeared without leaving the shadow of a trace behind them, not a fugitive, not a wounded man, not a corpse, nothing at all."

"It seems incredible. Whom did you talk to?"

"I saw ten people last night who, for a month, with no one to interfere with them except a few soldiers of the Landsturm placed in charge of Corvigny, have pursued a minute inquiry into all these problems, without establishing so much as a plausible theory. One thing alone is certain: the business was prepared long ago, down to the slightest detail.

The exact range had been taken of the forts, the cupolas, the church and the square; and the siege-gun had been placed in position before and accurately laid so that the eleven shells should strike the eleven objects aimed at. That's all. The rest is mystery."

"And what about the château? And Élisabeth?"

Paul had risen from his seat. The bugles were sounding the morning roll-call. The gun-fire was twice as intense as before. They both started for the square; and Paul continued:

"Here, too, the mystery is bewildering and perhaps worse. One of the cross-roads that run through the fields between Corvigny and Ornequin has been made a boundary by the enemy which no one here had the right to overstep under pain of death."

"Then Élisabeth. . . ?"

"I don't know, I know nothing more. And it's terrible, this shadow of death lying over everything, over every incident. It appears—I have not been able to find out where the rumor originated—that the village of Ornequin, near the château, no longer exists. It has been entirely destroyed, more than that, annihilated; and its four hundred inhabitants have been sent away into captivity. And then. . ." Paul shuddered and, lowering his voice, went on, "And then. . . what did they do at the château? You can see the house, you can still see it at a distance, with its walls and turrets standing. But what happened behind those walls? What has become of Élisabeth? For nearly four weeks she has been living in the midst of those brutes, poor thing, exposed to every outrage! . . ."

The sun had hardly risen when they reached the square. Paul was sent for by his colonel, who gave him the heartiest congratulations of the general commanding the division and told him that his name had been submitted for the military cross and for a commission as second lieutenant and that he was to take command of his section from now.

"That's all," said the colonel, laughing. "Unless you have any further request to make."

"I have two, sir."

"Go ahead."

"First, that my brother-in-law here, Bernard d'Andeville, may be at once transferred to my section as corporal. He's deserved it."

"Very well. And next?"

"My second request is that presently, when we move towards the frontier, my section may be sent to the Château d'Ornequin, which is on the direct route."

"You mean that it is to take part in the attack on the château?"

"The attack?" echoed Paul, in alarm. "Why, the enemy is concentrated along the frontier, four miles from the château!"

"So it was believed, yesterday. In reality, the concentration took place at the Château d'Ornequin, an excellent defensive position where the enemy is hanging desperately while waiting for his reinforcements to come up. The best proof is that he's answering our fire. Look at that shell bursting over there. . . and, farther off, that shrapnel. . . two. . . three of them. Those are the guns which located the batteries which we have set up on the surrounding hills and which are now peppering them like mad. They must have twenty guns there."

"Then, in that case," stammered Paul, tortured by a horrible thought, "in that case, that fire of our batteries is directed at. . ."

"At them, of course. Our seventy-fives have been bombarding the Château d'Ornequin for the last hour."

Paul uttered an exclamation of horror:

"Do you mean to say, sir, that we're bombarding Ornequin? . . ."

And Bernard d'Andeville, standing beside him, repeated, in an anguish-stricken voice:

"Bombarding Ornequin? Oh, how awful!"

The colonel asked, in surprise:

"Do you know the place? Perhaps it belongs to you? Is that so? And are any of your people there?"

"Yes, sir, my wife."

Paul was very pale. Though he made an effort to stand stock-still, in order to master his emotion, his hands trembled a little and his chin quivered.

On the Grand Jonas, three pieces of heavy artillery began thundering, three Rimailho guns, which had been hoisted into position by traction engines. And this, added to the stubborn work of the seventy-fives, assumed a terrible significance after Paul Delroze's words. The colonel and the group of officers around him kept silence. The situation was one of those in which the fatalities of war run riot in all their tragic horror, stronger than the forces of nature themselves and, like them, blind, unjust and implacable. There was nothing to be done. Not one of those men would have dreamt of asking for the gun-fire to cease or to slacken its activity. And Paul did not dream of it, either. He merely said:

"It looks as if the enemy's fire was slowing down. Perhaps they are retreating. . ."

Three shells bursting at the far end of the town, behind the church, belied this hope. The colonel shook his head:

"Retreating? Not yet. The place is too important to them; they are waiting for reinforcements and they won't give way until our regiments take part in the game. . . which won't be long now."

In fact, the order to advance was brought to the colonel a few moments later. The regiment was to follow the road and deploy in the meadows on the right.

"Come along, gentlemen," he said to his officers. "Sergeant Delroze's section will march in front. His objective will be the Château d'Ornequin. There are two little short cuts. Take both of them."

"Very well, sir."

All Paul's sorrow and rage were intensified in a boundless need for action; when he marched off with his men, he felt an inexhaustible strength, felt capable of conquering the enemy's position all by himself. He moved from one to the other with the untiring hurry of a sheep-dog hustling his flock. He never ceased advising and encouraging his men:

"You're one of the plucky ones, old chap, I know, you're no shirker. . . Nor you either. . . Only you think too much about your skin, you keep grumbling, when you ought to be cheerful. . . Who's downhearted, eh? There's a bit more collar-work to do and we're going to do it without looking behind us, what?"

Overhead, the shells followed their march in the air, whistling and moaning and exploding till they formed a sort of canopy of steel and grape-shot.

"Duck your heads! Lie down flat!" cried Paul.

He himself remained standing, indifferent to the flight of the enemy's shells. But with what terror he listened to our own, those coming from behind, from all the hills hard by, whizzing ahead of them to carry destruction and death. Where would this one fall? And that one, where would its murderous rain of bullets and splinters descend?

He was obsessed with the vision of his wife, wounded, dying, and kept on murmuring her name. For many days now, ever since the day when he learnt that Élisabeth had refused to leave the Château d'Ornequin, he could not think of her without a loving emotion that was never spoilt by any impulse of revolt, any movement of anger. He no longer mingled the detestable memories of the past with the charming reality of his love. When he thought of the hated mother, the image of the daughter no longer appeared before his mind. They were two creatures of a different race, having no connection one with the other. Élisabeth, full of courage, risking her life to obey a duty to which she attached a value greater than her life, acquired in Paul's eyes a singular dignity. She was indeed the woman whom he had loved and cherished, the woman whom he loved still.

Paul stopped. He had ventured with his men into an open piece of ground, probably marked down in advance, which the enemy was now peppering with shrapnel. A number of men were hit.

"Halt!" he cried. "Flat on your stomachs, all of you!"

He caught hold of Bernard:

"Lie down, kid, can't you? Why expose yourself unnecessarily? . . . Stay there. Don't move."

He held him to the ground with a friendly pressure, keeping his arm round Bernard's neck and speaking to him with gentleness, as though he were trying to display to the brother all the affection that rose to his heart for his dear Élisabeth. He forgot the harsh words which he had addressed to Bernard and uttered quite different words, throbbing with a fondness which he had denied the evening before:

"Don't move, youngster. You see, I had no business to bring you with me or to drag you into this hot place. I'm responsible for you and I'm not going to have you hurt."

The fire diminished in intensity. By crawling over the ground, the men reached a double row of poplars which led them, by a gentle ascent, towards a ridge intersected by a hollow road. Paul, on climbing the slope which overlooked the Ornequin plateau, saw the ruins of the village in the distance, with its shattered church, and, farther to the left, a wilderness of trees and stones whence rose the walls of a building. This was the château. On every side around were blazing farmhouses, haystacks and barns.

Behind the section, the French troops were scattering forward in all directions. A battery had taken up its position in the shelter of a wood close by and was firing incessantly. Paul could see the shells bursting over the château and among the ruins.

Unable to bear the sight any longer, he resumed his march at the head of his section. The enemy's guns had ceased thundering, had doubtless been reduced to silence. But, when they were well within two miles of Ornequin, the bullets whistled around them and Paul saw a detachment of Germans falling back upon the village, firing as they went. And the seventy-fives and Rimailhos kept on growling. The din was terrible.

Paul gripped Bernard by the arm and, in a quivering voice, said:

"If anything happens to me, tell Élisabeth that I beg her to forgive me. Do you understand? I beg her to forgive me."

He was suddenly afraid that fate would not allow him to see his wife again; and he realized that he had behaved to her with unpardonable cruelty, deserting her as though she were guilty of a fault which she had not committed and abandoning her to every form of distress and torment. And he walked on briskly, followed at a distance by his men.

But, at the spot where the short cut joins the high road, in sight of the Liseron, a cyclist rode up to him. The colonel had ordered that the section should wait for the main body of the regiment in order to make an attack in full force.

This was the cruelest test of all. Paul, a victim to ever-increasing excitement, trembled with fever and rage.

"Come, Paul," said Bernard, "don't work yourself into such a state! We shall get there in time."

"In time for what?" he retorted. "To find her dead or wounded? Or not to find her at all? Oh, hang it, why can't our guns stop their damned row? What are they shelling, now that the enemy's no longer replying? Dead bodies and demolished houses! . . ."

"What about the rearguard covering the German retreat?"

"Well, aren't we here, the infantry? This is our job. All we have to do is to send out our sharpshooters and follow up with a good bayonet-charge. . ."

At last the section set out again, reinforced by the remainder of the ninth company and under the command of the captain. A detachment of hussars galloped by, pricking towards the village to cut off the fugitives. The company swerved towards the château.

Opposite them, all was silent as the grave. Was it a trap? Was there not every reason to believe that enemy forces, strongly entrenched and barricaded as these were, would prepare to offer a last resistance? And yet there was nothing suspicious in the avenue of old oaks that led to the front court, not a sign of life to be seen or heard.

Paul and Bernard, still keeping ahead, with their fingers on the trigger of their rifles, searched the dim light of the underwood with a keen glance. Columns of smoke rose above the wall, which was now quite near, yawning with breach upon breach. As they approached, they heard moans, followed by the heart-rending sound of a death-rattle. It was the German wounded.

And suddenly the earth shook as though an inner upheaval had shattered its crust and from the other side of the wall came a tremendous explosion, or rather a series of explosions, like so many peals of thunder. The air was darkened with a cloud of sand and dust which sent forth all sorts of stones and rubbish. The enemy had blown up the château.

"That was meant for us, I expect," said Bernard. "We were to have been blown up at the same time. They were out in their calculations."

When they had passed the gate, the sight of the mined court-yard, of the shattered turrets, of the demolished château, of the out-houses in flames, of the dying in their last throes and the thickly stacked corpses of the dead startled them into recoiling.

"Forward! Forward!" shouted the colonel, galloping up. "There are troops that must have made off across the park."

Paul knew the road, which he had covered a few weeks earlier in such tragic circumstances. He rushed across the lawns, among blocks of stone and uprooted trees. But, as he passed in sight of a little lodge that stood at the entrance to the wood, he stopped, nailed to the ground. And Bernard and all the men stood stupefied, opening their mouths wide with horror.

Against the lodge, two corpses rested on their feet, fastened to rings in the wall by a single chain wound round their waists. Their bodies were bent over the chains and their arms hung to the ground.

They were the corpses of a man and a woman. Paul recognized Jérôme and Rosalie. They had been shot.

The chain continued beyond them. There was a third ring in the wall. The plaster was stained with blood and there were visible traces of bullets. There had been a third victim, without a doubt, and the body had been removed.

As he approached, Paul noticed a splinter of bomb-shell embedded in the plaster. Around the hole thus formed, between the plaster and the splinter, was a handful of fair hair with golden lights in it, hair torn from the head of Élisabeth.

VII

H. E. R. M.

Paul's first feeling was an immense need of revenge, then and there, at all costs, a need outweighing any sense of horror or despair. He gazed around him, as though all the wounded men who lay dying in the park were guilty of the monstrous crime:

"The cowards!" he snarled. "The murderers!"

"Are you sure," stammered Bernard, "are you sure it's Élisabeth's hair?"

"Why, of course I am. They've shot her as they shot the two others. I know them both: it's the keeper and his wife. Oh, the blackguards! . . ."

He raised the butt of his rifle over a German dragging himself in the grass and was about to strike him, when the Colonel came up to him:

"Hullo, Delroze, what are you doing? Where's your company?"

"Oh, sir, if you only knew! . . ."

He rushed up to his colonel. He looked like a madman and brandished his rifle as he spoke:

"They've killed her, sir, yes, they've shot my wife. . . Look, against the wall there, with the two people who were in her service. . . They've shot her. . . She was twenty years old, sir. . . Oh, we must kill them all like dogs!"

But Bernard was dragging him away:

"Don't let us waste time, Paul; we can take our revenge on those who are still fighting. . . I hear firing over there. Some of them are surrounded, I expect."

Paul hardly knew what he was doing. He started running again, drunk with rage and grief.

Ten minutes later, he had rejoined his company and was crossing the open space where his father had been stabbed. The chapel was in front of him. Farther on, instead of the little door that used to be in the wall, a great breach had been made, to admit the convoys of wagons for provisioning the castle. Eight hundred yards beyond it, a violent rifle-fire crackled over the fields, at the crossing of the road and the highway.

A few dozen retreating Germans were trying to force their way through the hussars who had come by the high road. They were attacked from behind by Paul's company, but succeeded in taking shelter in a square patch of trees and copsewood, where they defended themselves with fierce energy, retiring step by step and dropping one after the other.

"Why don't they surrender?" muttered Paul, who was firing continually and who was gradually being calmed by the heat of the fray. "You would think they were trying to gain time."

"Look over there!" said Bernard, in a husky voice.

Under the trees, a motor-car had just come from the frontier, crammed with German soldiers. Was it bringing reinforcements? No, the motor turned almost in its own length; and between it and the last of the combatants stood an officer in a long gray cloak, who, revolver in hand, exhorted them to persevere in their resistance, while he himself effected his retreat towards the car sent to his rescue.

"Look, Paul," Bernard repeated, "look!"

Paul was dumfounded. That officer to whom Bernard was calling his attention was. . . but no, it could not be. And yet. . .

"What do you mean to suggest, Bernard?" he asked.

"It's the same face," muttered Bernard, "the same face as yesterday, you know, Paul: the face of the woman who asked me those questions about you, Paul."

And Paul on his side recognized beyond the possibility of a doubt the mysterious individual who had tried to kill him at the little door leading out of the park, the creature who presented such an unconceivable resemblance to his father's murderess, to the woman of the portrait, to Hermine d'Andeville, Élisabeth's mother and Bernard's.

Bernard raised his rifle to fire.

"No, don't do that!" cried Paul, terrified at the movement.

"Why not?"

"Let's try and take him alive."

He darted forward in a mad rush of hatred, but the officer had run to the car. The German soldiers held out their hands and hoisted him into their midst. Paul shot the one who was seated at the wheel. The officer caught hold of it just as the car was about to strike a tree, changed the direction and, skilfully guiding the car past the intervening obstacles, drove it behind a bend in the ground and from there towards the frontier. He was saved.

As soon as he was beyond the range of the bullets, the German soldiers who were still fighting surrendered.

Paul was trembling with impotent fury. To him this individual represented every imaginable form of evil; and, from the first to the last

MAURICE LEBLANC

minute of that long series of tragedies, murders, attempts at spying and assassination, treacheries and deliberate shootings, all conceived with the same object and the same spirit, that one figure stood out as the very genius of crime.

Nothing short of the creature's death would have appeased Paul's hatred. It was he, the monster, Paul never entertained a doubt of it, who had ordered Élisabeth to be shot. Élisabeth shot! Oh, the shame of it! Oh, infernal vision that tormented him! . . .

"Who is he?" he cried. "How can we find out? How can we get at him and torture him and kill him?"

"Question a prisoner," said Bernard.

The captain considered it wiser to advance no farther and ordered the company to fall back, so as to remain in touch with the remainder of the regiment. Paul was told off specially to occupy the château with his section and to take the prisoners there.

He lost no time in questioning two or three non-commissioned officers and some of the soldiers, as they went. But he could obtain nothing but a mass of conflicting particulars from them, for they had arrived from Corvigny the day before and had only spent the night at the château. They did not even know the name of the officer in the flowing gray cloak for whom so many of them had sacrificed their lives. He was called the major; and that was all.

"But still," Paul insisted, "he was your actual commanding officer?"

"No. The leader of the rearguard detachment to which we belong is an Oberleutnant who was wounded by the exploding of the mines, when we ran away. We wanted to take him with us, but the major objected, leveling his revolver at us, telling us to march in front of him and threatening to shoot the first man who left him in the lurch. And just now, while we were fighting, he stood ten paces behind us and kept threatening us with his revolver to compel us to defend him. He shot three of us, as a matter of fact."

"He was reckoning on the assistance of the car, wasn't he?"

"Yes; and also on reinforcements which were to save us all, so he said. But only the car came; and it just saved him."

"The Oberleutnant would know his name, of course. Is he badly wounded?"

"He's got a broken leg. We made him comfortable in a lodge in the park."

"The lodge against which your people put to death. . . those civilians?"

"Yes."

They were nearing the lodge, a sort of little orangery into which the plants were taken in winter. Rosalie and Jérôme's bodies had been removed. But the sinister chain was still hanging on the wall, fastened to the three iron rings; and Paul once more beheld, with a shudder of dread, the marks left by the bullet and the little splinter of bomb-shell that kept Élisabeth's hair embedded in the plaster.

A French bomb-shell! An added horror to the atrocity of the murder!

It was therefore Paul who, on the day before, by capturing the armored motor-car and effecting his daring raid on Corvigny, thus opening the road to the French troops, had brought about the events that ended in his wife's being murdered! The enemy had revenged himself for his retreat by shooting the inhabitants of the château! Élisabeth fastened to the wall by a chain had been riddled with bullets. And, by a hideous irony, her corpse had received in addition the splinters of the first shells which the French guns had fired before night-fall, from the top of the hills near Corvigny.

Paul pulled out the fragments of shell and removed the golden strands, which he put away religiously. He and Bernard then entered the lodge, where the Red Cross men had established a temporary ambulance. They found the Oberleutnant lying on a truss of straw, well looked after and able to answer questions.

One point at once became quite clear, which was that the German troops which had garrisoned the Château d'Ornequin had, so to speak, never been in touch at all with those which, the day before, had retreated from Corvigny and the adjoining forts. The garrison had been evacuated immediately upon the arrival of the fighting troops, as though to avoid any indiscretion on the subject of what had happened during the occupation of the château.

"At that moment," said the Oberleutnant, who belonged to the fighting force, not to the garrison, "it was seven o'clock in the evening. Your seventy-fives had already got the range of the château; and we found no one there but a number of generals and other officers of superior rank. Their baggage-wagons were leaving and their motors were ready to leave. I was ordered to hold out as long as I could to blow up the château. The major had made all the arrangements beforehand."

"What was the major's name?"

"I don't know. He was walking about with a young officer whom even the generals addressed with respect. This same officer called me over to him and charged me to obey the major 'as I would the emperor.'"

"And who was the young officer?"

"Prince Conrad."

"A son of the Kaiser's?"

"Yes. He left the château yesterday, late in the day."

"And did the major spend the night here?"

"I suppose so; at any rate, he was there this morning. We fired the mines and left. . . a bit late, for I was wounded near this lodge. . . near the wall. . ."

Paul mastered his emotion and said:

"You mean, the wall against which your people shot three French civilians, don't you?"

"Yes."

"When were they shot?"

"About six o'clock in the afternoon, I believe, before we arrived from Corvigny."

"Who ordered them to be shot?"

"The major."

Paul felt the perspiration trickling from the top of his head down his neck and forehead. It was as he thought: Élisabeth had been shot by the orders of that nameless and more than mysterious individual whose face was the very image of the face of Hermine d'Andeville, Élisabeth's mother!

He went on, in a trembling voice:

"So there were three people shot? You're quite sure?"

"Yes, the people of the château. They had been guilty of treachery."

"A man and two women?"

"Yes."

"But there were only two bodies fastened to the wall of the lodge."

"Yes, only two. The major had the lady of the house buried by Prince Conrad's orders."

"Where?"

"He didn't tell me."

"But why was she shot?"

"I understand that she had got hold of some very important secrets."

"They could have taken her away and kept her as a prisoner."

"Certainly, but Prince Conrad was tired of her."

Paul gave a start:

"What's that you say?"

The officer resumed, with a smile that might mean anything:

"Well, damn it all, everybody knows Prince Conrad! He's the Don Juan of the family. He'd been staying at the château for some weeks and had time to make an impression, had he not? . . . And then. . . and then to get tired. . . Besides, the major maintained that the woman and her two servants had tried to poison the prince. So you see. . ."

He did not finish his sentence. Paul was bending over him and, with a face distorted with rage, took him by the throat and shouted:

"Another word, you dog, and I'll throttle the life out of you! Ah, you can thank your stars that you're wounded! . . . If you weren't. . . if you weren't. . . !"

And Bernard, beside himself with rage, joined in:

"Yes, you can think yourself lucky. As for your Prince Conrad, he's a swine, let me tell you. . . and I mean to tell *him* so to his face. . . He's a swine like all his beastly family and like the whole lot of you! . . ."

They left the Oberleutnant utterly dazed and unable to understand a word of this sudden outburst. But, once outside, Paul had a fit of despair. His nerves relaxed. All his anger and all his hatred were changed into infinite depression. He could hardly contain his tears.

"Come, Paul," exclaimed Bernard, "surely you don't believe a word. . . ?"

"No, no, and again no! But I can guess what happened. That drunken brute of a prince must have tried to make eyes at Élisabeth and to take advantage of his position. Just think! A woman, alone and defenseless: that was a conquest worth making! What tortures the poor darling must have undergone, what humiliations! . . . A daily struggle, with threats and brutalities. . . And, at the last moment, death, to punish her for her resistance. . ."

"We shall avenge her, Paul," said Bernard, in a low voice.

"We shall; but shall I ever forget that it was on my account, through my fault, that she stayed here? I will explain what I mean later on; and you will understand how hard and unjust I have been. . . And yet. . ."

He stood gloomily thinking. He was haunted by the image of the major and he repeated:

"And yet. . . and yet. . . there are things that seem so strange. . ."

ALL THAT AFTERNOON, FRENCH TROOPS kept streaming in through the valley of the Liseron and the village of Ornequin in order to resist any counter-attack by the enemy. Paul's section was resting; and he and Bernard took advantage of this to make a minute search in the park and among the ruins of the château. But there was no clue to reveal to them where Élisabeth's body lay hidden.

At five o'clock, they gave Rosalie and Jérôme a decent burial. Two crosses were set up on a little mound strewn with flowers. An army chaplain came and said the prayers for the dead. And Paul was moved to tears when he knelt on the grave of those two faithful servants whose devotion had been their undoing.

Then also Paul promised to avenge. And his longing for vengeance evoked in his mind, with almost painful intensity, the hated image of the major, that image which had now become inseparable from his recollections of the Comtesse d'Andeville.

He led Bernard away from the grave and asked:

"Are you sure that you were not mistaken in connecting the major and the supposed peasant-woman who questioned you at Corvigny?"

"Absolutely."

"Then come with me. I told you of a woman's portrait. We will go and look at it and you shall tell me what impression it makes upon you."

Paul had noticed that that part of the castle which contained Hermine d'Andeville's bedroom and boudoir had not been entirely demolished by the explosion of either the mines or shells. It was possible that the boudoir was still in its former condition.

The staircase had been destroyed; and they had to clamber up the shattered masonry in order to reach the first floor. Traces of the corridor were visible here and there. All the doors were gone; and the rooms presented an appearance of pitiful chaos.

"It's here," said Paul, pointing to an open place between two pieces of wall that remained standing as by a miracle.

It was indeed Hermine d'Andeville's boudoir, shattered and dilapidated, cracked from top to bottom and filled with plaster and rubbish, but quite recognizable and containing all the furniture which Paul had noticed on the evening of his marriage. The window-shutters darkened the room partly, but there was enough light for Paul to see the whereabouts of the wall opposite. And he at once exclaimed:

"The portrait has been taken away!"

It was a great disappointment to him and, at the same time, a proof of the great importance which his enemy attached to the portrait, which could only have been removed because it constituted an overwhelming piece of evidence.

"I assure you," said Bernard, "that this does not affect my opinion in the least. There was no need to verify my conviction about the major and that peasant-woman at Corvigny. Whose portrait was it?"

"I told you, a woman."

"What woman? Was it a picture which my father hung there, one of the pictures of his collection?"

"That was it," said Paul, welcoming the opportunity of throwing his brother-in-law off the scent.

Opening one of the shutters, he saw a mark on the wall of the rectangular space which the picture used to occupy; and he was able to perceive, from certain details, that the removal had been effected in a hurry. For instance, the gilt scroll had dropped from the frame and was lying on the floor. Paul picked it up stealthily so that Bernard should not see the inscription engraved upon it.

But, while he was examining the panel more attentively after Bernard had unfastened the other shutter, he gave an exclamation.

"What's the matter?" asked Bernard.

"There. . . look. . . that signature on the wall. . . where the picture was: a signature and a date."

It was written in pencil; two lines across the white plaster, at a man's height. The date, "Wednesday evening, 16 September, 1914," followed by the signature: "Major Hermann."

Major Hermann! Even before Paul was aware of it, his eyes had seized upon a detail in which all the significance of those two lines of writing was concentrated; and, while Bernard came forward to look in his turn, he muttered, in boundless surprise:

"Hermann! . . . Hermine! . . ."

The two words were almost alike. Hermine began with the same letters as the Christian or surname which the major had written, after his rank, on the wall. Major Hermann! The Comtesse Hermine! H, E, R, M: The four letters on the dagger with which Paul had nearly been killed! H, E, R, M: the four letters on the dagger of the spy whom he had captured in the church-steeple!

Bernard said:

"It looks to me like a woman's writing. But, if so. . ." And he continued thoughtfully, "If so. . . what conclusion are we to draw? Either the peasant-woman and Major Hermann are one and the same person, which means that the peasant-woman is a man or that the major is not, or else we are dealing with two distinct persons, a woman and a man. I believe that is how it is, in spite of the uncanny resemblance between that man and that woman. For, after all, how can we suppose that the same person can have written this signature yesterday evening, passed through the French lines and spoken to me at Corvigny disguised as a peasant-woman. . . and then be able to return here, disguised as a German major, blow up the house, take to flight and, after killing some of his own soldiers, make his escape in a motor-car?"

Paul, absorbed by his thoughts, did not answer. Presently he went into the adjoining room, which separated the boudoir from the set of rooms which his wife had occupied. Of these nothing remained except debris. But the room in between had not suffered so very much; and it was very easy to see, by the wash-hand-stand and the condition of the bed, that it was used as a bedroom and that some one had slept in it the night before.

On the table Paul found some German newspapers and a French one, dated 10 September, in which the *communiqué* telling of the great victory of the Marne was struck out with two great dashes in red pencil and annotated with the word "Lies!" followed by the initial H.

"We're in Major Hermann's room right enough," said Paul to Bernard.

"And Major Hermann," Bernard declared, "burnt some compromising papers last night. Look at that heap of ashes in the fire-place." He stooped and picked up a few envelopes, a few half-burnt sheets of paper containing consecutive words, nothing but incoherent sentences. On turning his eyes to the bed, however, he saw under the bolster a parcel of clothes hidden or perhaps forgotten in the hurry of departure. He pulled them out and at once cried: "I say, just look at this!"

"At what?" asked Paul, who was searching another part of the room.

"These clothes, look, peasant clothes, the clothes I saw on the woman at Corvigny. There's no mistaking them: they are the same brown color and the same sort of serge stuff. And then here's the black-lace scarf which I told you about. . ."

"What's that?" exclaimed Paul, running up to him.

"Here, see for yourself, it's a scarf of sorts and not one of the newest, either. How worn and torn it is! And the brooch I described to you is still in it. Do you see?"

Paul had noticed the brooch at once with the greatest horror. What a terrible significance it lent to the discovery of the clothes in the room occupied by Major Hermann, the room next to Hermine d'Andeville's boudoir! The cameo was carved with a swan with its wings outspread and was set in a gold snake with ruby eyes. Paul had known that cameo since his early boyhood, from seeing it in the dress of the woman who killed his father, and he knew it also because he had seen it again, with every smallest detail reproduced, in the Comtesse Hermine's portrait. And now he was finding the actual brooch, stuck in the black-lace scarf among the Corvigny peasant-woman's clothes and left behind in Major Hermann's room!

"This completes the evidence," said Bernard. "The fact that the clothes are here proves that the woman who asked me about you came back here last night; but what is the connection between her and that officer who is her living likeness? Is the person who questioned me about you the same as the individual who ordered Élisabeth to be shot two hours earlier? And who are these people? What band of murderers and spies have we run up against?"

"They are simply Germans," was Paul's reply. "To them spying and murdering are natural and permissible forms of warfare. . . in a war, mark you, which they began and are carrying on in the midst of a perfectly peaceful period. I have told you so before, Bernard: we have been the victims of war for nearly twenty years. My father's murder opened the tragedy. And to-day we are mourning our poor Élisabeth. And that is not the end of it."

"Still," said Bernard, "he has taken to flight."

"We shall see him again, be sure of that. If he doesn't come back, I will go and find him. And, when that day comes. . ."

There were two easy-chairs in the room. Paul and Bernard resolved to spend the night there and, without further delay, wrote their names on the wall of the passage. Then Paul went back to his men, in order to see that they were comfortably settled in the barns and out-houses that remained standing. Here the soldier who served as his orderly, a decent Auvergnat called Gériflour, told him that he had dug out two pairs of sheets and a couple of clean mattresses from a little house next to the guard-room and that the beds were ready. Paul accepted the offer for Bernard and himself. It was arranged that Gériflour and one of his companions should go to the château and sleep in the two easy-chairs.

The night passed without any alarm. It was a feverish and sleepless night for Paul, who was haunted by the thought of Élisabeth. In the morning he fell into a heavy slumber, disturbed by nightmares. The reveille woke him with a start. Bernard was waiting for him.

MAURICE LEBLANC

The roll was called in the courtyard of the château. Paul noticed that his orderly, Gériflour, and the other man were missing.

"They must be asleep," he said to Bernard. "Let's go and shake them awake."

They went back, through the ruins, to the first floor and along the demolished bedroom. In the room which Major Hermann had occupied they found Private Gériflour, huddled on the bed, covered with blood, dead. His friend was lying back in one of the chairs, also dead. There was no disorder, no trace of a struggle around the bodies. The two soldiers must have been killed in their sleep.

Paul at once saw the weapon with which they had been murdered. It was a dagger with the letters H, E, R, M. on the handle.

VIII

Élisabeth's Diary

This double murder, following upon a series of tragic incidents all of which were closely connected, was the climax to such an accumulation of horrors and of shocking disasters that the two young men did not utter a word or stir a limb. Death, whose breath they had already felt so often on the battlefield, had never appeared to them under a more hateful or forbidding guise.

Death! They beheld it, not as an insidious disease that strikes at hazard, but as a specter creeping in the shadow, watching its adversary, choosing its moment and raising its arm with deliberate intention. And this specter bore for them the very shape and features of Major Hermann.

When Paul spoke at last, his voice had the dull, scared tone that seems to summon up the evil powers of darkness:

"He came last night. He came and, as we had written our names on the wall, the names of Bernard d'Andeville and Paul Delroze which represent the names of two enemies in his eyes, he took the opportunity to rid himself of those two enemies. Persuaded that it was you and I who were sleeping in this room, he struck. . . and those whom he struck were poor Gériflour and his friend, who have died in our stead."

After a long pause, he whispered:

"They have died as my father died. . . and as Élisabeth died. . . and the keeper also and his wife; and by the same hand, by the same hand, Bernard, do you understand? . . . Yes, it's inadmissible, is it not? My brain refuses to admit it. . . And yet it is always the same hand that holds the dagger. . . then and now."

Bernard examined the dagger. At the sight of the four letters, he said:

"That stands for Hermann, I suppose? Major Hermann?"

"Yes," said Paul, eagerly. "Is it his real name, though? And who is he actually? I don't know. But what I do know is that the criminal who committed all those murders is the same who signs with these four letters, H, E, R, M."

After giving the alarm to the men of his section and sending to inform the chaplain and the surgeons, Paul resolved to ask for a private interview with his colonel and to tell him the whole of the secret story, hoping that it might throw some light on the execution of Élisabeth and the assassination of the two soldiers. But he learnt that the colonel and his regiment were fighting on the other side of the frontier and that the 3rd Company had been hurriedly sent for, all but a detachment which was to remain at the château under Sergeant Delroze's orders. Paul therefore made his own investigation with his men.

It yielded nothing. There was no possibility of discovering the least clue to the manner in which the murderer had made his way first into the park, next into the ruins and lastly into the bedroom. As no civilian had passed, were they to conclude that the perpetrator of the two crimes was one of the privates of the 3rd company? Obviously not. And yet what other theory was there to adopt?

Nor did Paul discover anything to tell him of his wife's death or of the place where she was buried. And this was the hardest trial of all.

He encountered the same ignorance among the German wounded as among the prisoners. They had all heard of the execution of a man and two women, but they had all arrived after the execution and after the departure of the troops that occupied the château.

He went on to the village, thinking that they might know something there; that the inhabitants had some news to tell of the lady of the château, of the life she led, of her martyrdom and death. But Ornequin was empty, with not a woman even, not an old man left in it. The enemy must have sent all the inhabitants into Germany, doubtless from the start, with the manifest object of destroying every witness to his actions during the occupation and of creating a desert around the château.

Paul in this way devoted three days to the pursuit of fruitless inquiries.

"And yet," he said to Bernard, "Élisabeth cannot have disappeared entirely. Even if I cannot find her grave, can I not find the least trace of her existence? She lived here. She suffered here. I would give anything for a relic of her."

They had succeeded in fixing upon the exact site of the room in which she used to sleep and even, in the midst of the ruins, the exact heap of stones and plaster that remained of it. It was all mixed up with the wreckage of the ground-floor rooms, into which the first-floor ceilings had been precipitated; and it was in this chaos, under the pile of walls and furniture reduced to dust and fragments, that one morning he picked up a little broken mirror, followed by a tortoise-shell hairbrush, a silver pen-knife and a set of scissors, all of which had belonged to Élisabeth.

But what affected him even more was the discovery of a thick diary, in which he knew that his wife, before her marriage, used to note down her expenses, the errands or visits that had to be remembered and, occasionally, some more private details of her life. Now all that was left of her diary was the binding, with the date, 1914, and the part containing the entries for the first seven months of the year. All the sheets for the last five months had been not torn out but removed separately from the strings that fastened them to the binding.

Paul at once thought to himself:

"They were removed by Élisabeth, removed at her leisure, at a time when there was no hurry and when she merely wished to use those pages for writing on from day to day. What would she want to write? Just those more personal notes which she used formerly to put down in her diary between the entry of a disbursement and a receipt. And as there can have been no accounts to keep since my departure and as her existence was nothing but a hideous tragedy, there is no doubt that she confided her distress to those pages, her complaints, possibly her shrinking from me."

That day, in Bernard's absence, Paul increased the thoroughness of his search. He rummaged under every stone and in every hole. The broken slabs of marble, the twisted lustres, the torn carpets, the beams blackened by the flames, he lifted them all. He persisted for hours. He divided the ruins into sections which he examined patiently in rotation; and, when the ruins refused to answer his questions, he renewed his minute investigations in the ground.

His efforts were useless; and Paul knew that they were bound to be so. Élisabeth must have attached far too much value to those pages not to have either destroyed them or hidden them beyond the possibility of discovery. Unless:

"Unless," he said to himself, "they have been stolen from her. The major must have kept a constant watch upon her. And, in that case, who knows?"

An idea occurred to Paul's mind. After finding the peasant-woman's clothes and black lace scarf, he had left them on the bed, attaching no further importance to them; and he now asked himself if the major, on the night when he had murdered the two soldiers, had not come with the intention of fetching away the clothes, or at least the contents of their pockets, which he had not been able to do because they were hidden under Private Gériflour, who was sleeping on the top of them. Now Paul seemed to remember that, when unfolding that peasant's skirt and bodice, he had noticed a rustling of paper in one of the pockets. Was it not reasonable to conclude that this was Élisabeth's diary, which had been discovered and stolen by Major Hermann?

Paul hastened to the room in which the murders had been committed, snatched up the clothes and looked through them:

"Ah," he at once exclaimed, with genuine delight, "here they are!"

There was a large, yellow envelope filled with the pages removed from the diary. These were crumpled and here and there torn; and Paul saw at a glance that the pages corresponded only with the months of August and September and that even some days in each of these months were missing.

And he saw Élisabeth's handwriting.

It was not a full or detailed diary. It consisted merely of notes, poor little notes in which a bruised heart found an outlet. At times, when they ran to greater length, an extra page had been added. The notes had been jotted down by day or night, anyhow, in ink and pencil; they were sometimes hardly legible; and they gave the impression of a trembling hand, of eyes veiled with tears and of a mind crazed with suffering.

Paul was moved to the very depths of his being. He was alone and he read:

Sunday, 2 August

"He ought not to have written me that letter. It is too cruel. And why does he suggest that I should leave Ornequin? The war? Does he think that, because there is a chance of war, I shall not have the courage to stay here and do my duty? How little he knows me! Then he must either think me a coward or believe me capable of suspecting my poor mother! . . . Paul, dear Paul, you ought not to have left me. . .

Monday, 3 August

"Jérôme and Rosalie have been kinder and more thoughtful than ever, now that the servants are gone. Rosalie begged and prayed that I should go away, too.

"'And what about yourselves, Rosalie?' I said. 'Will you go?'

"'Oh, we're people who don't matter, we have nothing to fear! Besides, our place is here.'

"I said that so was mine; but I saw that she could not understand.

"Jérôme, when I meet him, shakes his head and looks at me sadly.

Tuesday, 4 August

"I have not the least doubt of what my duty is. I would rather die than turn my back on it. But how am I to fulfil that duty and get at the truth? I am full of courage; and yet I am always crying, as though I had nothing better to do. The fact is that I am always thinking of Paul. Where is he? What has become of him? When Jérôme told me this morning that war was declared, I thought that I should faint. So Paul is going to fight. He will be wounded perhaps. He may be killed. God knows if my true place is not somewhere near him, in a town close to where he is fighting! What have I to hope for in staying here? My duty to my mother, yes, I know. Ah, mother, I beseech your forgiveness. . . but, you see, I love my husband and I am so afraid of anything happening to him! . . .

Thursday, 6 August

"Still crying. I grow unhappier every day. But I feel that, even if I became still more so, I would not desist. Besides, how can I go to him when he does not want to have anything more to do with me and does not even write? Love me? Why, he loathes me! I am the daughter of a woman whom he hates above all things in the world. How unspeakably horrible! If he thinks like that of my mother and if I fail in my task, we shall never see each other again! That is the life I have before me.

Friday, 7 August

"I have made Jérôme and Rosalie tell me all about mother. They only knew her for a few weeks, but they remember her quite well; and what they said made me feel so happy! She was so good, it seems, and so pretty; everybody worshiped her.

"'She was not always very cheerful,' said Rosalie. 'I don't know if it was her illness already affecting her spirits, but there was something about her, when she smiled, that went to one's heart.'

"My poor, darling mother!

Saturday, 8 August

"We heard the guns this morning, a long way off. They are fighting 25 miles away.

"Some French soldiers have arrived. I had seen some of them pretty often from the terrace, marching down the Liseron Valley. But these are going to stay at the house. The captain made his apologies. So as not to inconvenience me, he and his lieutenants will sleep and have their meals in the lodge where Jérôme and Rosalie used to live.

Sunday, 9 August

"Still no news of Paul. I have given up trying to write to him either. I don't want him to hear from me until I have all the proofs. But what am I to do? How can I get proofs of something that happened seventeen years ago? Hunt about, think and reflect as I may, I can find nothing.

Monday, 10 August

"The guns never ceased booming in the distance. Nevertheless, the captain tells me that there is nothing to make one expect an attack by the enemy on this side.

Tuesday, 11 August

"A sentry posted in the woods, near the little door leading out of the estate, has just been killed—stabbed with a knife. They think that he must have been trying to stop a man who wanted to get out of the park. But how did the man get in?

Wednesday, 12 August

"What can be happening? Here is something that has made a great impression on me and seems impossible to understand. There are other things besides which are just as perplexing, though I can't say why. I am much astonished that the captain and all his soldiers whom I meet appear so indifferent and should even be able to make jokes among themselves. I feel the sort of depression that comes over one when a storm is at hand. There must be something wrong with my nerves.

"Well, this morning. . ."

Paul stopped reading. The lower portion of the page containing the last few lines and the whole of the next page were torn out. It looked as if the major, after stealing Élisabeth's diary, had, for reasons best known to himself, removed the pages in which she set forth a certain incident.

The diary continued:

Friday, 14 August

"I felt I must tell the captain. I took him to the dead tree covered with ivy and asked him to lie down on the ground and listen. He did so very patiently and attentively. But he heard nothing and ended by saying:

"'You see, madame, that everything is absolutely normal.'

"'I assure you,' I answered, 'that two days ago there was a confused sound from this tree, just at this spot. And it lasted for several minutes.'

"He replied, smiling as he spoke:

"'We could easily have the tree cut down. But don't you think, madame, that in the state of nervous tension in which we all are we are liable to make mistakes; that we are subject to hallucinations? For, after all, where could the sound come from?'

"Of course, he was right. And yet I had heard and seen for myself. . .

Saturday, 15 August

"Yesterday, two German officers were brought in and were locked up in the wash-house, at the end of the yard. This morning, there was nothing in the wash-house but their uniforms. One can understand their breaking open the door. But the captain has found out that they made their escape in French uniforms and that they passed the sentries, saying that they had been sent to Corvigny.

"Who can have supplied them with those uniforms? Besides, they had to know the password: who can have given them that?

"It appears that a peasant woman called several days in succession with eggs and milk, a woman rather too well-dressed for her station, and that she hasn't been here to-day. But there is nothing to prove her complicity.

Sunday, 16 August

"The captain has been strongly urging me to go away. He is no longer cheerful. He seems very much preoccupied:

"'We are surrounded by spies,' he said. 'And there is every sign of the possibility of a speedy attack. Not a big attack, intended to force a way through to Corvigny, but an attempt to take the château by surprise. It is my duty to warn you, madame, that we may be compelled at any moment to fall back on Corvigny and that it would be most imprudent for you to stay.'

"I answered that nothing would change my resolution. Jérôme and Rosalie also implored me to leave. But what is the good? I intend to remain."

Once again Paul stopped. There was a page missing in this section of the diary; and the next page, the one headed 18 August, was torn at the top and the bottom and contained only a fragment of what Élisabeth had written on that day:

" . . . and that is why I have not spoken of it in the letter which I have just sent to Paul. He will know that I am staying on and the reasons for my decision; but he must not know of my hopes.

"Those hopes are still so vague and built on so insignificant a detail. Still, I feel overjoyed. I do not realize the meaning of that detail, but I feel its importance. The captain is hurrying about, increasing the patrols; the soldiers are polishing their arms and crying out for the battle; the enemy may be taking up his quarters at Èbrecourt, as they say: what do I care? I have only one thought: have I found the key? Am I on the right road? Let me think. . ."

The page was torn here, at the place where Élisabeth was about to explain things exactly. Was this a precautionary measure on Major Hermann's part? No doubt; but why?

The first part of the page headed 19 August was likewise torn. The nineteenth was the day before t on which the Germans had carried Ornequin, Corvigny and the whole district by assault. What had Élisabeth written on that Wednesday afternoon? What had she discovered? What was preparing in the darkness?

Paul felt a dread at his heart. He remembered that the first gunshot had thundered over Corvigny at two o'clock in the morning on Thursday and it was with an anxious mind that he read, on the second half of the page:

11 P.M.

"I have got up and opened my window. Dogs are barking on every side. They answer one another, stop, seem to be listening and then begin howling again as I have never heard them do before. When they cease, the silence becomes impressive and I listen in my turn to try and catch the indistinct sounds that keep them awake.

"Those sounds seem to my ears also to exist. It is something different from the rustling of the leaves. It has nothing to do with the ordinary interruption to the dead silence of the night. It comes from I can't tell where; and the impression it makes on me is so powerful that I ask myself at the same time whether I am just listening to the beating of my heart or whether I am hearing what might be the distant tramp of a marching army.

"Oh, I must be mad! A marching army! And our outposts on the frontier? And our sentries all around the château? Why, there would be fighting, firing! . . .

1 A.M.

"I did not stir from the window. The dogs were no longer barking. Everything was asleep. And suddenly I saw some one come from under the trees and go across the lawn. I at first imagined it was one of our soldiers. But, when whoever it was passed under my window, there was just enough light in the sky for me to make out a woman's figure. I thought for a moment of Rosalie. But no, the figure was taller and moved with a lighter and quicker step.

"I was on the point of waking Jérôme and giving the alarm. I did not, however. The figure had disappeared in the direction of the terrace. And all at once there came the cry of a bird, which struck me as strange. This was followed by a light that darted into the sky, like a shooting star springing from the ground.

"After that, nothing. Silence, general restfulness. Nothing more. And yet I dare not go back to bed. I am frightened, without knowing why. All sorts of dangers seem to come rushing from every corner of the horizon. They draw closer, they surround me, they hem me in, they suffocate me, crush me, I can't breathe. I'm frightened. . . I'm frightened. . ."

IX

A Sprig of Empire

Paul clutched with convulsive fingers the heart-breaking diary to which Élisabeth had confided her anguish:

"The poor angel!" he thought. "What she must have gone through! And this is only the beginning of the road that led to her death. . ."

He dreaded reading on. The hours of torture were near at hand, menacing and implacable, and he would have liked to call out to Élisabeth:

"Go away, go away! Don't defy Fate! I have forgotten the past. I love you."

It was too late. He himself, through his cruelty, had condemned her to suffer; and he must go on to the bitter end and witness every station of the Calvary of which he knew the last, terrifying stage.

He hastily turned the pages. There were first three blank leaves, those dated 20, 21 and 22 August: days of confusion during which she had been unable to write. The pages of the 23rd and 24th were missing. These no doubt recounted what had happened and contained revelations concerning the inexplicable invasion.

The diary began again at the middle of a torn page, the page belonging to Tuesday the 25th:

"'Yes, Rosalie, I feel quite well and I thank you for looking after me so attentively.'

"'Then there's no more fever?'

"'No, Rosalie, it's gone.'

"'You said the same thing yesterday, ma'am, and the fever came back. . . perhaps because of that visit. . . But the visit won't be to-day. . . it's not till to-morrow. . . I was told to let you know, ma'am. . . At 5 o'clock to-morrow. . .'

"I made no answer. What is the use of rebelling? None of the humiliating words that I shall have to hear will hurt me more than what lies before my eyes: the lawn invaded, horses picketed all over it, baggage wagons and caissons in the walks, half the trees felled, officers sprawling on the grass, drinking and singing, and a German flag flapping from the balcony of my window, just in front of me. Oh, the wretches!

"I close my eyes so as not to see. And that makes it more horrible still. . . Oh, the memory of that night. . . and, in the morning, when the sun rose, the sight of all those dead bodies! Some of the poor fellows were still alive, with those monsters dancing round them; and I could hear the cries of the dying men asking to be put out of their misery.

"And then. . . But I won't think of it or think of anything that can destroy my courage and my hope. . .

"Paul, I always have you in my mind as I write my diary. Something tells me that you will read it if anything happens to me; and so I must have strength to go on with it and to keep you informed from day to day. Perhaps you can already understand from my story what to me still seems very obscure. What is the connection between the past and the present, between the murder of long ago and the incomprehensible attack of the other night? I don't know. I have told you the facts in detail and also my theories. You will draw your conclusions and follow up the truth to the end.

Wednesday, 26 August

"There is a great deal of noise in the château. People are moving about everywhere, especially in the rooms above my bedroom. An hour ago, half a dozen motor vans and the same number of motor cars drove onto the lawn. The vans were empty. Two or three ladies sprang out of each of the cars, German women, waving their hands and laughing noisily. The officers ran up to welcome them; and there were loud expressions of delight. Then they all went to the house. What do they want?

"But I hear footsteps in the passage. . . It is 5 o'clock. . . Somebody is knocking at the door. . .

*   *   *   *   *

"There were five of them: he first and four officers who kept bowing to him obsequiously. He said to them, in a formal tone:

"'Attention, gentlemen. . . I order you not to touch anything in this room or in the other rooms reserved for madame. As for the rest, except in the two big drawing-rooms, it is yours. Keep anything here that you want and take away what you please. It is war and the law of war.'

"He pronounced those words, 'The law of war,' in a tone of fatuous conviction and repeated:

"'As for madame's private apartments, not a thing is to be moved. Do you understand? I know what is becoming.'

"He looked at me as though to say:

"'What do you think of that? There's chivalry for you! I could take it all, if I liked; but I'm a German and, as such, I know what's becoming.'

"He seemed to expect me to thank him. I said:

"'Is this the pillage beginning? That explains the empty motor vans.'

"'You don't pillage what belongs to you by the law of war,' he answered.

"'I see. And the law of war does not extend to the furniture and pictures in the drawing-rooms?'

"He turned crimson. Then I began to laugh:

"'I follow you,' I said. 'That's your share. Well chosen. Nothing but rare and valuable things. The refuse your servants can divide among them.'

"The officers turned round furiously. He became redder still. He had a face that was quite round, hair, which was too light, plastered down with grease and divided in the middle by a faultless parting. His forehead was low; and I was able to guess the effort going on behind it, to find a repartee. At last he came up to me and, in a voice of triumph, said:

"'The French have been beaten at Charleroi, beaten at Morange, beaten everywhere. They are retreating all along the line. The upshot of the war is settled.'

"Violent though my grief was, I did not wince. I whispered:

"'You low blackguard!'

"He staggered. His companions caught what I said; and I saw one put his hand on his sword-hilt. But what would he himself do? What would he say? I could feel that he was greatly embarrassed and that I had wounded his self-esteem.

"'Madame,' he said, 'I daresay you don't know who I am?'

"'Oh, yes!' I answered. 'You are Prince Conrad, a son of the Kaiser's. And what then?'

"He made a fresh attempt at dignity. He drew himself up. I expected threats and words to express his anger; but no, his reply was a burst of laughter, the affected laughter of a high and mighty lord, too indifferent, too disdainful to take offense, too intelligent to lose his temper.

"'The dear little Frenchwoman! Isn't she charming, gentlemen? Did you hear what she said? The impertinence of her! There's your true Parisian, gentlemen, with all her roguish grace.'

"And, making me a great bow, with not another word, he stalked away, joking as he went:

"'Such a dear little Frenchwoman! Ah, gentlemen, those little Frenchwomen! . . .'

* * * * *

"The vans were at work all day, going off to the frontier laden with booty. It was my poor father's wedding present to us, all his collections so patiently and fondly brought together; it was the dear setting in which Paul and I were to have lived. What a wrench the parting means to me!

"The war news is bad! I cried a great deal during the day.

"Prince Conrad came. I had to receive him, for he sent me word by Rosalie that, if I refused to see him, the inhabitants of Ornequin would suffer the consequences."

Here Élisabeth again broke off her diary. Two days later, on the 29th, she went on:

"He came yesterday. To-day also. He tries to appear witty and cultured. He talks literature and music, Goethe, Wagner and so on. . . I leave him to do his own talking, however; and this throws him in such a state of fury that he ended by exclaiming:

"'Can't you answer? It's no disgrace, even for a Frenchwoman, to talk to Prince Conrad of Prussia!'

"'A woman doesn't talk to her gaoler.'

"He protested briskly:

"'But, dash it all, you're not in prison!'

"'Can I leave the château?'

"'You can walk about. . . in the grounds. . .'

"'Between four walls, therefore, like a prisoner.'

"'Well, what do you want to do?'

"'To go away from here and live. . . wherever you tell me to: at Corvigny, for instance.'

"'That is to say, away from me!'

"As I did not answer, he bent forward a little and continued, in a low voice:

"'You hate me, don't you? Oh, I'm quite aware of it! I've made a study of women. Only, it's Prince Conrad whom you hate, isn't it? It's the German, the conqueror. For, after all, there's no reason why you should dislike the man himself. . . And, at this moment, it's the man who is in question, who is trying to please you. . . do you understand? . . . So. . .'

"I had risen to my feet and faced him. I did not speak a single word; but he must have seen in my eyes so great an expression of disgust that he stopped in the middle of his sentence, looking absolutely stupid. Then, his nature getting the better of him, he shook his fist at me, like a common fellow, and went off slamming the door and muttering threats. . ."

The next two pages of the diary were missing. Paul was gray in the face. He had never suffered to such an extent as this. It seemed to him as though his poor dear Élisabeth were still alive before his eyes and feeling his eyes upon her. And nothing could have upset him more than the cry of distress and love which marked the page headed:

1 September

"Paul, my own Paul, have no fear. Yes, I tore up those two pages because I did not wish you ever to know such revolting things. But that will not estrange you from me, will it? Because a savage dared to insult me, that is no reason, surely, why I should not be worthy of your love? Oh, the things he said to me, Paul, only yesterday: his offensive remarks, his hateful threats, his even more infamous promises. . . and then his rage! . . . No, I will not repeat them to you. In making a confidant of this diary, I meant to confide to you my daily

acts and thoughts. I believed that I was only writing down
the evidence of my grief. But this is something different;
and I have not the courage. . . Forgive my silence. It will be
enough for you to know the offense, so that you may avenge
me later. Ask me no more. . ."

And, pursuing this intention, Élisabeth now ceased to describe
Prince Conrad's daily visits in detail; but it was easy to perceive from her
narrative that the enemy persisted in hovering round her. It consisted of
brief notes in which she no longer let herself go as before, notes which
she jotted down at random, marking the days herself, without troubling
about the printed headings.

Paul trembled as he read on. And fresh revelations aggravated his dread:

Thursday

"Rosalie asks them the news every morning. The French
retreat is continuing. They even say that it has developed into
a rout and that Paris has been abandoned. The government
has fled. We are done for.

Seven o'clock in the evening

"He is walking under my windows as usual. He has with him
a woman whom I have already seen many times at a distance
and who always wears a great peasant's cloak and a lace scarf
which hides her face. But, as a rule, when he walks on the
lawn he is accompanied by an officer whom they call the
major. This man also keeps his head concealed, by turning up
the collar of his gray cloak.

Friday

"The soldiers are dancing on the lawn, while their band plays
German national hymns and the bells of Ornequin are
kept ringing with all their might. They are celebrating the
entrance of their troops into Paris. It must be true, I fear!
Their joy is the best proof of the truth.

Saturday

"Between my rooms and the boudoir where mother's portrait
used to hang is the room that was mother's bedroom. This is

now occupied by the major. He is an intimate friend of the prince and an important person, so they say. The soldiers know him only as Major Hermann. He does not humble himself in the prince's presence as the other officers do. On the contrary, he seems to address him with a certain familiarity.

"At this minute they are walking side by side on the gravel path. The prince is leaning on Major Hermann's arm. I feel sure that they are talking about me and that they are not at one. It looks almost as if Major Hermann were angry.

Ten o'clock in the morning

"I was right. Rosalie tells me that they had a violent scene.

Tuesday, 8 September

"There is something strange in the behavior of all of them. The prince, the major and the other officers appear to be nervous about something. The soldiers have ceased singing. There are sounds of quarreling. Can things be turning in our favor?"

Thursday

"The excitement is increasing. It seems that couriers keep on arriving at every moment. The officers have sent part of their baggage into Germany. I am full of hope. But, on the other hand. . .

"Oh, my dear Paul, if you knew the torture those visits cause me! . . . He is no longer the bland and honey-mouthed man of the early days. He has thrown off the mask. . . But, no, no, I will not speak of that! . . .

Friday

"The whole of the village of Ornequin has been packed off to Germany. They don't want a single witness to remain of what happened during the awful night which I described to you.

Sunday evening

"They are defeated and retreating far from Paris. He confessed as much, grinding his teeth and uttering threats against me as he spoke. I am the hostage on whom they are revenging themselves. . .

"Paul, if ever you meet him in battle, kill him like a dog. But do those people fight? Oh, I don't know what I'm saying! My head is going round and round. Why did I stay here? You ought to have taken me away, Paul, by force. . .

"Paul, what do you think he has planned? Oh, the dastard! They have kept twelve of the Ornequin villagers as hostages; and it is I, it is I who am responsible for their lives! . . . Do you understand the horror of it? They will live, or they will be shot, one by one, according to my behavior. . . The thing seems too infamous to believe. Is he only trying to frighten me? Oh, the shamefulness of such a threat! What a hell to find one's self in! I would rather die. . .

Nine o'clock in the evening

"Die? No! Why should I die? Rosalie has been. Her husband has come to an understanding with one of the sentries who will be on duty to-night at the little door in the wall, beyond the chapel. Rosalie is to wake me up at three in the morning and we shall run away to the big wood, where Jérôme knows of an inaccessible shelter. Heavens, if we can only succeed! . . .

Eleven o'clock

"What has happened? Why have I got up? It's only a nightmare. I am sure of that; and yet I am shaking with fever and hardly able to write. . . And why am I afraid to drink the glass of water by my bedside, as I am accustomed to do when I cannot sleep?

"Oh, such an abominable nightmare! How shall I ever forget what I saw while I slept? For I was asleep, that is certain. I had lain down to get a little rest before running away; and I saw that woman's ghost in a dream. . . A ghost? It must have been one, for only ghosts can enter through a bolted door; and her steps made so little noise as she crept over the floor that I scarcely heard the faintest rustling of her skirt.

"What had she come to do? By the glimmer of my night-light I saw her go round the table and walk up to my bed, cautiously, with her head lost in the darkness of the room. I was so frightened that I closed my eyes, in order that she might believe me to be asleep. But the feeling of her very presence and approach increased within me; and I was able clearly to follow all her doings. She stooped over me and looked at me for a long time, as though she did not know me and wanted to study my face. How was it that she did not hear the frantic beating of my heart? I could hear hers and also the regular movement of her breath. The agony I went through! Who was the woman? What was her object?

"She ceased her scrutiny and went away, but not very far. Through my eyelids I could half see her bending beside me, occupied in some silent task; and at last I became so certain that she was no longer watching me that I gradually yielded to the temptation to open my eyes. I wanted, if only for a second, to see her face and what she was doing.

"I looked; and Heaven only knows by what miracle I had the strength to keep back the cry that tried to force its way through my lips! The woman who stood there and whose features I was able to make out plainly by the light of the night-light was. . .

"Ah, I can't write anything so blasphemous! If the woman had been beside me, kneeling down, praying, and I had seen a gentle face smiling through its tears, I should not have trembled before that unexpected vision of the dead. But this distorted, fierce, infernal expression, hideous with hatred and wickedness: no sight in the world could have filled me with greater terror. And it is perhaps for this reason, because the sight was so extravagant and unnatural, that I did not cry out and that I am now almost calm. *At the moment when my eyes saw, I understood that I was the victim of a nightmare.*

"Mother, mother, you never wore and you never can wear that expression. You were kind and gentle, were you not? You used to smile; and, if you were still alive, you would now be wearing that same kind and gentle look? Mother, darling, since the terrible night when Paul recognized your portrait, I have often been back to that room, to learn to know my mother's face, which I had forgotten: I was so young, mother, when you died! And, though I was sorry that the painter had given you a different expression from the one I should have liked to see, at least it was not the wicked and malignant expression of just now. Why should you hate me? I am your daughter. Father has often told me that we had the same smile, you and I, and also that your eyes would grow moist with tears when you looked at me. So you do not loathe me, do you? And I did dream, did I not?

"Or, at least, if I was not dreaming when I saw a woman in my room, I was dreaming when that woman seemed to me to have your face. It was a delirious hallucination, it must have been. I had looked at your portrait so long and thought of you so much that I gave the stranger the features which I knew; and it was she, not you, who bore that hateful expression.

"And so I sha'n't drink the water. What she poured into it must have been poison. . . or perhaps a powerful sleeping-drug which would make me helpless against the prince. . . And I cannot but think of the woman who sometimes walks with him. . .

"As for me, I know nothing, I understand nothing, my thoughts are whirling in my tired brain. . .

"It will soon be three o'clock. . . I am waiting for Rosalie. It is a quiet night. There is not a sound in the house or outside. . .

"It is striking three. Ah, to be away from this! . . . To be free! . . ."

X

75 or 155?

Paul Delroze anxiously turned the page, as though hoping that the plan of escape might have proved successful; and he received, as it were, a fresh shock of grief on reading the first lines, written the following morning, in an almost illegible hand:

"We were denounced, betrayed. . . Twenty men were spying on our movements. . . They fell upon us like brutes. . . I am now locked up in the park lodge. A little lean-to beside it is serving as a prison for Jérôme and Rosalie. They are bound and gagged. I am free, but there are soldiers at the door. I can hear them speaking to one another.

Twelve mid-day

"It is very difficult for me to write to you, Paul. The sentry on duty opens the door and watches my every movement. They did not search me, so I was able to keep the leaves of my diary; and I write to you hurriedly, by scraps at a time, in a dark corner. . .

"My diary! Shall you find it, Paul? Will you know all that has happened and what has become of me? If only they don't take it from me! . . .

"They have brought me bread and water! I am still separated from Rosalie and Jérôme. They have not given them anything to eat.

Two o'clock

"Rosalie has managed to get rid of her gag. She is now speaking to me in an undertone through the wall. She heard what the men who are guarding us said and she tells me that Prince Conrad left last night for Corvigny; that the French are approaching and that the soldiers here are very uneasy. Are they going to defend themselves, or will they fall back towards the frontier? . . . It was Major Hermann who prevented our escape. Rosalie says that we are done for. . .

Half-past two

"Rosalie and I had to stop speaking. I have just asked her what she meant, why we should be done for. She maintains that Major Hermann is a devil:

"'Yes, devil,' she repeated. 'And, as he has special reasons for acting against you. . .'

"'What reasons, Rosalie?'

"'I will explain later. But you may be sure that if Prince Conrad does not come back from Corvigny in time to save us, Major Hermann will seize the opportunity to have all three of us shot. . .'"

Paul positively roared with rage when he saw the dreadful word set down in his poor Élisabeth's hand. It was on one of the last pages. After that there were only a few sentences written at random, across the paper, obviously in the dark, sentences that seemed breathless as the voice of one dying:

"The tocsin! . . . The wind carries the sound from Corvigny. . . What can it mean? . . . The French troops? . . . Paul, Paul, perhaps you are with them! . . .

"Two soldiers came in, laughing:

"'Lady's *kaput*! . . . All three *kaput*! . . . Major Hermann said so: they're *kaput*!'

"I am alone again. . . We are going to die. . . But Rosalie wants to talk to me and daren't. . .

Five o'clock

"The French artillery. . . Shells bursting round the château. . . Oh, if one of them could hit me! . . . I hear Rosalie's voice. . . What has she to tell me? What secret has she discovered?

"Oh, horror! Oh, the vile truth! Rosalie has spoken. Dear God, I beseech Thee, give me time to write. . . Paul, you could never imagine. . . You must be told before I die. . . Paul. . ."

The rest of the page was torn out; and the following pages, to the end of the month, were blank. Had Élisabeth had the time and the strength to write down what Rosalie had revealed to her?

This was a question which Paul did not even ask himself. What cared he for those revelations and the darkness that once again and for good shrouded the truth which he could no longer hope to discover? What cared he for vengeance or Prince Conrad or Major Hermann or all those savages who tortured and slew women? Élisabeth was dead. She had, so to speak, died before his eyes. Nothing outside that fact was worth a thought or an effort. Faint and stupefied by a sudden fit of cowardice, his eyes still fixed on the diary in which his poor wife had jotted down the phases of the most cruel martyrdom imaginable, he felt an immense longing for death and oblivion steal slowly over him. Élisabeth was calling to him. Why go on fighting? Why not join her?

Then some one tapped him on the shoulder. A hand seized the revolver which he was holding; and Bernard said:

"Drop that, Paul. If you think that a soldier has the right to kill himself at the present time, I will leave you free to do so when you have heard what I have to say."

Paul made no protest. The temptation to die had come to him, but almost without his knowing it; and, though he would perhaps have yielded to it, in a moment of madness, he was still in the state of mind in which a man soon recovers his consciousness.

"Speak," he said.

"It will not take long. Three minutes will give me time to explain. Listen to me. I see, from the writing, that you have found a diary kept by Élisabeth. Does it confirm what you knew?"

"Yes."

"When Élisabeth wrote it, was she threatened with death as well as Jérôme and Rosalie?"

"Yes."

"And all three were shot on the day when you and I arrived at Corvigny, that is to say, on Wednesday, the sixteenth?"

"Yes."

"It was between five and six in the afternoon, on the day before the Thursday when we arrived here, at the Château d'Ornequin?"

"Yes, but why these questions?"

"Why? Look at this, Paul. I took from you and I hold in my hand the splinter of shell which you removed from the wall of the lodge at the exact spot where Élisabeth was shot. Here it is. There was a lock of hair still sticking to it."

"Well?"

"Well, I had a talk just now with an adjutant of artillery, who was passing by the château; and the result of our conversation and of his inspection was that the splinter does not belong to a shell fired from a 75-centimeter gun, but to a shell fired from a 155-centimeter gun, a Rimailho."

"I don't understand."

"You don't understand, because you don't know or because you have forgotten what my adjutant reminded me of. On the Corvigny day, Wednesday the sixteenth, the batteries which opened fire and dropped a few shells on the château at the moment when the execution was taking place were all batteries of seventy-fives; and our one-five-five Rimailhos did not fire until the next day, Thursday, while we were marching against the château. Therefore, as Élisabeth was shot and buried at about 6 o'clock on the Wednesday evening, it is physically impossible for a splinter of a shell fired from a Rimailho to have taken off a lock of her hair, because the Rimailhos were not fired until the Thursday morning."

"Then you mean to say. . ." murmured Paul, in a husky voice.

"I mean to say, how can we doubt that the Rimailho splinter was picked up from the ground on the Thursday morning and deliberately driven into the wall among some locks of hair cut off on the evening before?"

"But you're crazy, Bernard! What object can there have been in that?"

Bernard gave a smile:

"Well, of course, the object of making people think that Élisabeth had been shot when she hadn't."

Paul rushed at him and shook him:

"You know something, Bernard, or you wouldn't be laughing! Can't you speak? How do you account for the bullets in the wall of the lodge? And the iron chain? And that third ring?"

"Just so. There were too many stage properties. When an execution takes place, does one see marks of bullets like that? And did you ever find Élisabeth's body? How do you know that they did not take pity on her after shooting Jérôme and his wife? Or who can tell? Some one may have interfered. . ."

Paul felt some little hope steal over him. Élisabeth, after being condemned to death by Major Hermann, had perhaps been saved by Prince Conrad, returning from Corvigny before the execution.

He stammered:

"Perhaps. . . yes. . . perhaps. . . And then there's this: Major Hermann knew of our presence at Corvigny—remember your meeting with that peasant woman—and wanted Élisabeth at any rate to be dead for us, so that we might give up looking for her. I expect Major Hermann arranged those properties, as you call them. How can I tell? Have I any right to hope?"

Bernard came closer to him and said, solemnly:

"It's not hope, Paul, that I'm bringing you, but a certainty. I wanted to prepare you for it. And now listen. My reason for asking those questions of the artillery adjutant was that I might check facts which I already knew. Yes, when I was at Ornequin village just now, a convoy of German prisoners arrived from the frontier. I was able to exchange a few words with one of them who had formed part of the garrison of the château. He had seen things, therefore. He knew. Well, Élisabeth was not shot. Prince Conrad prevented the execution."

"What's that? What's that?" cried Paul, overcome with joy. "You're quite sure? She's alive?"

"Yes, alive. . . They've taken her to Germany."

"But since then? For, after all, Major Hermann may have caught up with her and succeeded in his designs."

"No."

"How do you know?"

"Through that prisoner. The French lady whom he had seen here he saw this morning."

"Where?"

"Not far from the frontier, in a village just outside Èbrecourt, under the protection of the man who saved her and who is certainly capable of defending her against Major Hermann."

"What's that?" repeated Paul, but in a dull voice this time and with a face distorted with anger.

"Prince Conrad, who seems to take his soldiering in a very amateurish spirit—he is looked upon as an idiot, you know, even in his own family—has made Èbrecourt his headquarters and calls on Élisabeth every day. There is no fear, therefore. . ." But Bernard interrupted himself, and asked in amazement, "Why, what's the matter? You're gray in the face."

Paul took his brother-in-law by the shoulders and shouted:

"Élisabeth is lost. Prince Conrad has fallen in love with her—we heard that before, you know; and her diary is one long cry of distress—

he has fallen in love with her and he never lets go his prey. Do you understand? He will stop at nothing!"

"Oh, Paul, I can't believe. . ."

"At nothing, I tell you. He is not only an idiot, but a scoundrel and a blackguard. When you read the diary you will understand. . . But enough of words, Bernard. What we have to do is to act and to act at once, without even taking time to reflect."

"What do you propose?"

"To snatch Élisabeth from that man's clutches, to deliver her."

"Impossible."

"Impossible? We are not eight miles from the place where my wife is a prisoner, exposed to that rascal's insults, and you think that I am going to stay here with my arms folded? Nonsense! We must show that we have blood in our veins! To work, Bernard! And if you hesitate I shall go alone."

"You will go alone? Where?"

"To Èbrecourt. I don't want any one with me. I need no assistance. A German uniform will be enough. I shall cross the frontier in the dark. I shall kill the enemies who have to be killed and to-morrow morning Élisabeth shall be here, free."

Bernard shook his head and said, gently:

"My poor Paul!"

"What do you mean?"

"I mean that I should have been the first to agree and that we should have rushed to Élisabeth's rescue together, without counting the risk. Unfortunately. . ."

"What?"

"Well, it's this, Paul: there is no intention on our side of taking a more vigorous offensive. They've sent for reserve and territorial regiments; and we are leaving."

"Leaving?" stammered Paul, in dismay.

"Yes, this evening. Our division is to start from Corvigny this evening and go I don't know where. . . to Rheims, perhaps, or Arras. North and west, in short. So you see, my poor chap, your plan can't be realized. Come, buck up. And don't look so distressed. It breaks my heart to see you. After all, Élisabeth isn't in danger. She will know how to defend herself. . ."

Paul did not answer. He remembered Prince Conrad's abominable words, quoted by Élisabeth in her diary:

"It is war. It is the law, the law of war."

He felt the tremendous weight of that law bearing upon him, but he felt at the same time that he was obeying it in its noblest and loftiest phase, the sacrifice of the individual to everything demanded by the safety of the nation.

The law of war? No, the duty of war; and a duty so imperious that a man does not discuss it and that, implacable though it be, he must not even allow the merest quiver of a complaint to stir in his secret soul. Whether Élisabeth was faced by death or by dishonor did not concern Sergeant Paul Delroze and could not make him turn for a second from the path which he was ordered to follow. He was a soldier first and a man afterwards. He owed no duty save to France, his sorely-stricken and beloved country.

He carefully folded up Élisabeth's diary and went out, followed by his brother-in-law.

At nightfall he left the Château d'Ornequin.

XI

"Ysery, Misery"

Toul, Bar-le-Duc, Vitry-le-François. . . The little towns sped past as the long train carried Paul and Bernard westwards into France. Other, numberless trains came before or after theirs, laden with troops and munitions of war. They reached the outskirts of Paris and turned north, passing through Beauvais, Amiens and Arras.

It was necessary that they should arrive there first, on the frontier, to join the heroic Belgians and to join them as high up as possible. Every mile of ground covered was so much territory snatched from the invader during the long immobilized war that was in preparation.

Second Lieutenant Paul Delroze—he had received his new rank in the course of the railway journey—accomplished the northward march as it were in a dream, fighting every day, risking his life every minute, leading his men with irresistible dash, but all as though he were doing it without his own cognizance, in obedience to the automatic operation of a predetermined will.

While Bernard continued to stake his life with a laugh, as though in play, keeping up his comrade's courage with his own light-hearted pluck, Paul remained speechless and absent. Everything—fatigue, privations, the weather—seemed to him a matter of indifference.

Nevertheless, it was an immense delight, as he would sometimes confess to Bernard, to be going towards the fighting line. He had the feeling that he was making for a definite object, the only one that interested him: Élisabeth's deliverance. Even though he was attacking this frontier and not the other, the eastern frontier, he was still rushing with all the strength of his hatred against the detested enemy. Whether that enemy was defeated here or there made little difference. In either case, Élisabeth would be free.

"We shall succeed," said Bernard. "You may be sure that Élisabeth will outwit that swine. Meanwhile, we shall stampede the Huns, make a dash across Belgium, take Conrad in the rear and capture Èbrecourt. Doesn't the proposal make you smile? Oh, no, you never smile, do you, when you demolish a Hun? Not you! You've got a little way of laughing that tells me all about it. I say to myself, 'There's a bullet gone home,' or 'That's done it: he's got one at the end of his toothpick!' For you've a way of your own of sticking them. Ah, lieutenant, how fierce we grow! Simply through practise in killing! And to think that it makes us laugh!"

Roye, Lassigny, Chaulnes. . . Later, the Bassée Canal and the River Lys. . . And, later and at last, Ypres. Ypres! Here the two lines met, extended towards the sea. After the French rivers, after the Marne, the Aisne, the Oise and the Somme, a little Belgian stream was to run red with young men's blood. The terrible battle of the Yser was beginning.

Bernard, who soon won his sergeant's stripes, and Paul Delroze lived in this hell until the early days of December. Together with half a dozen Parisians, a volunteer soldier, a reservist and a Belgian called Laschen, who had escaped from Roulers and joined the French in order to get at the enemy more quickly, they formed a little band who seemed proof against fire. Of the whole section commanded by Paul, only these remained; and, when the section was re-formed, they continued to group together. They claimed all the dangerous expeditions. And each time, when their task was fulfilled, they met again, safe and sound, without a scratch, as though they brought one another luck.

During the last fortnight, the regiment, which had been pushed to the extreme point of the front, was flanked by the Belgian lines on the one side and the British lines on the other. Heroic assaults were delivered. Furious bayonet charges were made in the mud, even in the water of the flooded fields; and the Germans fell by the thousand and the ten thousand.

Bernard was in the seventh heaven:

"Tommy," he said to a little English soldier who was advancing by his side one day under a hail of shot and who did not understand a single word of French, "Tommy, no one admires the Belgians more than I do, but they don't stagger me, for the simple reason that they fight in our fashion; that is to say, like lions. The fellows who stagger me are you English beggars. You're different, you know. You have a way of your own of doing your work. . . and such work! No excitement, no fury. You keep all that bottled up. Oh, of course, you go mad when you retreat: that's when you're really terrible! You never gain as much ground as when you've lost a bit. Result: mashed Boches!"

He paused and then continued:

"I give you my word, Tommy, it fills us with confidence to have you by our side. Listen and I'll tell you a great secret. France is getting lots of applause just now; and she deserves it. We are all standing on our legs, holding our heads high and without boasting. We wear a smile on our faces and are quite calm, with clean souls and bright eyes. Well, the reason why we don't flinch, why we have confidence nailed to our hearts, is that you are with us. It's as I say, Tommy. Look here, do you know at what precise moment France felt just a little shaking at the pit of her stomach? During the retreat from Belgium? Not a bit of it! When Paris was within an ace of being sacked? Not at all. You give it up? Well, it was on the first day or two. At that time, you see, we knew, without saying so, without admitting it even to ourselves, that we were done for. There was no help for it. No time to prepare ourselves. Done for was what we were. And, though I say it as shouldn't, France behaved well. She marched straight to death without wincing, with her brightest smile and as gaily as if she were marching to certain victory. *Ave, Cæsar, morituri te salutant!* Die? Why not, since our honor demands it? Die to save the world? Right you are! And then suddenly London rings us up on the telephone. 'Hullo! Who are you?' 'It's England speaking.' 'Well?' 'Well, I'm coming in.' 'You don't mean it?' 'I do—with my last ship, with my last man, with my last shilling.' Then. . . oh, then there was a sudden change of front! Die? Rather not! No question of that now! Live, yes, and conquer! We two together will settle fate. From that day, France did not know a moment's uneasiness. The retreat? A trifle. Paris captured? A mere accident! One thing alone mattered: the final result. Fighting against England and France, there's nothing left for you Huns to do but go down on your knees. Here, Tommy, I'll start with that one: the big fellow at the foot of the tree. Down on your knees, you big fellow! . . . Hi! Tommy! Where are you off to? Calling you, are they? Good-by, Tommy. My love to England!"

It was on the evening of that day, as the 3rd company were skirmishing near Dixmude, that an incident occurred which struck the two brothers-in-law as very odd. Paul suddenly felt a violent blow in the right side, just above the hip. He had no time to bother about it. But, on retiring to the trenches, he saw that a bullet had passed through the holster of his revolver and flattened itself against the barrel. Now, judging from the position which Paul had occupied, the bullet must have been fired from behind him; that is to say, by a soldier belonging to his company or to some other company of his regiment. Was it an accident? A piece of awkwardness?

Two days later, it was Bernard's turn. Luck protected him, too. A bullet went through his knapsack and grazed his shoulder-blade.

And, four days after that, Paul had his cap shot through: and, this time again, the bullet came from the French lines.

There was no doubt about it therefore. The two brothers-in-law had evidently been aimed at; and the traitor, a criminal in the enemy's pay, was concealed in the French ranks.

"It's as sure as eggs," said Bernard. "You first, then I, then you again. There's a touch of Hermann about this. The major must be at Dixmude."

"And perhaps the prince, too," observed Paul.

"Very likely. In any case, one of their agents has slipped in amongst us. How are we to get at him? Tell the colonel?"

"If you like, Bernard, but don't speak of ourselves and of our private quarrel with the major. I did think for a moment of going to the colonel about it, but decided not to, as I did not want to drag in Élisabeth's name."

There was no occasion, however, for them to warn their superiors. Though the attempts on the lives of Paul and Bernard were not repeated, there were fresh instances of treachery every day. French batteries were located and attacked; their movements were forestalled; and everything proved that a spying system had been organized on a much more methodical and active scale than anywhere else. They felt certain of the presence of Major Hermann, who was evidently one of the chief pivots of the system.

"He is here," said Bernard, pointing to the German lines. "He is here because the great game is being played in those marshes and because there is work for him to do. And also he is here because we are."

"How would he know?" Paul objected.

And Bernard rejoined:

"How could he fail to know?"

One afternoon there was a meeting of the majors and the captains in the cabin which served as the colonel's quarters. Paul Delroze was summoned to attend it and was told that the general commanding the division had ordered the capture of a little house, standing on the left bank of the canal, which in ordinary times was inhabited by a ferryman. The Germans had strengthened and were holding it. The fire of their distant batteries, set up on a height on the other side, defended this block-house, which had formed the center of the fighting for some days. It had become necessary to take it.

"For this purpose," said the colonel, "we have called for a hundred volunteers from the African companies. They will set out to-night and deliver the assault to-morrow morning. Our business will be to support them at once and, once the attack has succeeded, to repel the counter-attacks, which are sure to be extremely violent because of the importance of the position. You all of you know the position, gentlemen. It is separated from us by the marshes which our African volunteers will enter to-night. . . up to their waists, one might say. But to the right of the marshes, alongside of the canal, runs a tow-path by which we will be able to come to the rescue. This tow-path has been swept by the guns on both sides and is free for a great part. Still, half a mile before the ferryman's house there is an old lighthouse which was occupied by the Germans until lately and which we have just destroyed with our gun-fire. Have they evacuated it entirely? Is there a danger of encountering an advance post there? It would be a good thing if we could find out; and I thought of you, Delroze."

"Thank you, sir."

"It's not a dangerous job, but it's a delicate one; and it will have to make certain. I want you to start to-night. If the old lighthouse is occupied, come back. If not, send for a dozen reliable men and hide them carefully until we come up. It will make an excellent base."

"Very well, sir."

Paul at once made his arrangements, called together his little band of Parisians and volunteers who, with the reservist and Laschen the Belgian, formed his usual command, warned them that he would probably want them in the course of the night and, at nine o'clock in the evening, set out, accompanied by Bernard d'Andeville.

The fire from the enemy's guns kept them for a long time on the bank of the canal, behind a huge, uprooted willow-trunk. Then an impenetrable darkness gathered round them, so much so that they could not even distinguish the water of the canal.

They crept rather than walked along, for fear of unexpected flashes of light. A slight breeze was blowing across the muddy fields and over the marshes, which quivered with the whispering of the reeds.

"It's pretty dreary here," muttered Bernard.

"Hold your tongue."

"As you please, lieutenant."

Guns kept booming at intervals for no reason, like dogs barking to make a noise amid the deep, nervous silence; and other guns at once barked back furiously, as if to make a noise in their turn and to prove that they were not asleep.

And once more peace reigned. Nothing stirred in space. It was as though the very grass of the marshes had ceased to wave. And yet Bernard and Paul seemed to perceive the slow progress of the African volunteers who had set out at the same time as themselves, their long halts in the middle of the icy waters, their stubborn efforts.

"Drearier and drearier," sighed Bernard.

"You're very impressionable to-night," said Paul.

"It's the Yser. You know what the men say: 'Yysery, misery!'"

They dropped to the ground suddenly. The enemy was sweeping the path and the marshes with search-lights. There were two more alarms; and at last they reached the neighborhood of the old lighthouse without impediment.

It was half-past eleven. With infinite caution they stole in between the demolished blocks of masonry and soon perceived that the post had been abandoned. Nevertheless, they discovered, under the broken steps of the staircase, an open trap-door and a ladder leading to a cellar which revealed gleams of swords and helmets. But Bernard, who was piercing the darkness from above with the rays of his electric lamp, declared:

"There's nothing to fear, they're dead. The Huns must have thrown them in, after the recent bombardment."

"Yes," said Paul. "And we must be prepared for the fact that they may send for the bodies. Keep guard on the Yser side, Bernard."

"And suppose one of the beggars is still alive?"

"I'll go down and see."

"Turn out their pockets," said Bernard, as he moved away, "and bring us back their note-books. I love those. They're the best indications of the state of their souls. . . or rather of their stomachs."

Paul went down. The cellar was a fairly large one. Half-a-dozen bodies lay spread over the floor, all lifeless and cold. Acting on Bernard's advice, he turned out the pockets and casually inspected the note-books. There was nothing interesting to attract his attention. But in the tunic of the sixth soldier whom he examined, a short, thin man, shot right through the head, he found a pocket-book bearing the name of Rosenthal and containing French and Belgian bank-notes and a packet of letters with Spanish, Dutch and Swiss postage stamps. The letters, all of which were in German, had been addressed to a German agent residing in France, whose name did not appear, and sent by him to Private Rosenthal, on whose body Paul discovered them. This private was to pass them on, together with a photograph, to a third person, referred to as his excellency.

"Secret Service," said Paul, looking through them. "Confidential information. . . Statistics. . . What a pack of scoundrels!"

But, on glancing at the pocket-book again, he saw an envelope which he tore open. Inside was a photograph; and Paul's surprise at the sight of it was so great that he uttered an exclamation. It represented the woman whose portrait he had seen in the locked room at Ornequin, the same woman, with the same lace scarf arranged in the identical way and with the same expression, whose hardness was not masked by its smile. And was this woman not the Comtesse Hermine d'Andeville, the mother of Élisabeth and Bernard?

The print bore the name of a Berlin photographer. On turning it over, Paul saw something that increased his stupefaction. There were a few words of writing:

"To Stéphane d'Andeville. 1902. "

Stéphane was the Comte d'Andeville's Christian name!

The photograph, therefore, had been sent from Berlin to the father of Élisabeth and Bernard in 1902, that is to say, four years after the Comtesse Hermine's death, so that Paul was faced with one of two solutions: either the photograph, taken before the Comtesse Hermine's death, was inscribed with the date of the year in which the count had received it; or else the Comtesse Hermine was still alive.

And, in spite of himself, Paul thought of Major Hermann, whose memory was suggested to his troubled mind by this portrait, as it had been by the picture in the locked room. Hermann! Hermine! And here was Hermine's image discovered by him on the corpse of a German spy, by the banks of the Yser, where the chief spy, who was certainly Major Hermann, must even now be prowling.

"Paul! Paul!"

It was his brother-in-law calling him. Paul rose quickly, hid the photograph, being fully resolved not to speak of it to Bernard, and climbed the ladder.

"Well, Bernard, what is it?"

"A little troop of Boches. . . I thought at first that they were a patrol, relieving the sentries, and that they would keep on the other side. But they've unmoored a couple of boats and are pulling across the canal."

"Yes, I can hear them."

"Shall we fire at them?" Bernard suggested.

"No, it would mean giving the alarm. It's better to watch them. Besides, that's what we're here for."

But at this moment there was a faint whistle from the tow-path. A similar whistle answered from the boat. Two other signals were exchanged at regular intervals.

A church clock struck midnight.

"It's an appointment," Paul conjectured. "This is becoming interesting. Follow me. I noticed a place below where I think we shall be safe against any surprise."

It was a back-cellar separated from the first by a brick wall containing a breach through which they easily made their way. They rapidly filled up the breach with bricks that had fallen from the ceiling and the walls.

They had hardly finished when a sound of steps was heard overhead and some words in German reached their ears. The troop of soldiers seemed to be fairly numerous. Bernard fixed the barrel of his rifle in one of the loop-holes in their barricade.

"What are you doing?" asked Paul.

"Making ready for them if they come. We can sustain a regular siege here."

"Don't be a fool, Bernard. Listen. Perhaps we shall be able to catch a few words."

"You may, perhaps. I don't know a syllable of German. . ."

A dazzling light suddenly filled the cellar. A soldier came down the ladder and hung a large electric lamp to a hook in the wall. He was joined by a dozen men; and the two brothers-in-law at once perceived that they had come to remove the dead.

It did not take long. In a quarter of an hour's time, there was nothing left in the cellar but one body, that of Rosenthal, the spy.

And an imperious voice above commanded:

"Stay there, you others, and wait for us. And you, Karl, go down first."

Some one appeared on the top rungs of the ladder. Paul and Bernard were astounded at seeing a pair of red trousers, followed by a blue tunic and the full uniform of a French private. The man jumped to the ground and cried:

"I'm here, *Excellenz*. You can come now."

And they saw Laschen, the Belgian, or rather the self-styled Belgian who had given his name as Laschen and who belonged to Paul's section.

They now knew where the three shots that had been fired at them came from. The traitor was there. Under the light they clearly distinguished his face, the face of a man of forty, with fat, heavy features and red-rimmed eyes. He seized the uprights of the ladder so as to hold it steady. An officer climbed down cautiously, wrapped in a wide gray cloak with upturned collar.

They recognized Major Hermann.

XII

MAJOR HERMANN

Resisting the surge of hatred that might have driven him to perform an immediate act of vengeance, Paul at once laid his hand on Bernard's arm to compel him to prudence. But he himself was filled with rage at the sight of that demon. The man who represented in his eyes every one of the crimes committed against his father and his wife, that man was there, in front of his revolver, and Paul must not budge! Nay more, circumstances had taken such a shape that, to a certainty, the man would go away in a few minutes, to commit other crimes, and there was no possibility of calling him to account.

"Good, Karl," said the major, in German, addressing the so-called Belgian. "Good. You have been punctual. Well, what news is there?"

"First of all, *Excellenz*," replied Karl, who seemed to treat the major with that deference mingled with familiarity which men show to a superior who is also their accomplice, "by your leave."

He took off his blue tunic and put on that of one of the dead Germans. Then, giving the military salute:

"That's better. You see, I'm a good German, *Excellenz*. I don't stick at any job. But this uniform chokes me.

"Well, *Excellenz*, it's too dangerous a trade, plied in this way. A peasant's smock is all very well; but a soldier's tunic won't do. Those beggars know no fear; I am obliged to follow them; and I run the risk of being killed by a German bullet."

"What about the two brothers-in-law?"

"I fired at them three times from behind and three times I missed them. Couldn't be helped: they've got the devil's luck; and I should only end by getting caught. So, as you say, I'm deserting; and I sent the youngster who runs between me and Rosenthal to make an appointment with you."

"Rosenthal sent your note on to me at headquarters."

"But there was also a photograph, the one you know of, and a bundle of letters from your agents in France. I didn't want to have those proofs found on me if I was discovered."

"Rosenthal was to have brought them to me himself. Unfortunately, he made a blunder."

"What was that, *Excellenz?*"

"Getting killed by a shell."

"Nonsense!"

"There's his body at your feet."

Karl merely shrugged his shoulders and said:

"The fool!"

"Yes, he never knew how to look after himself," added the major, completing the funeral oration. "Take his pocketbook from him, Karl. He used to carry it in an inside pocket of his woolen waistcoat."

The spy stooped and, presently, said:

"It's not there, *Excellenz.*"

"Then he put it somewhere else. Look in the other pockets."

Karl did so and said:

"It's not there either."

"What! This is beyond me! Rosenthal never parted with his pocketbook. He used to keep it to sleep with; he would have kept it to die with."

"Look for yourself, *Excellenz.*"

"But then. . . ?"

"Some one must have been here recently and taken the pocketbook."

"Who? Frenchmen?"

The spy rose to his feet, was silent for a moment and then, going up to the major, said in a deliberate voice:

"Not Frenchmen, *Excellenz*, but a Frenchman."

"What do you mean?"

"*Excellenz*, Delroze started on a reconnaissance not long ago with his brother-in-law, Bernard d'Andeville. I could not get to know in which direction, but I know now. He came this way. He must have explored the ruins of the lighthouse and, seeing some dead lying about, turned out their pockets."

"That's a bad business," growled the major. "Are you sure?"

"Certain. He must have been here an hour ago at most. Perhaps," added Karl, with a laugh, "perhaps he's here still, hiding in some hole. . ."

Both of them cast a look around them, but mechanically; and the movement denoted no serious fear on their part. Then the major continued, pensively:

"After all, that bundle of letters received by our agents, letters without names or addresses to them, doesn't matter so much. But the photograph is more important."

"I should think so, *Excellenz*! Why, here's a photograph taken in 1902; and we've been looking for it, therefore, for the last twelve years. I manage, after untold efforts, to discover it among the papers which Comte Stéphane d'Andeville left behind at the outbreak of war. And this photograph, which you wanted to take back from the Comte d'Andeville, to whom you had been careless enough to give it, is now in the hands of Paul Delroze, M. d'Andeville's son-in-law, Élisabeth d'Andeville's husband and your mortal enemy!"

"Well, I know all that," cried the major, who was obviously annoyed. "You needn't rub it in!"

"*Excellenz*, one must always look facts in the face. What has been your constant object with regard to Paul Delroze? To conceal from him the truth as to your identity and therefore to turn his attention, his enquiries, his hatred, towards Major Hermann. That's so, is it not? You went to the length of multiplying the number of daggers engraved with the letters H, E, R, M and even of signing 'Major Hermann' on the panel where the famous portrait hung. In fact, you took every precaution, so that, when you think fit to kill off Major Hermann, Paul Delroze will believe his enemy to be dead and will cease to think of you. And now what happens? Why, in that photograph he possesses the most certain proof of the connection between Major Hermann and the famous portrait which he saw on the evening of his marriage, that is to say, between the present and the past."

"True; but this photograph, found on the body of some dead soldier, would have no importance in his eyes unless he knew where it came from, for instance, if he could see his father-in-law."

"His father-in-law is fighting with the British army within eight miles of Paul Delroze."

"Do they know it?"

"No, but an accident may bring them together. Moreover, Bernard and his father correspond; and Bernard must have told his father what happened at the Château d'Ornequin, at least in so far as Paul Delroze was able to piece the incidents together."

"Well, what does that matter, so long as they know nothing of the other events? And that's the main thing. They could discover all our secrets through Élisabeth and find out who I am. But they won't look for her, because they believe her to be dead."

"Are you sure of that, *Excellenz*?"

MAURICE LEBLANC

"What's that?"

The two accomplices were standing close together, looking into each other's eyes, the major uneasy and irritated, the spy cunning.

"Speak," said the major. "What do you want to say?"

"Just this, *Excellenz*, that just now I was able to put my hand on Delroze's kit-bag. Not for long: two seconds, that's all; but long enough to see two things. . ."

"Hurry up, can't you?"

"First, the loose leaves of that manuscript of which you took care to burn the more important papers, but of which, unfortunately, you mislaid a considerable part."

"His wife's diary?"

"Yes."

The major burst into an oath:

"May I be damned for everlasting! One should burn everything in those cases. Oh, if I hadn't indulged that foolish curiosity! . . . And next?"

"Oh, hardly anything, *Excellenz*! A bit of a shell, yes, a little bit of a shell; but I must say that it looked to me very like the splinter which you ordered me to drive into the wall of the lodge, after sticking some of Élisabeth's hair to it. What do you think of that, *Excellenz*?"

The major stamped his foot with anger and let fly a new string of oaths and anathemas at the head of Paul Delroze.

"What do you think of that?" repeated the spy.

"You are right," cried the major. "His wife's diary will have given that cursed Frenchman a glimpse of the truth; and that piece of shell in his possession is a proof to him that his wife is perhaps still alive, which is the one thing I wanted to avoid. We shall never get rid of him now!" His rage seemed to increase. "Oh, Karl, he makes me sick and tired! He and his street-boy of a brother-in-law, what a pair of swankers! By God, I did think that you had rid me of them the night when we came back to their room at the château and found their names written on the wall! And you can understand that they won't let things rest, now that they know the girl isn't dead! They will look for her. They will find her. And, as she knows all our secrets. . . ! You ought to have made away with her, Karl!"

"And the prince?" chuckled the spy.

"Conrad is an ass! The whole of that family will bring us ill-luck and first of all to him who was fool enough to fall in love with that hussy.

You ought to have made away with her at once, Karl—I told you—and not to have waited for the prince's return."

Standing full in the light as he was, Major Hermann displayed the most appalling highwayman's face imaginable, appalling not because of the deformity of the features or any particular ugliness, but because of the most repulsive and savage expression, in which Paul once more recognized, carried to the very limits of paroxysm, the expression of the Comtesse Hermine, as revealed in her picture and the photograph. At the thought of the crime which had failed, Major Hermann seemed to suffer a thousand deaths, as though the murder had been a condition of his own life. He ground his teeth. He rolled his bloodshot eyes.

In a distraught voice, clutching the shoulder of his accomplice with his fingers, he shouted, this time in French:

"Karl, it is beginning to look as though we couldn't touch them, as though some miracle protected them against us. You've missed them three times lately. At the Château d'Ornequin you killed two others in their stead. I also missed him the other day at the little gate in the park. And it was in the same park, near the same chapel—you remember—sixteen years ago, when he was only a child, that you drove your knife into him. . . Well, you started your blundering on that day."

The spy gave an insolent, cynical laugh:

"What did you expect, *Excellenz*? I was on the threshold of my career and I had not your experience. Here were a father and a little boy whom we had never set eyes on ten minutes before and who had done nothing to us except annoy the Kaiser. My hand shook, I confess. You, on the other hand: ah, you made neat work of the father, you did! One little touch of your little hand and the trick was done!"

This time it was Paul who, slowly and carefully, slipped the barrel of his revolver into one of the breaches. He could no longer doubt, after Karl's revelations, that the major had killed his father. It was that creature whom he had seen, dagger in hand, on that tragic evening, that creature and none other! And the creature's accomplice of to-day was the accomplice of the earlier occasion, the satellite who had tried to kill Paul while his father was dying.

Bernard, seeing what Paul did, whispered in his ear:

"So you have made up your mind? We're to shoot him down?"

"Wait till I give the signal," answered Paul. "But don't you fire at him, aim at the spy."

In spite of everything, he was thinking of the inexplicable mystery of the bonds connecting Major Hermann with Bernard d'Andeville and his sister Élisabeth and he could not allow Bernard to be the one to carry out the act of justice. He himself hesitated, as one hesitates before performing an action of which one does not realize the full scope. Who was that scoundrel? What identity was Paul to ascribe to him? To-day, Major Hermann and chief of the German secret service; yesterday, Prince Conrad's boon companion, all-powerful at the Château d'Ornequin, disguising himself as a peasant-woman and prowling through Corvigny; long before that, an assassin, the Emperor's accomplice. . . and the lady of Ornequin: which of all these personalities, which were but different aspects of one and the same being, was the real one?

Paul looked at the major in bewilderment, as he had looked at the photograph and, in the locked room, at the portrait of Hermine d'Andeville. Hermann, Hermine! In his mind the two names became merged into one. And he noticed the daintiness of the hands, white and small as a woman's hands. The tapering fingers were decked with rings set with precious stones. The booted feet, too, were delicately formed. The colorless face showed not a trace of hair. But all this effeminate appearance was belied by the grating sound of a hoarse voice, by heaviness of gait and movement and by a sort of barbarous strength.

The major put his hands before his face and reflected for a few minutes. Karl watched him with a certain air of pity and seemed to be asking himself whether his master was not beginning to feel some kind of remorse at the thought of the crimes which he had committed. But the major threw off his torpor and, in a hardly audible voice, quivering with nothing but hatred, said:

"On their heads be it, Karl! On their heads be it for trying to get in our path! I put away the father and I did well. One day it will be the son's turn. And now. . . now we have the girl to see to."

"Shall I take charge of that, *Excellenz*?"

"No, I have a use for you here and I must stay here myself. Things are going very badly. But I shall go down there early in January. I shall be at Èbrecourt on the morning of the tenth of January. The business must be finished forty-eight hours after. And it shall be finished, that I swear to you."

He was again silent while the spy laughed loudly. Paul had stooped, so as to bring his eyes to the level of his revolver. It would be criminal to hesitate now. To kill the major no longer meant revenging himself and slaying his father's murderer: it meant preventing a further crime and saving Élisabeth. He had to act, whatever the consequences of his act might be. He made up his mind.

"Are you ready?" he whispered to Bernard.

"Yes. I am waiting for you to give the signal."

He took aim coldly, waiting for the propitious moment, and was about to pull the trigger, when Karl said, in German: "I say, *Excellenz*, do you know what's being prepared for the ferryman's house?"

"What?"

"An attack, just that. A hundred volunteers from the African companies are on their way through the marshes now. The assault will be delivered at dawn. You have only just time to let them know at headquarters and to find out what precautions they intend to take."

The major simply said:

"They are taken."

"What's that you say, *Excellenz*?"

"I say, that they are taken. I had word from another quarter; and, as they attach great value to the ferryman's house, I telephoned to the officer in command of the post that we would send him three hundred men at five o'clock in the morning. The African volunteers will be caught in a trap. Not one of them will come back alive."

The major gave a little laugh of satisfaction and turned up the collar of his cloak as he added:

"Besides, to make doubly sure, I shall go and spend the night there. . . especially as I am beginning to wonder whether the officer commanding the post did not chance to send some men here with instructions to take the papers off Rosenthal, whom he knew to be dead."

"But. . ."

"That'll do. Have Rosenthal seen to and let's be off."

"Am I to go with you, *Excellenz*?"

"No, there's no need. One of the boats will take me up the canal. The house is not forty minutes from here."

In answer to the spy's call, three soldiers came down and hoisted the dead man's body to the trap-door overhead. Karl and the major both remained where they were, at the foot of the ladder, while Karl turned the light of the lantern, which he had taken down from the wall, towards the trap-door.

Bernard whispered:

"Shall we fire now?"

"No," said Paul.

"But. . ."

"I forbid you."

When the operation was over, the major said to Karl:

"Give me a good light and see that the ladder doesn't slip."

He went up and disappeared from sight.

"All right," he said. "Hurry."

The spy climbed the ladder in his turn. Their footsteps were heard overhead. The steps moved in the direction of the canal and there was not a sound.

"What on earth came over you?" cried Bernard. "We shall never have another chance like that. The two ruffians would have dropped at the first shot."

"And we after them," said Paul. "There were twelve of them up there. We should have been doomed."

"But Élisabeth would have been saved, Paul! Upon my word, I don't understand you. Fancy having two monsters like that at our mercy and letting them go! The man who murdered your father and who is torturing Élisabeth was there; and you think of ourselves!"

"Bernard," said Paul Delroze, "you didn't understand what they said at the end, in German. The enemy has been warned of the attack and of our plans against the ferryman's house. In a little while, the hundred volunteers who are stealing up through the marsh will be the victims of an ambush laid for them. We've got to save them first. We have no right to sacrifice our lives before performing that duty. And I am sure that you agree with me."

"Yes," said Bernard. "But all the same it was a grand opportunity."

"We shall have another and perhaps soon," said Paul, thinking of the ferryman's house to which Major Hermann was now on his way.

"Well, what do you propose to do?"

"I shall join the detachment of volunteers. If the lieutenant in command is of my opinion, he will not wait until seven to deliver the assault, but attack at once. And I shall be of the party."

"And I?"

"Go back to the colonel. Explain the position to him and tell him that the ferryman's house will be captured this morning and that we shall hold it until reinforcements come up."

They parted with no more words and Paul plunged resolutely into the marshes.

The task which he was undertaking did not meet with the obstacles he expected. After forty minutes of rather difficult progress, he heard the murmur of voices, gave the password and told the men to take him to the lieutenant.

Paul's explanations at once convinced that officer: the job must either be abandoned or hurried on at once.

The column went ahead. At three o'clock, guided by a peasant who knew a path where the men sank no deeper than their knees, they succeeded in reaching the neighborhood of the house unperceived. Then, when the alarm had been given by a sentry, the attack began.

This attack, one of the finest feats of arms in the war, is too well known to need a detailed description here. It was extremely violent. The enemy, who was on his guard, made an equally vigorous defense. There was a tangle of barbed wire to be forced and many pitfalls to be overcome. A furious hand-to-hand fight took place first outside and then inside the house; and, by the time that the French had gained the victory after killing or taking prisoner the eighty-three Germans who defended it, they themselves had suffered losses which reduced their effective force by half.

Paul was the first to leap into the trenches, the line of which ran beside the house on the left and was extended in a semicircle as far as the Yser. He had an idea: before the attack succeeded and before it was even certain that it would succeed, he wanted to cut off all retreat on the part of the fugitives.

Driven back at first, he made for the bank, followed by three volunteers, stepped into the water, went up the canal and thus came to the other side of the house, where, as he expected, he found a bridge of boats.

At that moment, he saw a figure disappearing in the darkness.

"Stay here," he said to his men, "and let no one pass."

He himself jumped out of the water, crossed the bridge and began to run.

A searchlight was thrown on the canal bank and he again perceived the figure, thirty yards in front of him.

A minute later, he shouted:

"Halt, or I fire!"

And, as the man continued to run, he fired, but aimed so as not to hit him.

The fugitive stopped and fired his revolver four times, while Paul, stooping down, flung himself between his legs and brought him to the ground.

The enemy, seeing that he was mastered, offered no resistance. Paul rolled his cloak round him and took him by the throat. With the hand that remained free, he threw the light of his pocket-lamp full on the other's face.

His instinct had not deceived him: the man he held by the throat was Major Hermann.

XIII

THE FERRYMAN'S HOUSE

Paul Delroze did not speak a word. Pushing his prisoner in front of him, after tying the major's wrists behind his back, he returned to the bridge of boats in the darkness illumined by brief flashes of light.

The fighting continued. But a certain number of the enemy tried to run away; and, when the volunteers who guarded the bridge received them with a volley of fire, the Germans thought that they had been cut off; and this diversion hastened their defeat.

When Paul arrived, the combat was over. But the enemy was bound, sooner or later, to deliver a counter-attack, supported by the reinforcements that had been promised to the commandant; and the defense was prepared forthwith.

The ferryman's house, which had been strongly fortified by the Germans and surrounded with trenches, consisted of a ground floor and an upper story of three rooms, now knocked into one. At the back of this large room, however, was a recess with a sloping roof, reached by three steps, which at one time had done duty as a servant's attic. Paul, who was entrusted with the arrangement of this upper floor, brought his prisoner here. He laid him on the floor, bound him with a cord and fastened him to a beam; and, while doing so, he was seized with such a paroxysm of hatred that he took him by the throat as though to strangle him.

He mastered himself, however. After all, there was no hurry. Before killing the man or handing him over to the soldiers to be shot against the wall, why deny himself the supreme satisfaction of having an explanation with him?

When the lieutenant entered, Paul said, so as to be heard by all and especially by the major:

"I recommend that scoundrel to your care, lieutenant. It's Major Hermann, one of the chief spies in the German army. I have the proofs on me. Remember that, in case anything happens to me. And, if we should have to retreat. . ."

The lieutenant smiled:

"There's no question of that. We shall not retreat, for the very good reason that I would rather blow up the shanty first. And Major

Hermann, therefore, would be blown up with us. So make your mind easy."

The two officers discussed the defensive measures to be adopted; and the men quickly got to work.

First of all, the bridge of boats was unmade, trenches dug along the canal and the machine-guns turned to face the other way. Paul, on his first floor, had the sandbags moved from the one side of the house to the other and the less solid-looking portions of the wall shored up with beams.

At half-past five, under the rays of the German flashlights, several shells fell round about. One of them struck the house. The big guns began to sweep the towpath.

A few minutes before daybreak, a detachment of cyclists arrived by this path, with Bernard d'Andeville at their head. He explained that two companies and a section of sappers in advance of a complete battalion had started, but their progress was hampered by the enemy's shells and they were obliged to skirt the marshes, under the cover of the dyke supporting the towpath. This had slowed their march; and it would be an hour before they could arrive.

"An hour," said the lieutenant. "It will be stiff work. Still, we can do it. So. . ."

While he was giving new orders and placing the cyclists at their posts, Paul came up; and he was just going to tell Bernard of Major Hermann's capture, when his brother-in-law announced his news:

"I say, Paul, dad's with me!"

Paul gave a start:

"Your father is here? Your father came with you?"

"Just so; and in the most natural manner. You must know that he had been looking for an opportunity for some time. By the way, he has been promoted to interpreter lieutenant. . ."

Paul was no longer listening. He merely said to himself:

"M. d'Andeville is here. . . M. d'Andeville, the Comtesse Hermine's husband. He must know, surely. Is she alive or dead? Or has he been the dupe of a scheming woman to the end and does he still bear a loving recollection of one who has vanished from his life? But no, that's incredible, because there is that photograph, taken four years later and sent to him: sent to him from Berlin! So he knows; and then. . . ?"

Paul was greatly perplexed. The revelations made by Karl the spy had suddenly revealed M. d'Andeville in a startling light. And now circumstances were bringing M. d'Andeville into Paul's presence, at the very time when Major Hermann had been captured.

Paul turned towards the attic. The major was lying motionless, with his face against the wall.

"Your father has remained outside?" Paul asked his brother-in-law.

"Yes, he took the bicycle of a man who was riding near us and who was slightly wounded. Papa is seeing to him."

"Go and fetch him; and, if the lieutenant doesn't object. . ."

He was interrupted by the bursting of a shrapnel shell the bullets of which riddled the sandbags heaped up in the front of them. The day was breaking. They could see an enemy column looming out of the darkness a mile away at most.

"Ready there!" shouted the lieutenant from below. "Don't fire a shot till I give the order. No one to show himself!"

It was not until a quarter of an hour later and then only for four or five minutes that Paul and M. d'Andeville were able to exchange a few words. Their conversation, moreover, was so greatly hurried that Paul had no time to decide what attitude he should take up in the presence of Élisabeth's father. The tragedy of the past, the part which the Comtesse Hermine's husband played in that tragedy: all this was mingled in his mind with the defense of the block-house. And, in spite of their great liking for each other, their greeting was somewhat absent and distracted.

Paul was ordering a small window to be stopped with a mattress. Bernard was posted at the other end of the room.

M. d'Andeville said to Paul:

"You're sure of holding out, aren't you?"

"Absolutely, as we've got to."

"Yes, you've got to. I was with the division yesterday, with the English general to whom I am attached as interpreter, when the attack was decided on. The position seems to be of essential importance; and it is indispensable that we should stick to it. I saw that this gave me an opportunity of seeing you, Paul, as I knew that your regiment was to be here. So I asked leave to accompany the contingent that had been ordered to. . ."

There was a fresh interruption. A shell came through the roof and shattered the wall on the side opposite to the canal.

"Any one hurt?"

"No, sir."

M. d'Andeville went on:

"The strangest part of it was finding Bernard at your colonel's last night. You can imagine how glad I was to join the cyclists. It was my only chance of seeing something of my boy and of shaking you by the hand. . . And then I had no news of my poor Élisabeth; and Bernard told me. . ."

"Ah," said Paul quickly, "has Bernard told you all that happened at the château?"

"At least, as much as he knew; but there are a good many things that are difficult to understand; and Bernard says that you have more precise details. For instance, why did Élisabeth stay at the château?"

"Because she wanted to," said Paul. "I was not told of her decision until later, by letter."

"I know. But why didn't you take her with you, Paul?"

"When I left Ornequin, I made all the necessary arrangements for her to go."

"Good. But you ought not to have left Ornequin without her. All the trouble is due to that."

M. d'Andeville had been speaking with a certain acerbity, and, as Paul did not answer, he asked again:

"Why didn't you take Élisabeth away? Bernard said that there was something very serious, that you spoke of exceptional circumstances. Perhaps you won't mind explaining."

Paul seemed to suspect a latent hostility in M. d'Andeville; and this irritated him all the more on the part of a man whose conduct now appeared to him so perplexing:

"Do you think," he said, "that this is quite the moment?"

"Yes, yes, yes. We may be separated any minute. . ."

Paul did not allow him to finish. He turned abruptly towards his father-in-law and exclaimed:

"You are right, sir! It's a horrible idea. It would be terrible if I were not able to reply to your questions or you to mine. Élisabeth's fate perhaps depends on the few words which we are about to speak. For we must know the truth between us. A single word may bring it to light; and there is no time to be lost. We must speak out now. . . Whatever happens."

His excitement surprised M. d'Andeville, who asked:

"Wouldn't it be as well to call Bernard over?"

"No, no," said Paul, "on no account! It's a thing that he mustn't know about, because it concerns. . ."

"Because it concerns whom?" asked M. d'Andeville, who was more and more astonished.

A man standing near them was hit by a bullet and fell. Paul rushed to his assistance; but the man had been shot through the forehead and was dead. Two more bullets entered through an opening which was wider than it need be; and Paul ordered it to be partly closed up.

M. d'Andeville, who had been helping him, pursued the conversation:

"You were saying that Bernard must not hear because it concerns. . ."

"His mother," Paul replied.

"His mother? What do you mean? His mother? It concerns my wife? I don't understand. . ."

Through the loopholes in the wall they could see three enemy columns advancing, above the flooded fields, moving forward on narrow causeways which converged towards the canal opposite the ferryman's house.

"We shall fire when they are two hundred yards from the canal," said the lieutenant commanding the volunteers, who had come to inspect the defenses. "If only their guns don't knock the shanty about too much!"

"Where are our reinforcements?" asked Paul.

"They'll be here in thirty or forty minutes. Meantime the seventy-fives are doing good work."

The shells were flying through space in both directions, some falling in the midst of the German columns, others around the blockhouse. Paul ran to every side, encouraging and directing the men. From time to time he went to the attic and looked at Major Hermann, who lay perfectly still. Then Paul returned to his post.

He did not for a second cease to think of the duty incumbent on him as an officer and a combatant, nor for a second of what he had to say to M. d'Andeville. But these two mingled obsessions deprived him of all lucidity of mind! and he did not know how to come to an explanation with his father-in-law or how to unravel the tangled position. M. d'Andeville asked his question several times. He did not reply.

The lieutenant's voice was raised:

"Attention! . . . Present! . . . Fire! . . ."

The command was repeated four times over. The nearest enemy column, decimated by the bullets, seemed to waver. But the others came up with it; and it formed up again.

Two German shells burst against the house. The roof was carried away bodily, several feet of the frontage were demolished and three men killed.

MAURICE LEBLANC

After the storm, a calm. But Paul had so clear a sense of the danger which threatened them all that he was unable to contain himself any longer. Suddenly making up his mind, addressing M. d'Andeville without further preamble, he said:

"One word in particular. . . I must know. . . Are you quite sure that the Comtesse d'Andeville is dead?" And without waiting for the reply, he went on: "Yes, you think my question mad. It seems so to you because you do not know. But I am not mad; and I ask you to answer my question as you would do if I had the time to state the reasons that justify me in asking it. Is the Comtesse Hermine dead?"

M. d'Andeville, restraining his feelings and consenting to adopt the hypothesis which Paul seemed to insist on, said:

"Is there any reason that allows you to presume that my wife is still alive?"

"There are very serious reasons, I might say, incontestable reasons."

M. d'Andeville shrugged his shoulders and said, in a firm voice:

"My wife died in my arms. My lips touched her icy hands, felt that chill of death which is so horrible in those we love. I myself dressed her, as she had asked, in her wedding gown; and I was there when they nailed down the coffin. Anything else?"

Paul listened to him and thought to himself:

"Has he spoken the truth? Yes, he has; and still how can I admit. . . ?"

Speaking more imperiously, M. d'Andeville repeated:

"Anything else?"

"Yes," said Paul, "one more question. There was a portrait in the Comtesse d'Andeville's boudoir: was that her portrait?"

"Certainly, her full length portrait."

"Showing her with a black lace scarf over her shoulders?"

"Yes, the kind of scarf she liked wearing."

"And the scarf was fastened in front by a cameo set in a gold snake?"

"Yes, it was an old cameo which belonged to my mother and which my wife always wore."

Paul yielded to thoughtless impulse. M. d'Andeville's assertions seemed to him so many admissions; and, trembling with rage, he rapped out:

"Monsieur, you have not forgotten, have you, that my father was murdered? We often spoke of it, you and I. He was your friend. Well, the woman who murdered him and whom I saw, the woman whose image has stamped itself on my brain wore a black lace scarf round her shoulders and a cameo set in a gold snake. And I found this woman's portrait in your wife's room. Yes, I saw her portrait on my wedding evening. Do you understand now? Do you understand or don't you?"

It was a tragic moment between the two men. M. d'Andeville stood trembling, with his hands clutching his rifle.

"Why is he trembling?" Paul asked himself; and his suspicions increased until they became an actual accusation. "Is it a feeling of protest or his rage at being unmasked that makes him shake like that? And am I to look upon him as his wife's accomplice? For, after all. . ."

He felt a fierce grip twisting his arm. M. d'Andeville, gray in the face, blurted out:

"How dare you? How dare you suggest that my wife murdered your father? Why, you must be drunk! My wife, a saint in the sight of God and man! And you dare! Oh, I don't know what keeps me from smashing your face in!"

Paul released himself roughly. The two men, shaking with a rage which was increased by the din of the firing and the madness of their quarrel, were on the verge of coming to blows while the shells and bullets whistled all around them.

Then a new strip of wall fell to pieces. Paul gave his orders and, at the same time, thought of Major Hermann lying in his corner, to whom he could have brought M. d'Andeville like a criminal who is confronted with his accomplice. But why then did he not do so?

Suddenly remembering the photograph of the Comtesse Hermine which he had found on Rosenthal's body, he took it from his pocket and thrust it in front of M. d'Andeville's eyes:

"And this?" he shouted. "Do you know what this is? . . . There's a date on it, 1902, and you pretend that the Comtesse Hermine is dead! . . . Answer me, can't you? A photograph taken in Berlin and sent to you by your wife four years after her death!"

M. d'Andeville staggered. It was as though all his rage had evaporated and was changing into infinite stupefaction. Paul brandished before his face the overwhelming proof constituted by that bit of cardboard. And he heard M. d'Andeville mutter:

"Who can have stolen it from me? It was among my papers in Paris. . . Why didn't I tear it up? . . ." Then he added, in a very low whisper, "Oh, Hermine, Hermine, my adored one!"

Surely it was an avowal? But, if so, what was the meaning of an avowal expressed in those terms and with that declaration of love for a woman laden with crime and infamy?

The lieutenant shouted from the ground floor:

"Everybody into the trenches, except ten men. Delroze, keep the best shots and order independent firing."

The volunteers, headed by Bernard, hurried downstairs. The enemy was approaching the canal, in spite of the losses which he had sustained. In fact, on the right and left, knots of pioneers, constantly renewed, were already striving with might and main to collect the boats stranded on the bank. The lieutenant in command of the volunteers formed his men into a first line of defense against the imminent assault, while the sharpshooters in the house had orders to kill without ceasing under the storm of shells.

One by one, five of these marksmen fell.

Paul and M. d'Andeville were here, there and everywhere, while consulting one another as to the commands to be given and the things to be done. There was not the least chance, in view of their great inferiority in numbers, that they would be able to resist. But there was some hope of their holding out until the arrival of the reinforcements, which would ensure the possession of the blockhouse.

The French artillery, finding it impossible to secure an effective aim amid the confusion of the combatants, had ceased fire, whereas the German guns were still bombarding the house; and shells were bursting at every moment.

Yet another man was wounded. He was carried into the attic and laid beside Major Hermann, where he died almost immediately.

Outside, there was fighting on and even in the water of the canal, in the boats and around them. There were hand-to-hand contests amid general uproar, yells of execration and pain, cries of terror and shouts of victory. The confusion was so great that Paul and M. d'Andeville found it difficult to take aim.

Paul said to his father-in-law:

"I'm afraid we may be done for before assistance arrives. I am bound therefore to warn you that the lieutenant has made his arrangements to blow up the house. As you are here by accident, without any authorization that gives you the quality or duties of a combatant. . ."

"I am here as a Frenchman," said M. d'Andeville, "and I shall stay on to the end."

"Then perhaps we shall have time to finish what we have to say, sir. Listen to me. I will be as brief as I can. But if you should see the least glimmer of light, please do not hesitate to interrupt me."

He fully understood that there was a gulf of darkness between them and that, whether guilty or not, whether his wife's accomplice or her dupe, M. d'Andeville must know things which he, Paul, did not know and that these things could only be made plain by an adequate recital of what had happened.

He therefore began to speak. He spoke calmly and deliberately, while M. d'Andeville listened in silence. And they never ceased firing, quietly loading, aiming and reloading, as though they were at practise. All around and above them death pursued its implacable work.

Paul had hardly described his arrival at Ornequin with Élisabeth, their entrance into the locked room and his dismay at the sight of the portrait, when an enormous shell exploded over their heads, spattering them with shrapnel bullets.

The four volunteers were hit. Paul also fell, wounded in the neck; and, though he suffered no pain, he felt that all his ideas were gradually fading into a mist without his being able to retain them. He made an effort, however, and by some miracle of will was still able to exercise a remnant of energy that allowed him to keep his hold on certain reflections and impressions. Thus he saw his father-in-law kneeling beside him and succeeded in saying to him:

"Élisabeth's diary. . . You'll find it in my kit-bag in camp. . . with a few pages written by myself. . . which will explain. . . But first you must. . . Look, that German officer over there, bound up. . . he's a spy. . . Keep an eye on him. . . Kill him. . . If not, on the tenth of January. . . but you will kill him, won't you?"

Paul could speak no more. Besides, he saw that M. d'Andeville was not kneeling down to listen to him or help him, but that, himself shot, with his face bathed in blood, he was bending double and finally fell in a huddled heap, uttering moans that grew fainter and fainter.

A great calm now descended on the big room, while the rifles crackled outside. The German guns were no longer firing. The enemy's counter-attack must be meeting with success; and Paul, incapable of moving, lay awaiting the terrible explosion foretold by the lieutenant.

He pronounced Élisabeth's name time after time. He reflected that no danger threatened her now, because Major Hermann was also about to die. Besides, her brother Bernard would know how to defend her. But after a while this sort of tranquillity disappeared, changed into uneasiness and then into restless anxiety, giving way to a feeling of which every second that passed increased the torture. He could not tell whether he was haunted by a nightmare, by some morbid hallucination. It all happened on the side of the attic to which he had dragged Major Hermann. A soldier's dead body was lying between them. And it seemed, to his horror, as if the major had cut his bonds and were rising to his feet and looking around him.

Paul exerted all his strength to open his eyes and keep them open. But an ever thicker shadow veiled them; and through this shadow he perceived, as one sees a confused sight in the darkness, the major taking off his cloak, stooping over the body, removing its blue coat and buttoning it on himself. Then he put the dead man's cap on his head, fastened his scarf round his neck, took the soldier's rifle, bayonet and cartridges and, thus transfigured, stepped down the three wooden stairs.

It was a terrible vision. Paul would have been glad to doubt his eyes, to believe in some phantom image born of his fever and delirium. But everything confirmed the reality of what he saw; and it meant to him the most infernal suffering. The major was making his escape!

Paul was too weak to contemplate the position in all its bearings. Was the major thinking of killing him and of killing M. d'Andeville? Did the major know that they were there, both of them wounded, within reach of his hand? Paul never asked himself these questions. One idea alone obsessed his failing mind. Major Hermann was escaping. Thanks to his uniform, he would mingle with the volunteers! By the aid of some signal, he would get back to the Germans! And he would be free! And he would resume his work of persecution, his deadly work, against Élisabeth!

Oh, if the explosion had only taken place! If the ferryman's house could but be blown up and the major with it! . . .

Paul still clung to this hope in his half-conscious condition. Meanwhile his reason was wavering. His thoughts became more and more confused. And he swiftly sank into that darkness in which one neither sees nor hears. . .

THREE WEEKS LATER THE GENERAL commanding in chief stepped from his motor car in front of an old château in the Bourbonnais, now transformed into a military hospital. The officer in charge was waiting for him at the door.

"Does Second Lieutenant Delroze know that I am coming to see him?"

"Yes, sir."

"Take me to his room."

Paul Delroze was sitting up. His neck was bandaged; but his features were calm and showed no traces of fatigue. Much moved by the presence of the great chief whose energy and coolness had saved France, he rose to the salute. But the general gave him his hand and exclaimed, in a kind and affectionate voice:

"Sit down, Lieutenant Delroze. . . I say lieutenant, for you were promoted yesterday. No, no thanks. By Jove, we are still your debtors! So you're up and about?"

"Why, yes, sir. The wound wasn't much."

"So much the better. I'm satisfied with all my officers; but, for all that, we don't find fellows like you by the dozen. Your colonel has sent in a special report about you which sets forth such an array of acts of incomparable bravery that I have half a mind to break my own rule and to make the report public."

"No, please don't, sir."

"You are right, Delroze. It is the first attribute of heroism that it likes to remain anonymous; and it is France alone that must have all the glory for the time being. So I shall be content for the present to mention you once more in the orders of the day and to hand you the cross for which you were already recommended."

"I don't know how to thank you, sir."

"In addition, my dear fellow, if there's the least thing you want, I insist that you should give me this opportunity of doing it for you."

Paul nodded his head and smiled. All this cordial kindness and attentiveness were putting him at his ease.

"But suppose I want too much, sir?"

"Go ahead."

"Very well, sir, I accept. And what I ask is this: first of all, a fortnight's sick leave, counting from Saturday, the ninth of January, the day on which I shall be leaving the hospital."

"That's not a favor, that's a right."

"I know, sir. But I must have the right to spend my leave where I please."

MAURICE LEBLANC

"Very well."

"And more than that: I must have in my pocket a permit written in your own hand, sir, which will give me every latitude to move about as I wish in the French lines and to call for any assistance that can be of use to me."

The general looked at Paul for a moment, and said:

"That's a serious request you're making, Delroze."

"Yes, sir, I know it is. But the thing I want to undertake is serious too."

"All right, I agree. Anything more?"

"Yes, sir, Sergeant Bernard d'Andeville, my brother-in-law, took part as I did in the action at the ferryman's house. He was wounded like myself and brought to the same hospital, from which he will probably be discharged at the same time. I should like him to have the same leave and to receive permission to accompany me."

"I agree. Anything more?"

"Bernard's father, Comte Stéphane d'Andeville, second lieutenant interpreter attached to the British army, was also wounded on that day by my side. I have learnt that his wound, though serious, is not likely to prove fatal and that he has been moved to an English hospital, I don't know which. I would ask you to send for him as soon as he is well and to keep him on your staff until I come to you and report on the task which I have taken in hand."

"Very well. Is that all?"

"Very nearly, sir. It only remains for me to thank you for your kindness by asking you to give me a list of twenty French prisoners, now in Germany, in whom you take a special interest. Those twenty prisoners will be free in a fortnight from now at most."

"Eh? What's that?"

For all his coolness, the general seemed a little taken aback. He echoed:

"Free in a fortnight from now! Twenty prisoners!"

"I give you my promise, sir."

"Don't talk nonsense."

"It shall be as I say."

"Whatever the prisoners' rank? Whatever their social position?"

"Yes, sir."

"And by regular means, means that can be avowed?"

"By means to which there can be no possible objection."

The general looked at Paul again with the eye of a leader who is in the habit of judging men and reckoning them at their true value. He knew that the man before him was not a boaster, but a man of action and a man of his word, who went straight ahead and kept his promises. He replied:

"Very well, Delroze, you shall have your list to-morrow."

XIV

A Masterpiece of Kultur

On the morning of Sunday, the tenth of January, Lieutenant Delroze and Sergeant d'Andeville stepped on to the platform at Corvigny, went to call on the commandant of the town and then took a carriage in which they drove to the Château d'Ornequin.

"All the same," said Bernard, stretching out his legs in the fly, "I never thought that things would turn out as they have done when I was hit by a splinter of shrapnel between the Yser and the ferryman's house. What a hot corner it was just then! Believe me or believe me not, Paul, if our reinforcements hadn't come up, we should have been done for in another five minutes. We were jolly lucky!"

"We were indeed," said Paul. "I felt that next day, when I woke up in a French ambulance!"

"What I can't get over, though," Bernard continued, "is the way that blackguard of a Major Hermann made off. So you took him prisoner? And then you saw him unfasten his bonds and escape? The cheek of the rascal! You may be sure he got away safe and sound!"

Paul muttered:

"I haven't a doubt of it; and I don't doubt either that he means to carry out his threats against Élisabeth."

"Bosh! We have forty-eight hours before us, as he gave his pal Karl the tenth of January as the date of his arrival and he won't act until two days later."

"And suppose he acts to-day?" said Paul, in a husky voice.

Notwithstanding his anguish, however, the drive did not seem long to him. He was at last approaching—and this time really—the object from which each day of the last four months had removed him to a greater distance. Ornequin was on the frontier; and Èbrecourt was but a few minutes from the frontier. He refused to think of the obstacles which would intervene before he could reach Èbrecourt, discover his wife's retreat and save her. He was alive. Élisabeth was alive. No obstacles existed between him and her.

The Château d'Ornequin, or rather what remained of it—for even the ruins of the château had been subjected to a fresh bombardment in

November—was serving as a cantonment for territorial troops, whose first line of trenches skirted the frontier. There was not much fighting on this side, because, for tactical reasons, it was not to the enemy's advantage to push too far forward. The defenses were of equal strength; and a very active watch was kept on either side.

These were the particulars which Paul obtained from the territorial lieutenant with whom he lunched.

"My dear fellow," concluded the officer, after Paul had told him the object of his journey, "I am altogether at your service; but, if it's a question of getting from Ornequin to Èbrecourt, you can make up your mind that you won't do it."

"I shall do it all right."

"It'll have to be through the air then," said the officer, with a laugh.

"No."

"Or underground."

"Perhaps."

"There you're wrong. We wanted ourselves to do some sapping and mining. It was no use. We're on a deposit of rock in which it's impossible to dig."

It was Paul's turn to smile:

"My dear chap, if you'll just be kind enough to lend me for one hour four strong men armed with picks and shovels, I shall be at Èbrecourt to-night."

"I say! Four men to dig a six-mile tunnel through the rock in an hour!"

"That's ample. Also, you must promise absolute secrecy both as to the means employed and the rather curious discoveries to which they are bound to lead. I shall make a report to the general commanding in chief; but no one else is to know."

"Very well, I'll select my four fellows for you myself. Where am I to bring them to you?"

"On the terrace, near the donjon."

This terrace commands the Liseron from a height of some hundred and fifty feet and, in consequence of a loop in the river, is exactly opposite Corvigny, whose steeple and the neighboring hills are seen in the distance. Of the castle-keep nothing remains but its enormous base, which is continued by the foundation-walls, mingled with natural rocks, which support the terrace. A garden extends its clumps of laurels and spindle-trees to the parapet.

MAURICE LEBLANC

It was here that Paul went. Time after time he strode up and down the esplanade, leaning over the river and inspecting the blocks that had fallen from the keep under the mantle of ivy.

"Now then," said the lieutenant, on arriving with his men. "Is this your starting-point? I warn you we are standing with our backs to the frontier."

"Pooh!" replied Paul, in the same jesting tone. "All roads lead to Berlin!"

He pointed to a circle which he had marked out with stakes, and set the men to work:

"Go ahead, my lads."

They began to throw up, within a circle of three yards in circumference, a soil consisting of vegetable mold in which, in twenty minutes' time, they had dug a hole five feet deep. Here they came upon a layer of stones cemented together; and their work now became much more difficult, for the cement was of incredible hardness and they were only to break it up by inserting their picks into the cracks. Paul followed the operations with anxious attention.

After an hour, he told them to stop. He himself went down into the hole and then went on digging, but slowly and as though examining the effect of every blow that he struck.

"That's it!" he said, drawing himself up.

"What?" asked Bernard.

"The ground on which we are standing is only a floor of the big buildings that used to adjoin the old keep, buildings which were razed to the ground centuries ago and on the top of which this garden was laid out."

"Well?"

"Well, in clearing away the soil, I have broken through the ceiling of one of the old rooms. Look."

He took a stone, placed it right in the center of the narrower opening which he himself had made and let it drop. The stone disappeared. A dull sound followed almost immediately.

"All that need now be done is for the men to widen the entrance. In the meantime, we will go and fetch a ladder and lights: as much light as possible."

"We have pine torches," said the officer.

"That will do capitally."

Paul was right. When the ladder was let down and he had descended with the lieutenant and Bernard, they saw a very large hall, whose vaults were supported by massive pillars which divided it, like a church of irregular design, into two main naves, with narrower and lower side-aisles.

But Paul at once called his companions' attention to the floor of those two naves:

"A concrete flooring, do you see? . . . And, look there, as I expected, two rails running along one of the upper galleries! . . . And here are two more rails in the other gallery! . . ."

"But what does it all mean?" exclaimed Bernard and the lieutenant.

"It means simply this," said Paul, "that we have before us what is evidently the explanation of the great mystery surrounding the capture of Corvigny and its two forts."

"How?"

"Corvigny and its two forts were demolished in a few minutes, weren't they? Where did those gunshots come from, considering that Corvigny is fifteen miles from the frontier and that not one of the enemy's guns had crossed the frontier? They came from here, from this underground fortress."

"Impossible."

"Here are the rails on which they moved the two gigantic pieces which were responsible for the bombardment."

"I say! You can't bombard from the bottom of a cavern! Where are the embrasures?"

"The rails will take us there. Show a good light, Bernard. Look, here's a platform mounted on a pivot. It's a good size, eh? And here's the other platform."

"But the embrasures?"

"In front of you, Bernard."

"That's a wall."

"It's the wall which, together with the rock of the hill, supports the terrace above the Liseron, opposite Corvigny. And two circular breaches were made in the wall and afterwards closed up again. You can see the traces of the closing quite plainly."

Bernard and the lieutenant could not get over their astonishment:

"Why, it's an enormous work!" said the officer.

"Absolutely colossal!" replied Paul. "But don't be too much surprised, my dear fellow. It was begun sixteen or seventeen years ago, to my own knowledge. Besides, as I told you, part of the work was already done, because we are in the lower rooms of the old Ornequin buildings; and, having found them, all they had to do was to arrange them according to the object which they had in view. There is something much more astounding, though!"

"What is that?"

"The tunnel which they had to build in order to bring their two pieces here."

"A tunnel?"

"Well, of course! How do you expect they got here? Let's follow the rails, in the other direction, and we'll soon come to the tunnel."

As he anticipated, the two sets of rails joined a little way back and they saw the yawning entrance to a tunnel about nine feet wide and the same height. It dipped under ground, sloping very gently. The walls were of brick. No damp oozed through the walls; and the ground itself was perfectly dry.

"Èbrecourt branch-line," said Paul, laughing. "Seven miles in the shade. And that is how the stronghold of Corvigny was bagged. First, a few thousand men passed through, who killed off the little Ornequin garrison and the posts on the frontier and then went on to the town. At the same time, the two huge guns were brought up, mounted and trained upon sites located beforehand. When these had done their business, they were removed and the holes stopped up. All this didn't take two hours."

"But to achieve those two decisive hours the Kaiser worked for seventeen years, bless him!" said Bernard. "Well, let's make a start."

"Would you like my men to go with you?" suggested the lieutenant.

"No, thank you. It's better that my brother-in-law and I should go by ourselves. If we find, however, that the enemy has destroyed his tunnel, we will come back and ask for help. But it will astonish me if he has. Apart from the fact that he has taken every precaution lest the existence of the tunnel should be discovered, he is likely to have kept it intact in case he himself might want to use it again."

And so, at three o'clock in the afternoon, the two brothers-in-law started on their walk down the imperial tunnel, as Bernard called it. They were well armed, supplied with provisions and ammunition and resolved to pursue the adventure to the end.

In a few minutes, that is to say, two hundred yards farther on, the light of their pocket-lantern showed them the steps of a staircase on their right.

"First turning," remarked Paul. "I take it there must be at least three of them."

"Where does the staircase lead to?"

"To the château, obviously. And, if you want to know to what part, I say, to the room with the portrait. There's no doubt that this is the way by which Major Hermann entered the château on the evening of the day when we attacked it. He had his accomplice Karl with him. Seeing our names written on the wall, they stabbed the two men sleeping in the room, Private Gériflour and his comrade."

Bernard d'Andeville stopped short:

"Look here, Paul, you've been bewildering me all day. You're acting with the most extraordinary insight, going straight to the right place at which to dig, describing all that happened as if you had been there, knowing everything and foreseeing everything. I never suspected you of that particular gift. Have you been studying Sherlock Holmes?"

"Not even Arsène Lupin," said Paul, moving on again. "But I've been ill and I have thought things over. Certain passages in Élisabeth's diary, in which she spoke of her perplexing discoveries, gave me the first hint. I began by asking myself why the Germans had taken such pains to create a desert all around the château. And in this way, putting two and two together, drawing inference after inference, examining the past and the present, remembering my meeting with the German Emperor and a number of things which are all linked together, I ended by coming to the conclusion that there was bound to be a secret communication between the German and the French sides of the frontier, terminating at the exact place from which it was possible to fire on Corvigny. It seemed to me that, *a priori*, this place must be the terrace; and I became quite sure of it when, just now, I saw on the terrace a dead tree, overgrown with ivy, near which Élisabeth thought that she heard sounds coming from underground. From that moment, I had nothing to do but get to work."

"And your object is. . . ?" asked Bernard.

"I have only one object: to deliver Élisabeth."

"Your plan?"

"I haven't one. Everything will depend on circumstances; but I am convinced that I am on the right track."

In fact all his surmises were proving to be correct. In ten minutes they reached a space where another tunnel, also supplied with rails, branched off to the right.

"Second turning," said Paul. "Corvigny Road. It was down here that the Germans marched to the town and took our troops by surprise before they even had time to assemble; it was down here that the peasant-woman went who accosted you in the evening. The outlet must be at some distance from the town, perhaps in a farm belonging to the supposed peasant-woman."

"And the third turning?" said Bernard.

"Here it is."

"Another staircase?"

"Yes; and I have no doubt that it leads to the chapel. We may safely presume that, on the day when my father was murdered, the Emperor had come to examine the works which he had ordered and which were being executed under the supervision of the woman who accompanied him. The chapel, which at that time was not inside the walls of the park, is evidently one of the exits from the secret network of roads of which we are following the main thoroughfare."

Paul saw two more of these ramifications, which, judging from their position and direction, must issue near the frontier, thus completing a marvelous system of espionage and invasion.

"It's wonderful," said Bernard. "It's admirable. If this isn't Kultur, I should like to know what is. One can see that these people have the true sense of war. The idea of digging for twenty years at a tunnel intended for the possible bombardment of a tiny fortress would never have occurred to a Frenchman. It needs a degree of civilization to which we can't lay claim. Did you ever know such beggars!"

His enthusiasm increased still further when he observed that the roof of the tunnel was supplied with ventilating-shafts. But at last Paul enjoined him to keep silent or to speak in a whisper:

"You can imagine that, as they thought fit to preserve their lines of communication, they must have done something to make them unserviceable to the French. Èbrecourt is not far off. Perhaps there are listening-posts, sentries posted at the right places. These people leave nothing to chance."

One thing that lent weight to Paul's remark was the presence, between the rails, of those cast-iron slabs which covered the chambers of mines laid in advance, so that they could be exploded by electricity. The first was numbered five, the second four; and so on. Paul and Bernard avoided them carefully; and this delayed their progress, for they no longer dared switch on their lamps except at brief intervals.

At about seven o'clock they heard or rather they seemed to hear confused sounds of life and movement on the ground overhead. They felt deeply moved. The soil above them was German soil; and the echo brought the sounds of German life.

"It's curious, you know, that the tunnel isn't better watched and that we have been able to come so far without accident."

"We'll give them a bad mark for that," said Bernard. "Kultur has made a slip."

Meanwhile a brisker draught blew along the walls. The outside air entered in cool gusts; and they suddenly saw a distant light through the darkness. It was stationary. Everything around it seemed still, as though it were one of those fixed signals which are put up near a railway.

When they came closer, they perceived that it was the light of an electric arc-lamp, that it was burning inside a shed standing at the exit of the tunnel and its rays were cast upon great white cliffs and upon little mounds of sand and pebbles.

Paul whispered:

"Those are quarries. By placing the entrance to their tunnel there, they were able to continue their works in time of peace without attracting attention. You may be sure that those so-called quarries were worked very discreetly, in a compound to which the workmen were confined."

"What Kultur!" Bernard repeated.

He felt Paul's hand grip his arm. Something had passed in front of the light, like a shadow rising and falling immediately after.

With infinite caution they crawled up to the shed and raised themselves until their eyes were on a level with the windows. Inside were half a dozen soldiers, all lying down, or rather sprawling one across the other, among empty bottles, dirty plates, greasy paper wrappers and remnants of broken victuals. They were the men told off to guard the tunnel; and they were dead-drunk.

"More Kultur," said Bernard.

"We're in luck," said Paul, "and I now understand why the watch is so ill-kept: this is Sunday."

There was a telegraph-apparatus on a table and a telephone on the wall; and Paul saw under a glass case a switch-board with five brass handles, which evidently corresponded by electric wires with the five mine-chambers in the tunnel.

When they passed on, Bernard and Paul continued to follow the rails along the bed of a narrow channel, hollowed out of the rock, which led them to an open space bright with many lights. A whole village lay before them, consisting of barracks inhabited by soldiers whom they saw moving to and fro. They went outside it. They then noticed the sound of a motor-car and the blinding rays of two head-lights; and, after climbing a fence and passing through a shrubbery, they saw a large villa lit up from top to bottom.

The car stopped in front of the doorstep, where some footmen were standing, as well as a guard of soldiers. Two officers and a lady wrapped in furs alighted. When the car turned, the lights revealed a large garden, contained within very high walls.

"It is just as I thought," said Paul. "This forms the counterpart of the Château d'Ornequin. At either end there are strong walls which allow work to be done unobserved by prying eyes. The terminus is in the open air here, instead of underground, as it is down there; but at least the quarries, the work-yards, the barracks, the garrison, the villa belonging to the staff, the garden, the stables, all this military organization is surrounded by walls and no doubt guarded on the outside by sentries. That explains why one is able to move about so freely inside."

At that moment, a second motor-car set down three officers and then joined the other in the coach-house.

"There's a dinner-party on," said Bernard.

They resolved to approach as near as they could, under cover of the thick clumps of shrubs planted along the carriage-drive which surrounded the house.

They waited for some time; and then, from the sound of voices and laughter that came from the ground-floor, at the back, they concluded that this must be the scene of the banquet and that the guests were sitting down to dinner. There were bursts of song, shouts of applause. Outside, nothing stirred. The garden was deserted.

"The place seems quiet," said Paul. "I shall ask you to give me a leg up and to keep hidden yourself."

"You want to climb to the ledge of one of the windows? What about the shutters?"

"I don't expect they're very close. You can see the light shining through the middle."

"Well, but why are you doing it? There is no reason to bother about this house more than any other."

"Yes, there is. You yourself told me that one of the wounded prisoners said Prince Conrad had taken up his quarters in a villa outside Èbrecourt. Now this one, standing in the middle of a sort of entrenched camp and at the entrance to the tunnel, seems to me marked out. . ."

"Not to mention this really princely dinner-party," said Bernard, laughing. "You're right. Up you go."

They crossed the walk. With Bernard's assistance, Paul was easily able to grip the ledge above the basement floor and to hoist himself to the stone balcony.

"That's it," he said. "Go back to where we were and whistle in case of danger."

After bestriding the balustrade, he carefully loosened one of the shutters by passing first his fingers and then his hand through the intervening space; and he succeeded in unfastening the bolt. The curtains, being crossed inside, enabled him to move about unseen; but they were open at the top, leaving an inverted triangle through which he could see by climbing on to the balustrade.

He did so and then bent forward and looked.

The sight that met his eyes was such and gave him so horrible a blow that his legs began to shake beneath him. . .

XV

Prince Conrad Makes Merry

A table running parallel with the three windows of the room. An incredible collection of bottles, decanters and glasses, hardly leaving room for the dishes of cake and fruit. Ornamental side-dishes flanked by bottles of champagne. A basket of flowers surrounded by liqueur-bottles.

Twenty persons were seated at table, including half-a-dozen women in low-necked dresses. The others were officers, covered with gold lace and orders.

In the middle, facing the window, sat Prince Conrad, presiding over the banquet, with a lady on his right and another on his left. And it was the sight of these three, brought together in the most improbable defiance of the logic of things, that caused Paul to undergo a torture which was renewed from moment to moment.

That one of the two women should be there, on the prince's right, sitting stiff-backed in her plum-colored stuff gown, with a black-lace scarf half-hiding her short hair, was easy to understand. But the other woman, to whom Prince Conrad kept turning with a clumsy affectation of gallantry, that woman whom Paul contemplated with horror-struck eyes and whom he would have liked to strangle where she sat, what was she doing there? What was Élisabeth doing in the midst of those tipsy officers and dubious German women, beside Prince Conrad and beside the monstrous creature who was pursuing her with her hatred?

The Comtesse Hermine d'Andeville! Élisabeth d'Andeville! The mother and the daughter! There was no plausible argument that would allow Paul to apply any other description to the prince's two companions. And something happened to give this description its full value of hideous reality when, a moment later, Prince Conrad rose to his feet, with a glass of champagne in his hand, and shouted:

"*Hoch! Hoch! Hoch!* Here's to the health of our very wideawake friend!"

"*Hoch! Hoch! Hoch!* " shouted the band of guests. "The Comtesse Hermine!"

She took up a glass, emptied it at a draught and began to make a speech which Paul could not hear, while the others did their best to listen with a fervent attention which was all the more meritorious in view of their copious libations.

And Élisabeth also sat and listened. She was wearing a gray gown which Paul knew well, quite a simple frock, cut very high in the neck and with sleeves that came down to her wrists. But from her throat a wonderful necklace, consisting of four rows of large pearls, hung over her bodice; and this necklace Paul did not know.

"The wretch! The wretch!" he spluttered.

She was smiling. Yes, he saw on the younger woman's lips a smile provoked by something that Prince Conrad said as he bent over her. And the prince gave such a boisterous laugh that the Comtesse Hermine, who was still speaking, called him to order by tapping him on the hand with her fan.

The whole scene was a horrible one for Paul; and he suffered such scorching anguish that his one idea was to get away, to see no more, to abandon the struggle and to drive this hateful wife of his out of his life and out of his memory.

"She is a true daughter of the Comtesse Hermine," he thought, in despair.

He was on the point of going, when a little incident held him back. Élisabeth raised to her eyes a handkerchief which she held crumpled in the hollow of her hand and furtively wiped away a tear that was ready to flow. At the same time he perceived that she was terribly pale, not with a factitious pallor, which until then he had attributed to the crudeness of the light, but with a real and deathly pallor. It was as though all the blood had fled from her poor face. And, after all, what a melancholy smile was that which had twisted her lips in response to the prince's jest!

"But then what is she doing here?" Paul asked himself. "Am I not entitled to regard her as guilty and to suppose that her tears are due to remorse? She has become cowardly through fear, threats and the wish to live; and now she is crying."

He continued to insult her in his thoughts; but gradually he felt a great pity steal over him for the woman who had not had the strength to endure her intolerable trials.

Meanwhile, the Comtesse Hermine made an end of her speech. She drank again, swallowing bumper after bumper and each time flinging her glass behind her. The officers and their women followed her example. Enthusiastic *Hochs* were raised from every side; and, in a drunken fit of patriotism, the prince got on his feet and struck up *"Deutschland über Alles,"* the others joining in the chorus with a sort of frenzy.

Élisabeth had put her elbows on the table and her hands before her face, as though trying to isolate herself from her surroundings. But the prince, still standing and bawling, took her two arms and brutally forced them apart:

"None of your monkey-tricks, pretty one!"

She gave a movement of repulsion which threw him beside himself.

"What's all this? Sulking? And blubbering? A nice thing! And, bless my soul, what do I see? Madame's glass is full!"

He took the glass and, with a shaky hand, put it to Élisabeth's lips:

"Drink my health, child! The health of your lord and master! What's this? You refuse? . . . Ah, I see, you don't like champagne! Quite right! Down with champagne! What you want is hock, good Rhine wine, eh, baby? You're thinking of one of your country's songs: 'We held it once, your German Rhine! It babbled in our brimming glass!' Rhine wine, there!"

With one movement, the officers rose and started shouting:

Die Wacht am Rhein

"They shall not have our German Rhine,
Tho' like a flock of hungry crows
They shriek their lust. . ."

"No, they shan't have it," rejoined the prince, angrily, "but you shall drink it, little one!"

Another glass had been filled. Once more he tried to force Élisabeth to lift it to her lips; and, when she pushed it away, he began to whisper in her ear, while the wine dribbled over her dress.

Everybody was silent, waiting to see what would happen. Élisabeth turned paler than ever, but did not move. The prince, leaning over her, showed the face of a brute who alternately threatens, pleads, commands and insults. It was a heart-rending sight. Paul would have given his life to see Élisabeth yield to a fit of disgust and stab her insulter. Instead of that, she threw back her head, closed her eyes and half-swooning, accepted the chalice and swallowed a few mouthfuls.

The prince gave a shout of triumph as he waved the glass on high; then he put his lips, avidly, to the place at which she had drunk and emptied it at a draught.

"*Hoch! Hoch!*" he roared. "Up, comrades! Every one on his chair, with one foot on the table! Up, conquerors of the world! Sing the strength of Germany! Sing German gallantry!

> "'*The Rhine, the free, the German Rhine*
> *They shall not have while gallant boys*
> *Still tell of love to slender maids. . .*'

"Élisabeth, I have drunk Rhine wine from your glass. Élisabeth, I know what you are thinking. Her thoughts are of love, my comrades! I am the master! Oh, Parisienne! . . . You dear little Parisienne! . . . It's Paris we want! . . . Oh, Paris, Paris! . . ."

His foot slipped. The glass fell from his hand and smashed against the neck of a bottle. He dropped on his knees on the table, amid a crash of broken plates and glasses, seized a flask of liqueur and rolled to the floor, stammering:

"We want Paris. . . Paris and Calais. . . Papa said so. . . The Arc de Triomphe! . . . The Café Anglais! . . . A *cabinet particulier* at the Café Anglais! . . ."

The uproar suddenly stopped. The Comtesse Hermine's imperious voice was raised in command:

"Go away, all of you! Go home! And be quick about it, gentlemen, if you please."

The officers and the ladies soon made themselves scarce. Outside, on the other side of the house, there was a great deal of whistling. The cars at once drove up from the garage. A general departure took place.

Meanwhile the Countess had beckoned to the servants and, pointing to Prince Conrad, said:

"Carry him to his room."

The prince was removed at once. Then the Comtesse Hermine went up to Élisabeth.

Not five minutes had elapsed since the prince rolled under the table; and, after the din of the banquet, a great silence reigned in the disorderly room where the two women were now by themselves. Élisabeth had once more hidden her head in her hands and was weeping violently with sobs that shook her shoulders. The Comtesse Hermine sat down beside her and gently touched her on the arm.

The two women looked at each other without a word. It was a strange glance that they exchanged, a glance laden with mutual hatred.

MAURICE LEBLANC

Paul did not take his eyes from them. As he watched the two of them, he could not doubt that they had met before and that the words which they were about to speak were but the sequel and conclusion of some earlier discussion. But what discussion? And what did Élisabeth know of the Comtesse Hermine? Did she accept that woman, for whom she felt such loathing, as her mother?

Never were two human beings distinguished by a greater difference in physical appearance and above all by expressions of face denoting more opposite natures. And yet how powerful was the series of proofs that linked them together! These were no longer proofs, but rather the factors of so actual a reality that Paul did not even dream of discussing them. Besides, M. d'Andeville's confusion when confronted with the countess' photograph, a photograph taken in Berlin some years after her pretended death, showed that M. d'Andeville was an accessory to that pretended death and perhaps an accessory to many other things.

And Paul came back to the question provoked by the agonizing encounter between the mother and daughter: what did Élisabeth know of it all? What insight had she been able to obtain into the whole monstrous conglomeration of shame, infamy, treachery and crime? Was she accusing her mother? And, feeling herself crushed under the weight of the crimes, did she hold her responsible for her own lack of courage?

"Yes, of course she does," thought Paul. "But why so much hatred? There is a hatred between them which only death can quench. And the longing to kill is perhaps even more violent in the eyes of Élisabeth than in those of the woman who has come to kill her."

Paul felt this impression so keenly that he really expected one or the other to take some immediate action; and he began to cast about for a means of saving Élisabeth. But an utterly unforeseen thing happened. The Comtesse Hermine took from her pocket one of those large road-maps which motorists use, placed her finger at one spot, followed the red line of a road to another spot and, stopping, spoke a few words that seemed to drive Élisabeth mad with delight.

She seized the countess by the arm and began to talk to her feverishly, in words interrupted by alternate laughing and sobbing, while the countess nodded her head and seemed to be saying:

"That's all right. . . We are agreed. . . Everything shall be as you wish. . ."

Paul thought that Élisabeth was actually going to kiss her enemy's hand, for she seemed overcome with joy and gratitude; and he was anxiously wondering into what new trap the poor thing had fallen, when the countess rose, walked to a door and opened it.

She beckoned to some one outside and then came back again.

A man entered, dressed in uniform. And Paul now understood. The man whom the Comtesse Hermine was admitting was Karl the spy, her confederate, the agent of her designs, the man whom she was entrusting with the task of killing Élisabeth, whose last hour had struck.

Karl bowed. The Comtesse Hermine introduced the man to Élisabeth and then, pointing to the road and the two places on the map, explained what was expected of him. He took out his watch and made a gesture as though to say:

"It shall be done at such-and-such a time."

Thereupon, at the countess' suggestion, Élisabeth left the room.

Although Paul had not caught a single word of what was said, this brief scene was, for him, pregnant with the plainest and most terrifying significance. The countess, using her absolute power and taking advantage of the fact that Prince Conrad was asleep, was proposing a plan of escape to Élisabeth, doubtless a flight by motor-car, towards a spot in the neighboring district thought out in advance. Élisabeth was accepting this unhoped-for deliverance. And the flight would take place under the management and protection of Karl!

The trap was so well-laid and Élisabeth, driven mad with suffering, was rushing into it so confidently that the two accomplices, on being left alone, looked at each other and laughed. The trick was really too easy; and there was no merit in succeeding under such conditions.

There next took place between them, even before any explanation was entered into, a short pantomime: two movements, no more; but they were marked with diabolical cynicism. With his eyes fixed on the countess, Karl the spy opened his jacket and drew a dagger half-way out of its sheath. The countess made a sign of disapproval and handed the scoundrel a little bottle which he took with a shrug of the shoulders, apparently saying:

"As you please! It's all the same to me!"

Then, sitting side by side, they embarked on a lively conversation, the countess giving her instructions, while Karl expressed his approval or his dissent.

Paul had a feeling that, if he did not master his dismay, if he did not stop the disordered beating of his heart, Élisabeth was lost. To save her, he must keep his brain absolutely clear and take immediate resolutions, as circumstances demanded, without giving himself time to reflect or hesitate. And these resolutions he could only take at a venture and perhaps erroneously, because he did not really know the enemy's plans. Nevertheless he cocked his revolver.

He was at that moment presuming that, when Élisabeth was ready to start, she would return to the room and go away with the spy; but presently the countess struck a bell on the table and spoke a few words to the servant who appeared. The man went out. Paul heard two whistles, followed by the hum of an approaching motor.

Karl looked through the open door and down the passage. Then he turned to the countess, as though to say:

"Here she is. . . She's coming down the stairs. . ."

Paul now understood that Élisabeth would go straight to the car and that Karl would join her there. If so, it was a case for immediate action.

For a second he remained undecided. Should he take advantage of the fact that Karl was still there, burst into the room and shoot both him and the countess dead? It would mean saving Élisabeth, because it was only those two miscreants who had designs upon her life. But he dreaded the failure of so daring an attempt and, jumping from the balcony, he called Bernard.

"Élisabeth is going off in a motor-car. Karl is with her and has been told to poison her. Get out your revolver and come with me."

"What do you intend to do?"

"We shall see."

They went round the villa, slipping through the bushes that bordered the drive. The whole place, moreover, was deserted.

"Listen," said Bernard, "there's a car going off."

Paul, at first greatly alarmed, protested:

"No, no, it's only the noise of the engine."

In fact, when they came within sight of the front of the house, they saw at the foot of the steps a closed car surrounded by a group of some dozen soldiers. Its head-lamps, while lighting up one part of the garden, left the spot where Paul and Bernard stood in darkness.

A woman came down the steps and disappeared inside the car.

"Élisabeth," said Paul. "And here comes Karl. . ."

The spy stopped on the bottom step and gave his orders to the soldier who acted as chauffeur. Paul caught a syllable here and there.

Their departure was imminent. Another moment and, if Paul raised no obstacle, the car would carry off the assassin and his victim. It was a horrible minute, for Paul Delroze felt all the danger attending an interference which would not even possess the merit of being effective, since Karl's death would not prevent the Comtesse Hermine from pursuing her ends.

Bernard whispered:

"Surely you don't mean to carry away Élisabeth? There's a whole picket of sentries there."

"I mean to do only one thing, to do for Karl."

"And then?"

"Then they'll take us prisoners. We shall be questioned, cross-examined; there will be a scandal. Prince Conrad will take the matter up."

"And we shall be shot. I confess that your plan. . ."

"Can you propose a better one?"

He broke off. Karl the spy had flown into a rage and was storming at his chauffeur; and Paul heard him shout:

"You damned ass! You're always doing it! No petrol. . . Where do you think we shall find petrol in the middle of the night? There's some in the garage, is there? Then run and fetch it, you fat-head! . . . And where's my fur-coat? You've forgotten it? Go and get it at once. I shall drive the car myself. I've no use for fools like you! . . ."

The soldier started running. And Paul at once observed that he himself would be able to reach the garage, of which he saw the lights, without having to leave the protecting darkness.

"Come," he said to Bernard. "I have an idea: you'll see what it is."

With the sound of their footsteps deadened by a grassy lawn, they made for that part of the out-houses containing the stables and motor-sheds, which they were able to enter unseen by those without. The soldier was in a back-room, the door of which was open. From their hiding-place they saw him take from a peg a great goat-skin coat, which he threw over his shoulder, and lay hold of four tins of petrol. Thus laden, he left the back-room and passed in front of Paul and Bernard.

The trick was soon done. Before he had time to cry out, he was knocked down, rendered motionless and gagged.

"That's that," said Paul. "Now give me his great-coat and his cap. I would rather have avoided this disguise; but, if you want to be sure of a thing, you mustn't stick at the means."

"Then you're going to risk it?" asked Bernard. "Suppose Karl doesn't recognize his chauffeur?"

"He won't even think of looking at him."

"But if he speaks to you?"

"I shan't answer. Besides, once we are outside the grounds, I shall have nothing to fear from him."

"And what am I to do?"

"You? Bind your prisoner carefully and lock him up in some safe place. Then go back to the shrubbery beyond the window with the balcony. I hope to join you there with Élisabeth some time during the middle of the night; and we shall simply have to go back by the tunnel. If by accident you don't see me return. . ."

"Well?"

"Well, then go back alone before it gets light."

"But. . ."

Paul was already moving away. He was in the mood in which a man refuses to consider the actions which he has decided to perform. Moreover, the event seemed to prove that he was right. Karl received him with abusive language, but without paying the least attention to this supernumerary for whom he could not show enough contempt. The spy put on his fur-coat, sat down at the wheel and began to handle the levers while Paul took his seat beside him.

The car was starting, when a voice from the doorstep called, in a tone of command:

"Karl! Stop!"

Paul felt a moment's anxiety. It was the Comtesse Hermine. She went up to the spy and, lowering her voice, said, in French:

"I want you, Karl, to be sure. . . But your driver doesn't know French, does he?"

"He hardly knows German, *Excellenz*. He's an idiot. You can speak freely."

"What I was going to say is, don't use more than ten drops out of the bottle, else. . ."

"Very well, *Excellenz*. Anything more?"

"Write to me in a week's time if everything has gone off well. Write to our Paris address and not before: it would be useless."

"Then you're going back to France, *Excellenz*?"

"Yes, my plan is ripe."

"The same plan?"

"Yes. The weather is in our favor. It has been raining for days and the staff have told me that they mean to act on their side. So I shall be there to-morrow evening; and it will only need a touch of the thumb. . ."

"That's it, a touch of the thumb, no more. I've worked at it myself and everything's ready. But you spoke to me of another plan, to complete the first; and I confess that that one. . ."

"It's got to be done. Luck is turning against us. If I succeed, it will be the end of the run on the black."

"And have you the Kaiser's consent?"

"I didn't ask for it. It's one of those undertakings one doesn't talk about."

"But this one is terribly dangerous, *Excellenz*."

"Can't be helped."

"Sha'n't you want me over there, *Excellenz*?"

"No. Get rid of the chit for us. That will be enough for the present. Good-bye."

"Good-bye, *Excellenz*."

The spy released the brakes. The car started.

The drive which ran round the central lawn led to a lodge which stood beside the garden-gate and which served as a guard-room. The high walls surrounding the grounds rose on either side of it.

An officer came out of the lodge. Karl gave the pass-word, "Hohenstaufen." The gate was opened and the motor dashed down a high-road which first passed through the little town of Èbrecourt and next wound among low hills.

So Paul Delroze, at an hour before midnight, was alone in the open country, with Élisabeth and Karl the spy. If he succeeded in mastering the spy, as he did not doubt that he could, Élisabeth would be free. There would then remain nothing to do but to return to Prince Conrad's villa, with the aid of the pass-word, and pick up Bernard there. Once the adventure was completed in accordance with Paul's designs, the tunnel would bring back all the three of them to the Château d'Ornequin.

Paul therefore gave way to the delight that was stealing over him. Élisabeth was with him, under his protection: Élisabeth, whose courage, no doubt, had yielded under the weight of her trials, but who had a claim upon his indulgence because her misfortunes were due to his fault. He forgot, he wished to forget all the ugly phases in the tragedy, in order to think only of the end that was near at hand, his wife's triumph and deliverance.

He watched the road attentively, so as not to miss his way when returning, and planned out his attack, fixing it at the first stop which they would have to make. He resolved that he would not kill the spy, but that he would stun him with a blow of his fist and, after knocking him down and binding him, throw him into some wood by the road-side.

They came to a fair-sized market-town, then two villages and then a town where they had to stop and show the car's papers. It was past eleven.

Then once more they were driving along country lanes which ran through a series of little woods whose trees lit up as they passed.

At that moment, the light of the lamps began to fail. Karl slackened speed. He growled:

"You dolt, can't you even keep your lamps alight? Have you got any carbide?"

Paul did not reply. Karl went on cursing his luck. Suddenly, he put on the brakes, with an oath:

"You blasted idiot! One can't go on like this. . . Here, stir your stumps and light up."

Paul sprang from his seat, while the car drew up by the road-side. The time had come to act.

He first attended to the lamps, keeping an eye upon the spy's movements and taking care to stand outside the rays. Karl got down, opened the door of the car, and started a conversation which Paul could not hear. Then he came back to where Paul was:

"Well, pudding-head, haven't you done yet?"

Paul had his back turned to him, attending to his work and waiting for the propitious moment when the spy, coming two steps nearer, would be within his reach.

A minute elapsed. He clenched his fists. He foresaw the exact movement which he would have to make and was on the point of making it, when suddenly he felt himself seized round the body from behind and brought to the ground without being able to offer the least resistance.

"Thunder and lightning!" cried the spy, holding him down with his knee. "So that's why you wouldn't answer? . . . It struck me somehow that you were behaving queerly. . . And then I never gave it another thought. . . It was the lamp, just now, that threw a light on your side-face. . . But who is the fellow I've got hold of? Some dog of a Frenchman, may be?"

Paul had stiffened his muscles and believed for a moment that he would succeed in escaping from the other's grip. The enemy's strength was yielding; Paul gradually seemed to master him; and he exclaimed:

"Yes, a Frenchman, Paul Delroze, the one you used to try and kill, the husband of Élisabeth, your victim. . . Yes, it's I; and I know who you are: you're Laschen, the sham Belgian; you're Karl the spy."

He stopped. The spy, who had only weakened his effort to draw a dagger from his belt, was now raising it against him:

"Ah, Paul Delroze! . . . God's truth, this'll be a lucky trip! . . . First the husband and then the wife. . . Ah, so you came running into my clutches! . . . Here, take this, my lad! . . ."

Paul saw the gleam of a blade flashing above his face. He closed his eyes, uttering Élisabeth's name.

Another second; and three shots rang out in rapid succession. Some one was firing from behind the group formed by the two adversaries.

The spy swore a hideous oath. His grip became relaxed. The weapon in the hand trembled and he fell flat on the ground, moaning:

"Oh, the cursed woman! . . . That cursed woman! . . . I ought to have strangled her in the car. . . I knew this would happen. . ."

His voice failed him. He stammered:

"I've got it this time. . . Oh, that cursed woman! . . . And the pain. . . !"

Then he was silent. A few convulsions, a dying gasp and that was all.

Paul had leapt to his feet. He ran to the woman who had saved his life and who was still holding her revolver in her hand:

"Élisabeth!" he cried, wild with delight.

But he stopped, with his arms outstretched. In the dark, the woman's figure did not seem to him to be Élisabeth's, but a taller and broader figure. He blurted out, in a tone of infinite anguish:

"Élisabeth. . . is it you? . . . Is it really you? . . ."

And at the same time he intuitively knew the answer which he was about to hear:

"No," said the woman, "Mme. Delroze started a little before us, in another motor. Karl and I were to join her."

Paul remembered that car, of which he and Bernard had thought that he heard the sound when going round the villa. As the two starts had taken place with an interval of a few minutes at most between them, he cried:

"Let us be quick then and lose no time. . . By putting on speed, we shall be sure to catch them. . ."

But the woman at once objected:

"It's impossible, because the two cars have taken different roads."

"What does that matter, if they lead to the same point. Where are they taking Mme. Delroze?"

"To a castle belonging to the Comtesse Hermine."

"And where is that castle?"

"I don't know."

"You don't know? But this is terrible! At least, you know its name.

"No, I don't. Karl never told me."

XVI

The Impossible Struggle

In the terrible state of distress into which those last words threw him, Paul felt the need of some immediate action, even as he had done at the sight of the banquet given by Prince Conrad. Certainly, all hope was lost. His plan, which was to use the tunnel before the alarm was raised, his plan was shattered. Granting that he succeeded in finding Élisabeth and delivering her, a very unlikely contingency, at what moment would this take place? And how was he afterwards to escape the enemy and return to France?

No, henceforward space and time were both against him. His defeat was such that there was nothing for it but to resign himself and await the final blow.

And yet he did not flinch. He saw that any weakness would be irreparable. The impulse that had carried him so far must be continued unchecked and with more vigor than ever.

He walked up to the spy. The woman was stooping over the body and examining it by the light of one of the lamps which she had taken down.

"He's dead, isn't he?" asked Paul.

"Yes, he's dead. Two bullets hit him in the back." And she murmured, in a broken voice, "It's horrible, what I've done. I've killed him myself! But it's not a murder, sir, is it? And I had the right to, hadn't I? . . . But it's horrible all the same. . . I've killed Karl!"

Her face, which was young and still rather pretty, though common, was distorted. Her eyes seemed glued to the corpse.

"Who are you?" asked Paul.

She replied, sobbing:

"I was his sweetheart. . . and better than that. . . or rather worse. He had taken an oath that he would marry me. . . But Karl's oath! He was such a liar, sir, such a coward! . . . Oh, the things I know of him! . . . I myself, simply through holding my tongue, gradually became his accomplice. He used to frighten me so! I no longer loved him, but I was afraid of him and obeyed him. . . with such loathing, at the end! . . . And he knew how I loathed him. He used often to say, 'You are quite capable of killing me some day or other.' No, sir, I did think of it, but I should never have had the courage. It was only just now, when I saw that he was going to stab you. . . and above all when I heard your name. . ."

"My name? What has that to do with it?"

"You are Madame Delroze's husband."

"Well?"

"Well, I know her. Not for long, only since to-day. This morning, Karl, on his way from Belgium, passed through the town where I was and took me to Prince Conrad's. He told me I was to be lady's maid to a French lady whom we were going to take to a castle. I knew what that meant. I should once more have to be his accomplice, to inspire confidence. And then I saw that French lady, I saw her crying; and she was so gentle and kind that I felt sorry for her. I promised to rescue her. . . Only, I never thought that it would be in this way, by killing Karl. . ."

She drew herself up suddenly and said, in a hard voice:

"But it had to be, sir. It was bound to happen, for I knew too much about him. It had to be he or I. . . It was he. . . and I can't help it and I'm not sorry. . . He was the wickedest wretch on earth; and, with people like him, one mustn't hesitate. No, I am not sorry."

Paul asked:

"He was devoted to the Comtesse Hermine, was he not?"

She shuddered and lowered her voice to reply:

"Oh, don't speak of her, please! She is more terrible still; and she is still alive. Ah, if she should ever suspect!"

"Who is the woman?"

"How can I tell? She comes and goes, she is the mistress wherever she may be. . . People obey her as they do the Emperor. Everybody fears her. . . as they do her brother."

"Her brother?"

"Yes, Major Hermann."

"What's that? Do you mean to say that Major Hermann is her brother?"

"Why, of course! Besides, you have only to look at him. He is the very image of the Comtesse Hermine!"

"Have you ever seen them together?"

"Upon my word, I can't remember. Why do you ask?"

Time was too precious for Paul to insist. The woman's opinion of the Comtesse Hermine did not matter much. He asked:

"She is staying at the prince's?"

"For the present, yes. The prince is on the first floor, at the back; she is on the same floor, but in front."

"If I let her know that Karl has had an accident and that he has sent me, his chauffeur, to tell her, will she see me?"

"Certainly."

"Does she know Karl's chauffeur, whose place I took?"

"No. He was a soldier whom Karl brought with him from Belgium."

Paul thought for a moment and then said:

"Lend me a hand."

They pushed the body towards the ditch by the road-side, rolled it in and covered it with dead branches.

"I shall go back to the villa," he said. "You walk on until you come to the first cluster of houses. Wake the people and tell them the story of how Karl was murdered by his chauffeur and how you ran away. The time which it will take to inform the police, to question you and to telephone to the villa is more than I need."

She took alarm:

"But the Comtesse Hermine?"

"Have no fear there. Granting that I do not deprive her of her power of doing mischief, how could she suspect you, when the police-investigations will hold me alone to account for everything? Besides, we have no choice."

And, without more words, he started the engine, took his seat at the wheel and, in spite of the woman's frightened entreaties, drove off.

He drove off with the same eagerness and decision as though he were fulfilling the conditions of some new plan of which he had fixed every detail beforehand and as though he felt sure of its success.

"I shall see the countess," he said to himself. "She will either be anxious as to Karl's fate and want me to take her to him at once or she will see me in one of the rooms in the villa. In either case I shall find a method of compelling her to reveal the name of the castle in which Élisabeth is a prisoner. I shall even compel her to give me the means of delivering her and helping her to escape."

But how vague it all was! The obstacles in the way! The impossibilities! How could he expect circumstances to be so complaisant as first to blind the countess' eyes to the facts and next to deprive her of all assistance? A woman of her stamp was not likely to let herself be taken in by words or subdued by threats.

No matter, Paul would not entertain the thought of failure. Success lay at the end of his undertaking; and in order to achieve it more quickly he increased the pace, rushing his car like a whirlwind along the roads and hardly slackening speed as he passed through villages and towns.

"Hohenstaufen!" he cried to the sentry posted outside the wall.

The officer of the picket, after questioning him, sent him on to the sergeant in command of the post at the front-door. The sergeant was the only one who had free access to the villa; and he would inform the countess.

"Very well," said Paul. "I'll put up my car first."

In the garage, he turned off his lights; and, as he went towards the villa, he thought that it might be well, before going back to the sergeant, to look up Bernard and learn if his brother-in-law had succeeded in discovering anything.

He found him behind the villa, in the clumps of shrubs facing the window with the balcony.

"You're by yourself?" said Bernard, anxiously.

"Yes, the job failed. Élisabeth was in an earlier motor."

"What an awful thing!"

"Yes, but it can be put right. And you. . . what about the chauffeur?"

"He's safely hidden away. No one will see him. . . at least not before the morning, when other chauffeurs come to the garage."

"Very well. Anything else?"

"There was a patrol in the grounds an hour ago. I managed to keep out of sight."

"And then?"

"Then I made my way as far as the tunnel. The men were beginning to stir. Besides, there was something that made them jolly well pull themselves together!"

"What was that?"

"The sudden arrival of a certain person of our acquaintance, the woman I met at Corvigny, who is so remarkably like Major Hermann."

"Was she going the rounds?"

"No, she was leaving."

"Yes, I know, she means to leave."

"She has left."

"Oh, nonsense! I can't believe that. There was no immediate hurry about her departure for France."

"I saw her go, though."

"How? By what road?"

"The tunnel, of course! Do you imagine that the tunnel serves no further purpose? That was the road she took, before my eyes, under the most comfortable conditions, in an electric trolley driven by a brakesman. No doubt, since the object of her journey was, as you say, to get to France, they shunted her on to the Corvigny branch. That was two hours ago. I heard the trolley come back."

The disappearance of the Comtesse Hermine was a fresh blow to Paul. How was he now to find, how to deliver Élisabeth? What clue could he trust in this darkness, in which each of his efforts was ending in disaster?

He pulled himself together, made an act of will and resolved to persevere in the adventure until he attained his object. He asked Bernard if he had seen nothing more.

"No, nothing."

"Nobody going or coming in the garden?"

"No. The servants have gone to bed. The lights are out."

"All the lights?"

"All except one, there, over our heads."

The light was on the first floor, at a window situated above the window through which Paul had watched Prince Conrad's supper-party. He asked:

"Was that light put on while I was up on the balcony?"

"Yes, towards the end."

"From what I was told," Paul muttered, "that must be Prince Conrad's room. He's drunk and had to be carried upstairs."

"Yes, I saw some shadows at that time; and nothing has moved since."

"He's evidently sleeping off his champagne. Oh, if one could only see, if one could get into the room!"

"That's easily done," said Bernard.

"How?"

"Through the next room, which must be the dressing-room. They've left the window open, no doubt to give the prince a little air."

"But I should want a ladder. . ."

"There's one hanging on the wall of the coach-house. Shall I get it for you?"

"Yes, do," said Paul eagerly. "Be quick."

A whole new scheme was taking shape in his mind, similar in some respects to his first plan of campaign and likely, he thought, to lead to a successful issue.

He made certain that the approaches to the villa on either side were deserted and that none of the soldiers on guard had moved away from the front-door. Then, when Bernard was back, he placed the ladder in position and leant it against the wall. They went up.

The open window belonged, as they expected, to the dressing-room and the light from the bedroom showed through the open door. Not a sound came from that other room except a loud snoring. Paul put his head through the doorway.

Prince Conrad was lying fast asleep across his bed, like a loose-jointed doll, clad in his uniform, the front of which was covered with stains. He was sleeping so soundly that Paul was able to examine the room at his ease. There was a sort of little lobby between it and the passage, with a door at either end. He locked and bolted both doors, so that they were now alone with Prince Conrad, while it was impossible for them to be heard from the outside.

"Come on," said Paul, when they had apportioned the work to be done.

And he placed a twisted towel over the prince's face and tried to insert the ends into his mouth while Bernard bound his wrists and ankles with some more towels. All this was done in silence. The prince offered no resistance and uttered not a cry. He had opened his eyes and lay staring at his aggressors with the air of a man who does not understand what is happening to him, but is seized with increasing dread as he becomes aware of his danger.

"Not much pluck about William's son and heir," chuckled Bernard. "Lord, what a funk he's in! Hi, young-fellow-my-lad, pull yourself together! Where's your smelling-bottle?"

Paul had at last succeeded in cramming half the towel into his mouth. He lifted him up and said:

"Now let's be off."

"What do you propose to do?"

"Take him away."

"Where to?"

"To France."

"To France?"

"Well, of course. We've got him; he'll have to help us."

"They won't let him through."

"And the tunnel?"

"Out of the question. They're keeping too close a watch now."

"We shall see."

He took his revolver and pointed it at Prince Conrad:

"Listen to me," he said. "Your head is too muddled, I dare say, to take in any questions. But a revolver is easy to understand, isn't it? It talks a very plain language, even to a man who is drunk and shaking all over with fright. Well, if you don't come with me quietly, if you attempt to struggle or to make a noise, if my friend and I are in danger for a single moment, you're done for. You can feel the barrel of my revolver on your temple: Well, it's there to blow out your brains. Do you agree to my conditions?"

The prince nodded his head.

"Good," said Paul. "Bernard, undo his legs, but fasten his arms along his body. . . That's it. . . And now let's be off."

The descent of the ladder was easily accomplished and they walked through the shrubberies to the fence which separated the garden from the yard containing the barracks. Here they handed the prince across to each other, like a parcel, and then, taking the same road as when they came, they reached the quarries.

The night was bright enough to allow them to see their way; and, moreover, they had in front of them a diffused glow which seemed to rise from the guard-house at the entrance to the tunnel. And indeed all the lights there were burning; and the men were standing outside the shed, drinking coffee.

A soldier was pacing up and down in front of the tunnel, with his rifle on his shoulder.

"We are two," whispered Bernard. "There are six of them; and, at the first shot fired, they will be joined by some hundreds of Boches who are quartered five minutes away. It's a bit of an unequal struggle, what do you say?"

What increased the difficulty to the point of making it insuperable was that they were not really two but three and that their prisoner hampered them most terribly. With him it was impossible to hurry, impossible to run away. They would have to think of some stratagem to help them.

Slowly, cautiously, stealing along in such a way that not a stone rolled from under their footsteps or the prince's, they described a circle around the lighted space which brought them, after an hour, close to the tunnel, under the rocky slopes against which its first buttresses were built.

"Stay there," said Paul to Bernard, speaking very low, but just loud enough for the prince to hear. "Stay where you are and remember my instructions. First of all, take charge of the prince, with your revolver in your right hand and with your left hand on his collar. If he struggles, break his head. That will be a bad business for us, but just as bad for him. I shall go back to a certain distance from the shed and draw off the five men on guard. Then the man doing sentry down there will either join the rest, in which case you go on with the prince, or else he will obey orders and remain at his post, in which case you fire at him and wound him. . . and go on with the prince."

"Yes, I shall go on, but the Boches will come after me and catch us up."

"No, they won't."

"If you say so. . ."

"Very well, that's understood. And you, sir," said Paul to the prince, "do you understand? Absolute submission; if not, the least carelessness, a mere mistake may cost you your life."

Bernard whispered in his brother-in-law's ear:

"I've picked up a rope; I shall fasten it round his neck; and, if he jibs, he'll feel a sharp tug to recall him to the true state of things. Only, Paul, I warn you that, if he takes it into his head to struggle, I am incapable of killing him just like that, in cold blood."

"Don't worry. He's too much afraid to struggle. He'll go with you like a lamb to the other end of the tunnel. When you get there, lock him up in some corner of the château, but don't tell any one who he is."

"And you, Paul?"

"Never mind about me."

"Still. . ."

"We both stand the same risk. We're going to play a terribly dangerous game and there's every chance of our losing it. But, if we win, it means Élisabeth's safety. So we must go for it boldly. Good-bye, Bernard, for the present. In ten minutes everything will be settled one way or the other."

They embraced and Paul walked away.

As he had said, this one last effort could succeed only through promptness and audacity; and it had to be made in the spirit in which a man makes a desperate move. Ten minutes more would see the end of the adventure. Ten minutes and he would be either victorious or a dead man.

Every action which he performed from that moment was as orderly and methodical as if he had had time to think it out carefully and to ensure its inevitable success, whereas in reality he was forming a series of separate decisions as he went along and as the tragic circumstances seemed to call for them.

Taking a roundabout way and keeping to the slopes of the mounds formed by the sand thrown up in the works, he reached the hollow communication-road between the quarries and the garrison-camp. On the last of these rounds, his foot struck a block of stone which gave way beneath him. On stooping and groping with his hands, he perceived that this block held quite a heap of sand and pebbles in position behind it.

"That's what I want," he said, without a moment's reflection.

And, giving the stone a mighty kick, he sent the heap shooting into the road with a roar like an avalanche.

Paul jumped down among the stones, lay flat on his chest and began to scream for help, as though he had met with an accident.

From where he lay, it was impossible, owing to the winding of the road, to hear him in the barracks; but the least cry was bound to carry as far as the shed at the mouth of the tunnel, which was only a hundred yards away at most. The soldiers on guard came running along at once.

He counted only five of them. In an almost unintelligible voice, he gave incoherent, gasping replies to the corporal's questions and conveyed the impression that he had been sent by Prince Conrad to bring back the Comtesse Hermine.

Paul was quite aware that his stratagem had no chance of succeeding beyond a very brief space of time; but every minute gained was of inestimable value, because Bernard would make use of it on his side to take action against the sixth man, the sentry outside the tunnel, and to make his escape with Prince Conrad. Perhaps that man would come as well. Or else perhaps Bernard would get rid of him without using his revolver and therefore without attracting attention.

And Paul, gradually raising his voice, was spluttering out vague explanations, which only irritated without enlightening the corporal, when a shot rang out, followed by two others.

For the moment the corporal hesitated, not knowing for certain where the sound came from. The men stood away from Paul and listened. Thereupon he passed through them and walked straight on, without their realizing, in the darkness, that it was he who was moving away. Then, at the first turn, he started running and reached the shed in a few strides.

Twenty yards in front of him, at the mouth of the tunnel, he saw Bernard struggling with Prince Conrad, who was trying to escape. Near them, the sentry was dragging himself along the ground and moaning.

Paul saw clearly what he had to do. To lend Bernard a hand and with him attempt to run the risk of flight would have been madness, because their enemies would inevitably have caught them up and in any case Prince Conrad would have been set free. No, the essential thing was to stop the rush of the five other men, whose shadows were already appearing at the bend in the road, and thus to enable Bernard to get away with the prince.

Half-hidden behind the shed, he aimed his revolver at them and cried: "Halt!"

The corporal did not obey and ran on into the belt of light. Paul fired. The German fell, but only wounded, for he began to command in a savage tone:

"Forward! Go for him! Forward, can't you, you funks!"

The men did not stir a step. Paul seized a rifle from the stack which they had made of theirs near the shed and, while taking aim at them, was able to give a glance backwards and to see that Bernard had at last mastered Prince Conrad and was leading him well into the tunnel.

"It's only a question of holding out for five minutes," thought Paul, "so that Bernard may go as far as possible."

And he was so calm at this moment that he could have counted those minutes by the steady beating of his pulse.

"Forward! Rush at him! Forward!" the corporal kept clamoring, having doubtless seen the figures of the two fugitives, though without recognizing Prince Conrad.

Rising to his knees, he fired a revolver-shot at Paul, who replied by breaking his arm with a bullet. And yet the corporal went on shouting at the top of his voice:

"Forward! There are two of them making off through the tunnel! Forward! Here comes help!"

It was half-a-dozen soldiers from the barracks, who had run up at the sound of the shooting. Paul had now made his way into the shed. He broke a window-pane and fired three shots. The soldiers made for shelter; but others arrived, took their orders from the corporal and dispersed; and Paul saw them scrambling up the adjoining slopes in order to head him off. He fired his rifle a few more times; but what was the good? All hope of resistance had long since disappeared.

He persevered, however, killing his adversaries at intervals, firing incessantly and thus gaining all the time possible. But he saw that the enemy was maneuvering with the object of first circumventing him and then making for the tunnel and chasing the fugitives.

Paul set his teeth. He was really aware of each second that passed, of each of those inappreciable seconds which increased Bernard's distance.

Three men disappeared down the yawning mouth of the tunnel; then a fourth; then a fifth. Moreover, the bullets were now beginning to rain upon the shed.

Paul made a calculation:

"Bernard must be six or seven hundred yards away. The three men pursuing him have gone fifty yards. . . seventy-five yards now. That's all right."

A serried mass of Germans were coming towards the shed. It was evidently not believed that Paul was alone, so quickly did he fire. This time there was nothing for it but to surrender.

"It's time," he thought. "Bernard is outside the danger-zone."

He suddenly rushed at the board containing the handles which corresponded with the mine-chambers in the tunnel, smashed the glass with the butt-end of his rifle and pulled down the first handle and the second.

The earth seemed to shake. A thunderous roar rolled under the tunnel and spread far and long, like a reverberating echo.

The way was blocked between Bernard d'Andeville and the eager pack that was trying to catch him. Bernard could take Prince Conrad quietly to France.

Then Paul walked out of the shed, raising his arms in the air and crying, in a cheerful voice:

"*Kamerad! Kamerad!*"

Ten men surrounded him in a moment; and the officer who commanded them shouted, in a frenzy of rage:

"Let him be shot! . . . At once. . . at once! . . . Let him be shot! . . ."

MAURICE LEBLANC

XVII

The Law of the Conqueror

B rutally handled though he was, Paul offered no resistance; and, while they were pushing him with needless violence towards a perpendicular part of the cliff, he continued his inner calculations:

"It is mathematically certain that the two explosions took place at distances of three hundred and four hundred yards, respectively. I can therefore also take it as certain that Bernard and Prince Conrad were on the far side and that the men in pursuit were on this side. So all is for the best."

Docilely and with a sort of chaffing complacency he submitted to the preparations for his execution. The twelve soldiers entrusted with it were already drawn up in line under the bright rays of an electric search-light and were only waiting for the order. The corporal whom he had wounded early in the fight dragged himself up to him and snarled:

"Shot! . . . You're going to be shot, you dirty *Franzose*!"

He answered, with a laugh:

"Not a bit of it! Things don't happen as quickly as all that."

"Shot!" repeated the other. "*Herr Leutnant* said so."

"Well, what's he waiting for, your *Herr Leutnant*?"

The lieutenant was making a rapid investigation at the entrance to the tunnel. The men who had gone down it came running back, half-asphyxiated by the fumes of the explosion. As for the sentry, whom Bernard had been forced to get rid of, he was losing blood so profusely that it was no use trying to obtain any fresh information from him.

At that moment, news arrived from the barracks, where they had just learnt, through a courier sent from the villa, that Prince Conrad had disappeared. The officers were ordered to double the guard and to keep a good lookout, especially at the approaches.

Of course, Paul had counted on this diversion or some other of the same kind which would delay his execution. The day was beginning to break and he had little doubt that, Prince Conrad having been left dead drunk in his bedroom, one of his servants had been told to keep a watch on him. Finding the doors locked, the man must have given the alarm. This would lead to an immediate search.

But what surprised Paul was that no one suspected that the prince had been carried off through the tunnel. The sentry was lying unconscious and was unable to speak. The men had not realized that, of the two fugitives seen at a distance, one was dragging the other along. In short, it was thought that the prince had been assassinated. His murderers must have flung his body into some corner of the quarries and then taken to flight. Two of them had succeeded in escaping. The third was a prisoner. And nobody for a second entertained the least suspicion of an enterprise whose audacity simply surpassed imagination.

In any case there could no longer be any question of shooting Paul without a preliminary inquiry, the results of which must first be communicated to the highest authorities. He was taken to the villa, where he was divested of his German overcoat, carefully searched and lastly was locked up in a bedroom under the protection of four stalwart soldiers.

He spent several hours in dozing, glad of this rest, which he needed so badly, and feeling very easy in his mind, because, now that Karl was dead, the Comtesse Hermine absent and Élisabeth in a place of safety, there was nothing for him to do but to await the normal course of events.

At ten o'clock he was visited by a general who endeavored to question him and who, receiving no satisfactory replies, grew angry, but with a certain reserve in which Paul observed the sort of respect which people feel for noted criminals. And he said to himself:

"Everything is going as it should. This visit is only a preliminary to prepare me for the coming of a more serious ambassador, a sort of plenipotentiary."

He gathered from the general's words that they were still looking for the prince's body. They were now in fact looking for it beyond the immediate precincts, for a new clue, provided by the discovery and the revelations of the chauffeur whom Paul and Bernard had imprisoned in the garage, as well as by the departure and return of the motor car, as reported by the sentries, widened the field of investigation considerably.

At twelve o'clock Paul was provided with a substantial meal. The attentions shown to him increased. Beer was served with the lunch and afterwards coffee.

"I shall perhaps be shot," he thought, "but with due formality and not before they know exactly who the mysterious person is whom they have the honor of shooting, not to mention the motives of his enterprise and the results obtained. Now I alone am able to supply the details. Consequently. . ."

He so clearly felt the strength of his position and the necessity in which his enemies stood to contribute to the success of his plan that he was not surprised at being taken, an hour later, to a small drawing-room in the villa, before two persons all over gold lace, who first had him searched once more and then saw that he was fastened up with more elaborate care than ever.

"It must," he thought, "be at least the imperial chancellor coming all the way from Berlin to see me. . . unless indeed. . ."

Deep down within himself, in view of the circumstances, he could not help foreseeing an even more powerful intervention than the chancellor's; and, when he heard a motor car stop under the windows of the villa and saw the fluster of the two gold-laced individuals, he was convinced that his anticipations were being fully confirmed.

Everything was ready. Even before any one appeared, the two individuals drew themselves up and stood to attention; and the soldiers, stiffer still, looked like dolls out of a Noah's ark.

The door opened. And a whirlwind entrance took place, amid a jingling of spurs and saber. The man who arrived in this fashion at once gave an impression of feverish haste and of imminent departure. What he intended to do he must accomplish within the space of a few minutes.

At a sign from him, all those present quitted the room.

The Emperor and the French officer were left face to face. And the Emperor immediately asked, in an angry voice:

"Who are you? What did you come to do? Who are your accomplices? By whose orders were you acting?"

It was difficult to recognize in him the figure represented by his photographs and the illustrations in the newspapers, for the face had aged into a worn and wasted mask, furrowed with wrinkles and disfigured with yellow blotches.

Paul was quivering with hatred, not so much a personal hatred aroused by the recollection of his own sufferings as a hatred made up of horror and contempt for the greatest criminal imaginable. And, despite his absolute resolve not to depart from the usual formulas and the rules of outward respect, he answered:

"Let them untie me!"

The Emperor started. It was the first time certainly that any one had spoken to him like that; and he exclaimed:

"Why, you're forgetting that a word will be enough to have you shot! And you dare! Conditions! . . ."

Paul remained silent. The Emperor strode up and down, with his hand on the hilt of his sword, which he dragged along the carpet. Twice he stopped and looked at Paul; and, when Paul did not move an eyelid, he resumed his march, with an increasing display of indignation. And, all of a sudden, he pressed the button of an electric bell:

"Untie him!" he said to the men who hurried into the room.

When released from his bonds, Paul rose up and stood like a soldier in the presence of his superior officer.

The room was emptied once again. Then the Emperor went up to Paul and, leaving a table as a barrier between them, asked, still in a harsh voice:

"Prince Conrad?"

Paul answered:

"Prince Conrad is not dead, sir; he is well."

"Ah!" said the Kaiser, evidently relieved. And, still reluctant to come to the point, he continued: "That does not affect matters in so far as you are concerned. Assault. . . espionage. . . not to speak of the murder of one of my best servants. . ."

"Karl the spy, sir? I killed him in self-defense."

"But you did kill him? Then for that murder and for the rest you shall be shot."

"No, sir. Prince Conrad's life is security for mine."

The Emperor shrugged his shoulders:

"If Prince Conrad is alive he will be found."

"No, sir, he will not be found."

"There is not a place in Germany where my searching will fail to find him," he declared, striking the table with his fist.

"Prince Conrad is not in Germany, sir."

"Eh? What's that? Then where is he?"

"In France."

"In France!"

"Yes, sir, in France, at the Château d'Ornequin, in the custody of my friends. If I am not back with them by six o'clock to-morrow evening, Prince Conrad will be handed over to the military authorities."

The Emperor seemed to be choking, so much so that his anger suddenly collapsed and that he did not even seek to conceal the violence of the blow. All the humiliation, all the ridicule that would fall upon him and upon his dynasty and upon the empire if his son were a prisoner, the loud laughter that would ring through the whole world at the news, the assurance which the possession of such a hostage would give to the enemy; all this showed in his anxious look and in the stoop of his shoulders.

Paul felt the thrill of victory. He held that man as firmly as you hold under your knee the beaten foe who cries out for mercy; and the balance of the forces in conflict was so definitely broken in his favor that the Kaiser's very eyes, raised to Paul's, gave him a sense of his triumph.

The Emperor was able to picture the various phases of the drama enacted during the previous night: the arrival through the tunnel, the kidnapping by the way of the tunnel, the exploding of the mines to ensure the flight of the assailants; and the mad daring of the adventure staggered him. He murmured:

"Who are you?"

Paul relaxed slightly from his rigid attitude. He placed a quivering hand upon the table between them and said, in a grave tone:

"Sixteen years ago, sir, in the late afternoon of a September day, you inspected the works of the tunnel which you were building from Èbrecourt to Corvigny under the guidance of a person—how shall I describe her—of a person highly placed in your secret service. At the moment when you were leaving a little chapel which stands in the Ornequin woods, you met two Frenchmen, a father and son—you remember, sir? It was raining—and the meeting was so disagreeable to you that you allowed a gesture of annoyance to escape you. Ten minutes later, the lady who accompanied you returned and tried to take one of the Frenchmen, the father, back with her to German territory, alleging as a pretext that you wished to speak to him. The Frenchman refused. The woman murdered him before his son's eyes. His name was Delroze. He was my father."

The Kaiser had listened with increasing astonishment. It seemed to Paul that his color had become more jaundiced than ever. Nevertheless he kept his countenance under Paul's gaze. To him the death of that M. Delroze was one of those minor incidents over which an emperor does not waste time. Did he so much as remember it?

He therefore declined to enter into the details of a crime which he had certainly not ordered, though his indulgence for the criminal had made him a party to it, and he contented himself, after a pause, with observing:

"The Comtesse Hermine is responsible for her own actions."

"And responsible only to herself," Paul retorted, "seeing that the police of her country refused to let her be called to account for this one."

The Emperor shrugged his shoulders, with the air of a man who scorns to discuss questions of German morality and higher politics. He looked at his watch, rang the bell, gave notice that he would be ready to leave in a few minutes and, turning to Paul, said:

"So it was to avenge your father's death that you carried off Prince Conrad?"

"No, sir, that is a question between the Comtesse Hermine and me; but with Prince Conrad I have another matter to settle. When Prince Conrad was staying at the Château d'Ornequin, he pestered with his attentions a lady living in the house. Finding himself rebuffed by her, he brought her here, to his villa, as a prisoner. The lady bears my name; and I came to fetch her."

It was evident from the Emperor's attitude that he knew nothing of the story and that his son's pranks were a great source of worry to him.

"Are you sure?" he asked. "Is the lady here?"

"She was here last night, sir. But the Comtesse Hermine resolved to do away with her and gave her into the charge of Karl the spy, with instructions to take her out of Prince Conrad's reach and poison her."

"That's a lie!" cried the Emperor. "A damnable lie!"

"There is the bottle which the Comtesse Hermine handed to Karl the spy."

"And then? And then?" said the Kaiser, in an angry voice.

"Then, sir, as Karl the spy was dead and as I did not know the place to which my wife had been taken, I came back here. Prince Conrad was asleep. With the aid of one of my friends, I brought him down from his room and sent him into France through the tunnel."

"And I suppose, in return for his liberty, you want the liberty of your wife?"

"Yes, sir."

"But I don't know where she is!" exclaimed the Emperor.

"She is in a country house belonging to the Comtesse Hermine. Perhaps, if you would just think, sir. . . a country house a few hours off by motor car, say, a hundred or a hundred and twenty miles at most."

The Emperor, without speaking, kept tapping the table angrily with the pommel of his sword. Then he said:

"Is that all you ask?"

"No, sir."

"What? You want something more?"

"Yes, sir, the release of twenty French prisoners whose names appear on a list given me by the French commander-in-chief."

This time the Emperor sprang to his feet with a bound:

"You're mad! Twenty prisoners! And officers, I expect? Commanders of army corps? Generals?"

"The list also contains the names of privates, sir."

The Emperor refused to listen. His fury found expression in wild gestures and incoherent words. His eyes shot terrible glances at Paul. The idea of taking his orders from that little French subaltern, himself a captive and yet in a position to lay down the law, must have been fearfully unpleasant. Instead of punishing his insolent enemy, he had to argue with him and to bow his head before his outrageous proposals. But he had no choice. There was no means of escape. He had as his adversary one whom not even torture would have caused to yield.

And Paul continued:

"Sir, my wife's liberty against Prince Conrad's liberty would really not be a fair bargain. What do you care, sir, whether my wife is a prisoner or free? No, it is only reasonable that Prince Conrad's release should be the object of an exchange which justifies it. And twenty French prisoners are none too many. . . Besides, there is no need for this to be done publicly. The prisoners can come back to France, one by one, if you prefer, as though in exchange for German prisoners of the same rank. . . so that. . ."

The irony of these conciliatory words, intended to soften the bitterness of defeat and to conceal the blow struck at the imperial pride under the guise of a concession! Paul thoroughly relished those few minutes. He received the impression that this man, upon whom a comparatively slight injury to his self-respect inflicted so great a torment, must be suffering more seriously still at seeing his gigantic scheme come to nothing under the formidable onslaught of destiny.

"I am nicely revenged," thought Paul to himself. "And this is only the beginning!"

The capitulation was at hand. The Emperor declared:

"I shall see. . . I will give orders. . ."

Paul protested:

"It would be dangerous to wait, sir. Prince Conrad's capture might become known in France. . ."

"Well," said the Emperor, "bring Prince Conrad back and your wife shall be restored to you the same day."

But Paul was pitiless. He insisted on being treated with entire confidence:

"No, sir," he said, "I do not think that things can happen just like that. My wife is in a most horrible position; and her very life is at stake. I must ask to be taken to her at once. She and I will be in France this evening. It is imperative that we should be in France this evening."

He repeated the words in a very firm tone and added:

"As for the French prisoners, sir, they can be returned under such conditions as you may be pleased to state. I will give you a list of their names with the places at which they are interned."

Paul took a pencil and a sheet of paper. When he had finished writing, the Emperor snatched the list from him and his face immediately became convulsed. At each name he seemed to shake with impotent rage. He crumpled the paper into a ball, as though he had resolved to break off the whole arrangement. But, all of a sudden, abandoning his resistance, with a hurried movement, as though feverishly determined to have done with an exasperating business, he rang the bell three times.

An orderly officer entered with a brisk step and brought his heels together before the Kaiser.

The Emperor reflected a few seconds longer. Then he gave his commands:

"Take Lieutenant Delroze in a motor car to Schloss Hildensheim and bring him back with his wife to the Èbrecourt outposts. On this day week, meet him at the same point on our lines. He will be accompanied by Prince Conrad and you by the twenty French prisoners whose names are on this list. You will effect the exchange in a discreet manner, which you will fix upon with Lieutenant Delroze. That will do. Keep me informed by personal reports."

This was uttered in a jerky, authoritative tone, as though it were a series of measures which the Emperor had adopted of his own initiative, without undergoing pressure of any kind and by the mere exercise of his imperial will.

And, having thus settled the matter, he walked out, carrying his head high, swaggering with his sword and jingling his spurs.

MAURICE LEBLANC

"One more victory to his credit! What a play-actor!" thought Paul, who could not help laughing, to the officer's great horror.

He heard the Emperor's motor drive away. The interview had lasted hardly ten minutes.

A moment later he himself was outside, hastening along the road to Hildensheim.

XVIII

HILL 132

What a ride it was! And how gay Paul Delroze felt! He was at last attaining his object; and this time it was not one of those hazardous enterprises which so often end in cruel disappointment, but the logical outcome and reward of his efforts. He was beyond the reach of the least shade of anxiety. There are victories—and his recent victory over the Emperor was one of them—which involve the disappearance of every obstacle. Élisabeth was at Hildensheim Castle and he was on his way to the castle and nothing would stop him.

He seemed to recognize by the daylight features in the landscape which had been hidden from him by the darkness of the night before: a hamlet here, a village there, a river which he had skirted. He saw the string of little road-side woods, and he saw the ditch by which he had fought with Karl the spy.

It took hardly more than another hour to reach the hill which was topped by the feudal fortress of Hildensheim. It was surrounded by a wide moat, spanned by a draw-bridge. A suspicious porter made his appearance, but a few words from the officer caused the doors to be flung open.

Two footmen hurried down from the castle and, in reply to Paul's question, said that the French lady was walking near the pond. He asked the way and said to the officer:

"I shall go alone. We shall start very soon."

It had been raining. A pale winter sun, stealing through the heavy clouds, lit up the lawns and shrubberies. Paul went along a row of hot-houses and climbed an artificial rockery whence trickled the thin stream of a waterfall which formed a large pool set in a frame of dark fir trees and alive with swans and wild duck.

At the end of the pool was a terrace adorned with statues and stone benches. And there he saw Élisabeth.

Paul underwent an indescribable emotion. He had not spoken to his wife since the outbreak of war. Since that day, Élisabeth had suffered the most horrible trials and had suffered them for the simple reason that she wished to appear in her husband's eyes as a blameless wife, the daughter of a blameless mother.

And now he was about to meet her again at a time when none of the accusations which he had brought against the Comtesse Hermine could be rebuffed and when Élisabeth herself had roused Paul to such a pitch of indignation by her presence at Prince Conrad's supper-party! . . .

But how long ago it all seemed! And how little it mattered! Prince Conrad's blackguardism, the Comtesse Hermine's crimes, the ties of relationship that might unite the two women, all the struggles which Paul had passed through, all his anguish, all his rebelliousness, all his loathing, were but so many insignificant details, now that he saw at twenty paces from him his unhappy darling whom he loved so well. He no longer thought of the tears which she had shed and saw nothing but her wasted figure, shivering in the wintry wind.

He walked towards her. His steps grated on the gravel path; and Élisabeth turned round.

She did not make a single gesture. He understood, from the expression of her face, that she did not see him, really, that she looked upon him as a phantom rising from the mists of dreams and that this phantom must often float before her deluded eyes.

She even smiled at him a little, such a sad smile that Paul clasped his hands and was nearly falling on his knees:

"Élisabeth. . . Élisabeth," he stammered.

Then she drew herself up and put her hand to her heart and turned even paler than she had been the evening before, seated between Prince Conrad and Comtesse Hermine. The image was emerging from the realm of mist; the reality grew plainer before her eyes and in her brain. This time she saw Paul!

He ran towards her, for she seemed on the point of falling. But she recovered herself, put out her hands to make him stay where he was and looked at him with an effort as though she would have penetrated to the very depths of his soul to read his thoughts.

Paul, trembling with love from head to foot, did not stir. She murmured:

"Ah, I see that you love me. . . that you have never ceased to love me! . . . I am sure of it now. . ."

She kept her arms outstretched, however, as though against an obstacle, and he himself did not attempt to come closer. All their life and all their happiness lay in their eyes; and, while her gaze wildly encountered his, she went on:

"They told me that you were a prisoner. Is it true, then? Oh, how I have implored them to take me to you! How low I have stooped! I have even had to sit down to table with them and laugh at their jokes and wear jewels and pearl necklaces which he has forced upon me. All this in order to see you! . . . And they kept on promising. And then, at length, they brought me here last night and I thought that they had tricked me once more. . . or else that it was a fresh trap. . . or that they had at last made up their minds to kill me. . . And now here you are, here you are, Paul, my own darling! . . ."

She took his face in her two hands and, suddenly, in a voice of despair:

"But you are not going just yet? You will stay till to-morrow, surely? They can't take you from me like that, after a few minutes? You're staying, are you not? Oh, Paul, all my courage is gone. . . don't leave me! . . ."

She was greatly surprised to see him smile:

"What's the matter? Why, my dearest, how happy you look!"

He began to laugh and this time, drawing her to him with a masterful air that admitted of no denial, he kissed her hair and her forehead and her cheeks and her lips; and he said:

"I am laughing because there is nothing to do but to laugh and kiss you. I am laughing also because I have been imagining so many silly things. Yes, just think, at that supper last night, I saw you from a distance. . . and I suffered agonies: I accused you of I don't know what. . . Oh, what a fool I was!"

She could not understand his gaiety; and she said again:

"How happy you are! How can you be so happy?"

"There is no reason why I should not be," said Paul, still laughing.

"Come, look at things as they are: you and I are meeting after unheard-of misfortunes. We are together; nothing can separate us; and you wouldn't have me be glad?"

"Do you mean to say that nothing can separate us?" she asked, in a voice quivering with anxiety.

"Why, of course! Is that so strange?"

"You are staying with me? Are we to live here?"

"No, not that! What an idea! You're going to pack up your things at express speed and we shall be off."

"Where to?"

"Where to? To France, of course. When you think of it, that's the only country where one's really comfortable."

MAURICE LEBLANC

And, when she stared at him in amazement, he said:

"Come, let's hurry. The car's waiting; and I promised Bernard—yes, your brother Bernard—that we should be with him to-night. . . Are you ready? But why that astounded look? Do you want to have things explained to you? But, my very dearest, it will take hours and hours to explain everything that's happened to yourself and me. You've turned the head of an imperial prince. . . and then you were shot. . . and then. . . and then. . . Oh, what does it all matter? Must I force you to come away with me?"

All at once she understood that he was speaking seriously; and, without taking her eyes from him, she asked:

"Is it true? Are we free?"

"Absolutely free."

"We're going back to France?"

"Immediately."

"We have nothing more to fear?"

"Nothing."

The tension from which she was suffering suddenly relaxed. She in her turn began to laugh, yielding to one of those fits of uncontrollable mirth which find vent in every sort of childish nonsense. She could have sung, she could have danced for sheer joy. And yet the tears flowed down her cheeks. And she stammered:

"Free! . . . it's all over! . . . Have I been through much? . . . Not at all! . . . Oh, you know that I had been shot? Well, I assure you, it wasn't so bad as all that. . . I will tell you about it and lots of other things. . . And you must tell me, too. . . But how did you manage? You must be cleverer than the cleverest, cleverer than the unspeakable Conrad, cleverer than the Emperor! Oh, dear, how funny it is, how funny! . . ."

She broke off and, seizing him forcibly by the arm, said:

"Let us go, darling. It's madness to remain another second. These people are capable of anything. They look upon no promise as binding. They are scoundrels, criminals. Let's go. . . Let's go. . ."

They went away.

Their journey was uneventful. In the evening, they reached the lines on the front, facing Èbrecourt.

The officer on duty, who had full powers, had a reflector lit and himself, after ordering a white flag to be displayed, took Élisabeth and Paul to the French officer who came forward.

The officer telephoned to the rear. A motor car was sent; and, at nine o'clock, Paul and Élisabeth pulled up at the gates of Ornequin and Paul asked to have Bernard sent for. He met him half-way:

"Is that you, Bernard?" he said. "Listen to me and don't let us waste a minute. I have brought back Élisabeth. Yes, she's here, in the car. We are off to Corvigny and you're coming with us. While I go for my bag and yours, you give instructions to have Prince Conrad closely watched. He's safe, isn't he?"

"Yes."

"Then hurry. I want to get at the woman whom you saw last night as she was entering the tunnel. Now that she's in France, we'll hunt her down."

"Don't you think, Paul, that we should be more likely to find her tracks by ourselves going back into the tunnel and searching the place where it opens at Corvigny?"

"We can't afford the time. We have arrived at a phase of the struggle that demands the utmost haste."

"But, Paul, the struggle is over, now that Élisabeth is saved."

"The struggle will never be over as long as that woman lives."

"Well, but who is she?"

Paul did not answer.

At ten o'clock they all three alighted outside the station at Corvigny. There were no more trains. Everybody was asleep. Paul refused to be put off, went to the military guard, woke up the adjutant, sent for the station-master, sent for the booking-clerk and, after a minute inquiry, succeeded in establishing the fact that on that same Monday morning a woman supplied with a pass in the name of Mme. Antonin had taken a ticket for Château-Thierry. She was the only woman traveling alone. She was wearing a Red Cross uniform. Her description corresponded at all points with that of the Comtesse Hermine.

"It's certainly she," said Paul, when they had taken their rooms for the night at the hotel near the station. "There's no doubt about it. It's the only way she could go from Corvigny. And it's the way that we shall go to-morrow morning, at the same time that she did. I hope that she will not have time to carry out the scheme that has brought her to France. In any case, this is a great opportunity; and we must make the most of it."

"But who is the woman?" Bernard asked again.

"Who is she? Ask Élisabeth to tell you. We have an hour left in which to discuss certain details and then we must go to bed. We need rest, all three of us."

MAURICE LEBLANC

They started on the Tuesday morning. Paul's confidence was unshaken. Though he knew nothing of the Comtesse Hermine's intentions, he felt sure that he was on the right road. And, in fact, they were told several times that a Red Cross nurse, traveling first-class and alone, had passed through the same stations on the day before.

They got out at Château-Thierry late in the afternoon. Paul made his inquiries. On the previous evening, the nurse had driven away in a Red Cross motor car which was waiting at the station. This car, according to the papers carried by the driver, belonged to one of the ambulances working to the rear of Soissons; but the exact position of the ambulance was not known.

This was near enough for Paul, however. Soissons was in the battle line.

"Let's go to Soissons," he said.

The order signed by the commander-in-chief which he had on him gave him full power to requisition a motor car and to enter the fighting zone. They reached Soissons at dinner-time.

The outskirts, ruined by the bombardment, were deserted. The town itself seemed abandoned for the greater part. But as they came nearer to the center a certain animation prevailed in the streets. Companies of soldiers passed at a quick pace. Guns and ammunition wagons trotted by. In the hotel to which they went on the Grande Place, a hotel containing a number of officers, there was general excitement, with much coming and going and even a little disorder.

Paul and Bernard asked the reason. They were told that, for some days past, we had been successfully attacking the slopes opposite Soissons, on the other side of the Aisne. Two days before, some battalions of light infantry and African troops had taken Hill 132 by assault. On the following day, we held the positions which we had won and carried the trenches on the Dent de Crouy. Then, in the course of the Monday night at a time when the enemy was delivering a violent counter-attack, a curious thing happened. The Aisne, which was swollen as the result of the heavy rains, overflowed its banks and carried away all the bridges at Villeneuve and Soissons.

The rise of the Aisne was natural enough; but, high though the river was, it did not explain the destruction of the bridges; and this destruction, coinciding with the German counter-attack and apparently due to suspect reasons which had not yet been cleared up, had complicated the position of the French troops by making the dispatch of reinforcements almost impossible. Our men had held the hill all day, but with difficulty and with great losses. At this moment, a part of the artillery was being moved back to the right bank of the Aisne.

Paul and Bernard did not hesitate in their minds for a second. In all this they recognized the Comtesse Hermine's handiwork. The destruction of the bridges, the German attacks, those two incidents which happened on the very night of her arrival were, beyond a doubt, the outcome of a plan conceived by her, the execution of which had been prepared for the time when the rains were bound to swell the river and proved the collaboration existing between the countess and the enemy's staff.

Besides, Paul remembered the sentences which she had exchanged with Karl the spy outside the door of Prince Conrad's villa:

"I am going to France. . . everything is ready. The weather is in our favor; and the staff have told me. . . So I shall be there to-morrow evening; and it will only need a touch of the thumb. . ."

She had given that touch of the thumb. All the bridges had been tampered with by Karl or by men in his pay and had now broken down.

"It's she, obviously enough," said Bernard. "And, if it is, why look so anxious? You ought to be glad, on the contrary, because we are now positively certain of laying hold of her."

"Yes, but shall we do so in time? When she spoke to Karl, she uttered another threat which struck me as much more serious. As I told you, she said, 'Luck is turning against us. If I succeed, it will be the end of the run on the black.' And, when the spy asked her if she had the Emperor's consent, she answered that it was unnecessary and that this was one of the undertakings which one doesn't talk about. You understand, Bernard, it's not a question of the German attack or the destruction of the bridges: that is honest warfare and the Emperor knows all about it. No, it's a question of something different, which is intended to coincide with other events and give them their full significance. The woman can't think that an advance of half a mile or a mile is an incident capable of ending what she calls the run on the black. Then what is at the back of it all? I don't know; and that accounts for my anxiety."

Paul spent the whole of that evening and the whole of the next day, Wednesday the 13th, in making prolonged searches in the streets of the town or along the banks of the Aisne. He had placed himself in communication with the military authorities. Officers and men took part in his investigations. They went over several houses and questioned a number of the inhabitants.

Bernard offered to go with him; but Paul persisted in refusing:

"No. It is true, the woman doesn't know you; but she must not see your sister. I am asking you therefore to stay with Élisabeth, to keep her from going out and to watch over her without a moment's intermission, for we have to do with the most terrible enemy imaginable."

The brother and sister therefore passed the long hours of that day with their faces glued to the window-panes. Paul came back at intervals to snatch a meal. He was quivering with hope.

"She's here," he said. "She must have left those who were with her in the motor car, dropped her nurse's disguise and is now hiding in some hole, like a spider behind its web. I can see her, telephone in hand, giving her orders to a whole band of people, who have taken to earth like herself and made themselves invisible like her. But I am beginning to perceive her plan and I have one advantage over her, which is that she believes herself in safety. She does not know that her accomplice, Karl, is dead. She does not know of Élisabeth's release. She does not know of our presence here. I've got her, the loathsome beast, I've got her."

The news of the battle, meanwhile, was not improving. The retreating movement on the left bank continued. At Crouy, the severity of their losses and the depth of the mud stopped the rush of the Moroccan troops. A hurriedly-constructed pontoon bridge went drifting down-stream.

When Paul made his next appearance, at six o'clock in the evening, there were a few drops of blood on his sleeve. Élisabeth took alarm.

"It's nothing," he said, with a laugh. "A scratch; I don't know how I got it."

"But your hand; look at your hand. You're bleeding!"

"No, it's not my blood. Don't be frightened. Everything's all right."

Bernard said:

"You know the commander-in-chief came to Soissons this morning."

"Yes, so it seems. All the better. I should like to make him a present of the spy and her gang. It would be a handsome gift."

He went away for another hour and then came back and had dinner.

"You look as though you were sure of things now," said Bernard.

"One can never be sure of anything. That woman is the very devil."

"But you know where she's hiding?"

"Yes."

"And what are you waiting for?"

"I'm waiting for nine o'clock. I shall take a rest till then. Wake me up at a little before nine."

The guns never ceased booming in the distant darkness. Sometimes a shell would fall on the town with a great crash. Troops passed in every direction. Then there would be brief intervals of silence, in which the sounds of war seemed to hang in suspense; and it was those minutes which perhaps were most formidable and significant.

Paul woke of himself. He said to his wife and Bernard:

"You know, you're coming, too. It will be rough work, Élisabeth, very rough work. Are you certain that you're equal to it?"

"Oh, Paul. . . But you yourself are looking so pale."

"Yes," he said, "it's the excitement. Not because of what is going to happen. But, in spite of all my precautions, I shall be afraid until the last moment that the adversary will escape. A single act of carelessness, a stroke of ill-luck that gives the alarm. . . and I shall have to begin all over again. . . Never mind about your revolver, Bernard."

"What!" cried Bernard. "Isn't there going to be any fighting in this expedition of yours?"

Paul did not reply. According to his custom, he expressed himself during or after action. Bernard took his revolver.

The last stroke of nine sounded as they crossed the Grande Place, amid a darkness stabbed here and there by a thin ray of light issuing from a closed shop. A group of soldiers were massed in the forecourt of the cathedral, whose shadowy bulk they felt looming overhead.

Paul flashed the light from an electric lamp upon them and asked the one in command:

"Any news, sergeant?"

"No, sir. No one has entered the house and no one has gone out."

The sergeant gave a low whistle. In the middle of the street, two men emerged from the surrounding gloom and approached the group.

"Any sound in the house?"

"No, sergeant."

"Any light behind the shutters?"

"No, sergeant."

Then Paul marched ahead and, while the others, in obedience to his instructions, followed him without making the least noise, he stepped on resolutely, like a belated wayfarer making for home.

They stopped at a narrow-fronted house, the ground-floor of which was hardly distinguishable in the darkness of the night. Three steps led to the door. Paul gave four sharp taps and, at the same time, took a key from his pocket and opened the door.

He switched on his electric lamp again in the passage and, while his companions continued as silent as before, turned to a mirror which rose straight from the flagged floor. He gave four little taps on the mirror and then pushed it, pressing one side of it. It masked the aperture of a staircase which led to the basement; and Paul sent the light of his lantern down the well.

This appeared to be a signal, the third signal agreed upon, for a voice from below, a woman's voice, but hoarse and rasping in its tones, asked:

"Is that you, Daddy Walter?"

The moment had come to act. Without answering, Paul rushed down the stairs, taking four steps at a time. He reached the bottom just as a massive door was closing, almost barring his access to the cellar.

He gave a strong push and entered.

The Comtesse Hermine was there, in the semi-darkness, motionless, hesitating what to do.

Then suddenly she ran to the other end of the cellar, seized a revolver on the table, turned round and fired.

The hammer clicked, but there was no report.

She repeated the action three times; and the result, was three times the same.

"It's no use going on," said Paul, with a laugh. "The charge has been removed."

The countess uttered a cry of rage, opened the drawer of the table and, taking another revolver, pulled the trigger four times, without producing a sound.

"You may as well drop it," laughed Paul. "This one has been emptied, too; and so has the one in the other drawer: so have all the firearms in the house, for that matter."

Then, when she stared at him in amazement, without understanding, dazed by her own helplessness, he bowed and introduced himself, just in two words, which meant so much:

"Paul Delroze."

XIX

HOHENZOLLERN

The cellar, though smaller, looked like one of those large vaulted basement halls which prevail in the Champagne district. Walls spotlessly clean, a smooth floor with brick paths running across it, a warm atmosphere, a curtained-off recess between two wine vats, chairs, benches and rugs all went to form not only a comfortable abode, out of the way of the shells, but also a safe refuge for any one who stood in fear of indiscreet visits.

Paul remembered the ruins of the old lighthouse on the bank of the Yser and the tunnel from Ornequin to Èbrecourt. So the struggle was still continuing underground: a war of trenches and cellars, a war of spying and trickery, the same unvarying, stealthy, disgraceful, suspicious, criminal methods.

Paul had put out his lantern, and the room was now only dimly lit by an oil lamp hanging from the ceiling, whose rays, thrown downward by an opaque shade, cast a white circle in which the two of them stood by themselves. Élisabeth and Bernard remained in the background, in the shadow.

The sergeant and his men had not appeared, but they could be heard at the foot of the stairs.

The countess did not move. She was dressed as on the evening of the supper at Prince Conrad's villa. Her face showed no longer any fear or alarm, but rather an effort of thought, as though she were trying to calculate all the consequences of the position now revealed to her. Paul Delroze? With what object was he attacking her? His intention—and this was evidently the idea that gradually caused the Comtesse Hermine's features to relax—his intention no doubt was to procure his wife's liberty.

She smiled. Élisabeth a prisoner in Germany: what a trump card for herself, caught in a trap but still able to command events!

At a sign from Paul, Bernard stepped forward and Paul said to the countess:

"My brother-in-law. Major Hermann, when he lay trussed up in the ferryman's house, may have seen him, just as he may have seen me. But, in any case, the Comtesse Hermine—or, to be more exact, the

Comtesse d'Andeville—does not know or at least has forgotten her son, Bernard d'Andeville."

She now seemed quite reassured, still wearing the air of one fighting with equal or even more powerful weapons. She displayed no confusion at the sight of Bernard, and said, in a careless tone:

"Bernard d'Andeville is very like his sister Élisabeth, of whom circumstances have allowed me to see a great deal lately. It is only three days since she and I were having supper with Prince Conrad. The prince is very fond of Élisabeth, and he is quite right, for she is charming. . . and so amiable!"

Paul and Bernard both made the same movement, which would have ended in their flinging themselves upon the countess, if they had not succeeded in restraining their hatred. Paul pushed aside his brother-in-law, of whose intense anger he was conscious, and replied to his adversary's challenge in an equally casual tone:

"Yes, I know all about it; I was there. I was even present at her departure. Your friend Karl offered me a seat in his car and we went off to your place at Hildensheim: a very handsome castle, which I should have liked to see more thoroughly. . . But it is not a safe house to stay at; in fact, it is often deadly; and so. . ."

The countess looked at him with increasing disquiet. What did he mean to convey? How did he know these things? She resolved to frighten him in his turn, so as to gain some idea of the enemy's plans, and she said, in a hard voice:

"Yes, deadly is the word. The air there is not good for everybody."

"A poisonous air."

"Just so."

"And are you nervous about Élisabeth?"

"Frankly, yes. The poor thing's health is none of the best, as it is; and I shall not be easy. . ."

"Until she's dead, I suppose?"

She waited a second or two and then retorted, speaking very clearly, so that Paul might take in the meaning of her words:

"Yes, until she is dead. . . And that can't be far off. . . if it has not happened already."

There was a pause of some length. Once more, in the presence of that woman, Paul felt the same craving to commit murder, the same craving to gratify his hatred. She must be killed. It was his duty to kill her, it was a crime not to obey that duty.

Élisabeth was standing three paces back, in the dark. Slowly, without a word, Paul turned in her direction, pressed the spring of his lantern and flashed the light full on his wife's face.

Not for a moment did he suspect the violent effect which his action would have on the Comtesse Hermine. A woman like her was incapable of making a mistake, of thinking herself the victim of an hallucination or the dupe of a resemblance. No, she at once accepted the fact that Paul had delivered his wife and that Élisabeth was standing in front of her. But how was so disastrous an event possible? Élisabeth, whom three days before she had left in Karl's hands; Élisabeth, who at this very moment ought to be either dead or a prisoner in a German fortress, the access to which was guarded by more than two million German soldiers: Élisabeth was here! She had escaped Karl in less than three days! She had fled from Hildensheim Castle and passed through the lines of those two million Germans!

The Comtesse Hermine sat down with distorted features at the table that served her as a rampart and, in her fury, dug her clenched fists into her cheeks. She realized the position. The time was past for jesting or defiance. The time was past for bargaining. In the hideous game which she was playing, the last chance of victory had suddenly slipped from her grasp. She must yield before the conqueror; and that conqueror was Paul Delroze.

She stammered:

"What do you propose to do? What is your object? To murder me?"

He shrugged his shoulders:

"We are not murderers. You are here to be tried. The penalty which you will suffer will be the sentence passed upon you after a lawful trial, in which you will be able to defend yourself."

A shiver ran through her; and she protested:

"You have no right to try me; you are not judges."

At that moment there was a noise on the stairs. A voice cried:

"Eyes front!"

And, immediately after, the door, which had remained ajar, was flung open, admitting three officers in their long cloaks.

Paul hastened towards them and gave them chairs in that part of the room which the light did not reach. A fourth arrived, who was also received by Paul and took a seat to one side, a little farther away.

Élisabeth and Paul were close together.

Paul went back to his place in front and, standing beside the table, said:

"There are your judges. I am the prosecutor."

And forthwith, without hesitation, as though he had settled beforehand all the counts of the indictment which he was about to deliver, speaking in a tone deliberately free from any trace of anger or hatred, he said:

"You were born at Hildensheim Castle, of which your grandfather was the steward. The castle was given to your father after the war of 1870. Your name is really Hermine: Hermine von Hohenzollern. Your father used to boast of that name of Hohenzollern, though he had no right to it; but the extraordinary favor in which he stood with the old Emperor prevented any one from contesting his claim. He served in the campaign of 1870 as a colonel and distinguished himself by the most outrageous acts of cruelty and rapacity. All the treasures that adorn Hildensheim Castle come from France; and, to complete the brazenness of it, each object bears a note giving the place from which it came and the name of the owner from whom it was stolen. In addition, in the hall there is a marble slab inscribed in letters of gold with the name of all the French villages burnt by order of His Excellency Colonel Count Hohenzollern. The Kaiser has often visited the castle. Each time he passes in front of that marble slab he salutes."

The countess listened without paying much heed. This story obviously seemed to her of but indifferent importance. She waited until she herself came into question.

Paul continued:

"You inherited from your father two sentiments which dominate your whole existence. One of these is an immoderate love for the Hohenzollern dynasty, with which your father appears to have been connected by the hazard of an imperial or rather a royal whim. The other is a fierce and savage hatred for France, which he regretted not to have injured as deeply as he would have liked. Your love for the dynasty you concentrated wholly, as soon as you had achieved womanhood, upon the man who represents it now, so much so that, after entertaining the unlikely hope of ascending the throne, you forgave him everything, even his marriage, even his ingratitude, to devote yourself to him body and soul. Married by him first to an Austrian prince, who died a mysterious death, and then to a Russian prince, who died an equally mysterious death, you worked solely for the greatness of your idol. At the time when war was declared between England and the Transvaal, you were in the Transvaal. At the time of the Russo-Japanese war, you were in Japan. You were everywhere: at Vienna, when the Crown Prince Rudolph was assassinated; at Belgrade when King Alexander and Queen Draga were assassinated. But I will not linger over the part played by you in diplomatic events. It is time that I came to your favorite occupation, the work which for the last twenty years you have carried on against France."

An expression of wickedness and almost of happiness distorted the Comtesse Hermine's features. Yes, indeed, that was her favorite occupation. She had devoted all her strength to it and all her perverse intelligence.

"And even so," added Paul, "I shall not linger over the gigantic work of preparation and espionage which you directed. I have found one of your accomplices, armed with a dagger bearing your initials, even in a village of the Nord, in a church-steeple. All that happened was conceived, organized and carried out by yourself. The proofs which I collected, your correspondent's letters and your own letters, are already in the possession of the court. But what I wish to lay special stress upon is that part of your work which concerns the Château d'Ornequin. It will not take long: a few facts, linked together by murders, will be enough."

There was a further silence. The countess prepared to listen with a sort of anxious curiosity. Paul went on:

"It was in 1894 that you suggested to the Emperor the piercing of a tunnel from Èbrecourt to Corvigny. After the question had been studied by the engineers, it was seen that this work, this '*kolossal*' work, was not possible and could not be effective unless possession was first obtained of the Château d'Ornequin. As it happened, the owner of the property was in a very bad state of health. It was decided to wait. But, as he seemed in no hurry to die, you came to Corvigny. A week later, he died. Murder the first."

"You lie! You lie!" cried the countess. "You have no proof. I defy you to produce a proof."

Paul, without replying, continued:

"The château was put up for sale and, strange to say, without the least advertisement, secretly, so to speak. Now what happened was that the man of business whom you had instructed bungled the matter so badly that the château was declared sold to the Comte d'Andeville, who took up his residence there in the following year, with his wife and his two children. This led to anger and confusion and lastly a resolve to start work, nevertheless, and to begin boring at the site of a little chapel which, at that time, stood outside the walls of the park. The Emperor came often to Èbrecourt. One day, on leaving the chapel, he was met and recognized by my father and myself. Two minutes later, you were accosting my father. He was stabbed and killed. I myself received a wound. Murder the second. A month later, the Comtesse d'Andeville was seized with a mysterious illness and went down to the south to die."

"You lie!" cried the countess, again. "Those are all lies! Not a single proof! . . ."

"A month later," continued Paul, still speaking very calmly, "M. d'Andeville, who had lost his wife, took so great a dislike to Ornequin that he decided never to go back to it. Your plan was carried out at once. Now that the château was free, it became necessary for you to obtain a footing there. How was it done? By buying over the keeper, Jérôme, and his wife. That wretched couple, who certainly had the excuse that they were not Alsatians, as they pretended to be, but of Luxemburg birth, accepted the bribe. Thenceforth you were at home, free to come to Ornequin as and when you pleased. By your orders, Jérôme even went to the length of keeping the death of the Comtesse Hermine, the real Comtesse Hermine, a secret. And, as you also were a Comtesse Hermine and as no one knew Mme. d'Andeville, who had led a secluded life, everything went off well. Moreover, you continued to multiply your precautions. There was one, among others, that baffled me. A portrait of the Comtesse d'Andeville hung in the boudoir which she used to occupy. You had a portrait painted of yourself, of the same size, so as to fit the frame inscribed with the name of the countess; and this portrait showed you under the same outward aspect, wearing the same clothes and ornaments. In short, you became what you had striven to appear from the outset and indeed during the lifetime of Mme. d'Andeville, whose dress you were even then beginning to copy: you became the Comtesse Hermine d'Andeville, at least during the period of your visits to Ornequin. There was only one danger, the possibility of M. d'Andeville's unexpected return. To ward this off with certainty, there was but one remedy, murder. You therefore managed to become acquainted with M. d'Andeville, which enabled you to watch his movements and correspond with him. Only, something happened on which you had not reckoned. I mean to say that a feeling which was really surprising in a woman like yourself began gradually to attach you to the man whom you had chosen as a victim. I have placed among the exhibits a photograph of yourself which you sent to M. d'Andeville from Berlin. At that time, you were hoping to induce him to marry you; but he saw through your schemes, drew back and broke off the friendship."

The countess had knitted her brows. Her lips were distorted. The lookers-on divined all the humiliation which she had undergone and all the bitterness which she had retained in consequence. At the same time, she felt no shame, but rather an increasing surprise at thus seeing her life divulged down to the least detail and her murderous past dragged from the obscurity in which she believed it buried.

"When war was declared," Paul continued, "your work was ripe. Stationed in the Èbrecourt villa, at the entrance to the tunnel, you were ready. My marriage to Élisabeth d'Andeville, my sudden arrival at the château, my amazement at seeing the portrait of the woman who had killed my father: all this was told you by Jérôme and took you a little by surprise. You had hurriedly to lay a trap in which I, in my turn, was nearly assassinated. But the mobilization rid you of my presence. You were able to act. Three weeks later, Corvigny was bombarded, Ornequin taken, Élisabeth a prisoner of Prince Conrad's. . . That, for you, was an indescribable period. It meant revenge; and also, thanks to you, it meant the great victory, the accomplishment—or nearly so—of the great dream, the apotheosis of the Hohenzollerns! Two days more and Paris would be captured; two months more and Europe was conquered. The intoxication of it! I know of words which you uttered at that time and I have read lines written by you which bear witness to an absolute madness: the madness of pride, the madness of boundless power, the madness of cruelty; a barbarous madness, an impossible, superhuman madness. . . And then, suddenly, the rude awakening, the battle of the Marne! Ah, I have seen your letters on this subject, too! And I know no finer revenge. A woman of your intelligence was bound to see from the first, as you did see, that it meant the breakdown of every hope and certainty. You wrote that to the Emperor, yes, you wrote it! I have a copy of your letter. . . Meanwhile, defense became necessary. The French troops were approaching. Through my brother-in-law, Bernard, you learnt that I was at Corvigny. Would Élisabeth be delivered, Élisabeth who knew all your secrets? No, she must die. You ordered her to be executed. Everything was made ready. And, though she was saved, thanks to Prince Conrad, and though, in default of her death, you had to content yourself with a mock execution intended to cut short my inquiries, at least she was carried off like a slave. And you had two victims for your consolation: Jérôme and Rosalie. Your accomplices, smitten with tearful remorse by Élisabeth's tortures, tried to escape with her. You dreaded their evidence against you: they were shot. Murders the third and fourth. And the next day there were two more, two soldiers whom you had killed, taking them for Bernard and myself. Murders the fifth and sixth."

Thus was the whole drama reconstructed in all its tragic phases and in accordance with the order of the events and murders. And it was a horrible thing to look upon this woman, guilty of so many crimes, walled in by destiny, trapped in this cellar, face to face with her mortal enemies. And yet how was it that she did not appear to have lost all hope? For such was the case; and Bernard noticed it.

"Look at her," he said, going up to Paul. "She has twice already consulted her watch. Any one would think that she was expecting a miracle or something more, a direct, inevitable aid which is to arrive at a definite hour. See, her eyes are glancing about. . . She is listening for something. . ."

"Order all the soldiers at the foot of the stairs to come in," Paul answered. "There is no reason why they should not hear what I have still to say."

And, turning towards the countess, he said, in tones which gradually betrayed more feeling:

"We are coming to the last act. All this part of the contest you conducted under the aspect of Major Hermann, which made it easier for you to follow the armies and play your part as chief spy. Hermann, Hermine. . . The Major Hermann whom, when necessary, you passed off as your brother was yourself, Comtesse Hermine. And it was you whose conversation I overheard with the sham Laschen, or rather Karl the spy, in the ruins of the lighthouse on the bank of the Yser. And it was you whom I caught and bound in the attic of the ferryman's house. Ah, what a fine stroke you missed that day! Your three enemies lay wounded, within reach of your hand, and you ran away without seeing them, without making an end of them! And you knew nothing further about us, whereas we knew all about your plans. An appointment for the 10th of January at Èbrecourt, that ill-omened appointment which you made with Karl while telling him of your implacable determination to do away with Élisabeth. And I was there, punctually, on the 10th of

January! I looked on at Prince Conrad's supper-party! And I was there, after the supper, when you handed Karl the poison. I was there, on the driver's seat of the motor-car, when you gave Karl your last instructions. I was everywhere! And that same evening Karl died. And the next night I kidnaped Prince Conrad. And the day after, that is to say, two days ago, holding so important a hostage and thus compelling the Emperor to treat with me, I dictated conditions of which the first was the immediate release of Élisabeth. The Emperor gave way. And here you see us!"

In all this speech, a speech which showed the Comtesse Hermine with what implacable energy she had been hunted down, there was one word which overwhelmed her as though it related the most terrible of catastrophes. She stammered:

"Dead? You say that Karl is dead?"

"Shot down by his mistress at the moment when he was trying to kill me," cried Paul, once again mastered by his hatred. "Shot down like a mad dog! Yes, Karl the spy is dead; and even after his death he remained the traitor that he had been all his life. You were asking for my proofs: I discovered them on Karl's person! It was in his pocket-book that I read the story of your crimes and found copies of your letters and some of the originals as well. He foresaw that sooner or later, when your work was accomplished, you would sacrifice him to secure your own safety; and he revenged himself in advance. He avenged himself just as Jérôme the keeper and his wife Rosalie revenged themselves, when about to be shot by your orders, by revealing to Élisabeth the mysterious part which you played at the Château d'Ornequin. So much for your accomplices! You kill them, but they destroy you. It is no longer I who accuse you, it is they. Your letters and their evidence are in the hands of your judges. What answer have you to make?"

Paul was standing almost against her. They were separated at the most by a corner of the table; and he was threatening her with all his anger and all his loathing. She retreated towards the wall, under a row of pegs from which hung skirts and blouses, a whole wardrobe of various disguises. Though surrounded, caught in a trap, confounded by an accumulation of proofs, unmasked and helpless, she maintained an attitude of challenge and defiance. The game did not yet seem lost. She had some trump cards left in her hand; and she said:

"I have no answer to make. You speak of a woman who has committed murders; and I am not that woman. It is not a question of proving that the Comtesse Hermine is a spy and a murderess: it is a question of proving that I am the Comtesse Hermine. Who can prove that?"

"*I* can!"

Sitting apart from the three officers whom Paul had mentioned as constituting the court was a fourth, who had listened as silently and impassively as they. He stepped forward. The light of the lamp shone on his face. The countess murmured:

"Stéphane d'Andeville. . . Stéphane. . ."

It was the father of Élisabeth and Bernard. He was very pale, weakened by the wounds which he had received and from which he was only beginning to recover.

He embraced his children. Bernard expressed his surprise and delight at seeing him there.

"Yes," he said, "I had a message from the commander-in-chief and I came the moment Paul sent for me. Your husband is a fine fellow, Élisabeth. He told me what had happened when we met a little while ago. And I now see all that he has done. . . to crush that viper!"

He had taken up his stand opposite the countess; and his hearers felt beforehand the full importance of the words which he was about to speak. For a moment, she lowered her head before him. But soon her eyes once more flashed defiance; and she said:

"So you, too, have come to accuse me? What have you to say against me? Lies, I suppose? Infamies? . . ."

There was a long pause after those words. Then, speaking slowly, he said:

"I come, in the first place, as a witness to give the evidence as to your identity for which you were asking just now. You introduced yourself to me long ago by a name which was not your own, a name under which you succeeded in gaining my confidence. Later, when you tried to bring about a closer relationship between us, you revealed to me who you really were, hoping in this way to dazzle me with your titles and your connections. It is therefore my right and my duty to declare before God and man that you are really and truly the Countess Hermine von Hohenzollern. The documents which you showed me were genuine. And it was just because you were the Countess von Hohenzollern that I broke off relations which in any case were painful and disagreeable to me, for reasons which I should have been puzzled to state. That is my evidence."

"It is infamous evidence!" she cried, in a fury. "Lying evidence, as I said it would be! Not a proof!"

"Not a proof?" echoed the Comte d'Andeville, moving closer to her and shaking with rage. "What about this photograph, signed by yourself, which you sent me from Berlin? This photograph in which you had the impudence to dress up like my wife? Yes, you, you! You did this thing! You thought that, by trying to make your picture resemble that of my poor loved one, you would rouse in my breast feelings favorable to yourself! And you did not feel that what you were doing was the worst insult, the worst outrage that you could offer to the dead! And you dared, you, you, after what had happened. . ."

Like Paul Delroze a few minutes before, the count was standing close against her, threatening her with his hatred. She muttered, in a sort of embarrassment:

"Well, why not?"

He clenched his fists and said:

"As you say, why not? I did not know at the time what you were. . . and I knew nothing of the tragedy. . . of the tragedy of the past. . . It is only to-day that I have been able to compare the facts. And, whereas I repulsed you at that time with a purely instinctive repulsion, I accuse you now with unparalleled execration. . . now when I know, yes, know, with absolute certainty. Long ago, when my poor wife was dying, time after time the doctor said to me, 'It's a strange illness. She has bronchitis and pneumonia, I know; and yet there are things which I don't understand, symptoms—why conceal it?—symptoms of poisoning.' I used to protest. The theory seemed impossible! My wife poisoned? And by whom? By you, Comtesse Hermine, by you! I declare it to-day. By you! I swear it, as I hope to be saved. Proofs? Why, your whole life bears witness against you. Listen, there is one point on which Paul Delroze failed to shed light. He did not understand why, when you murdered his father, you wore clothes like those of my wife. Why did you? For this hateful reason that, even at that time, my wife's death was resolved upon and that you already wished to create in the minds of those who might see you a confusion between the Comtesse d'Andeville and yourself. The proof is undeniable. My wife stood in your way: you killed her. You guessed that, once my wife was dead, I should never come back to Ornequin; and you killed my wife. Paul Delroze, you have spoken of six murders. This is the seventh: the murder of the Comtesse d'Andeville."

The count had raised his two clenched fists and was shaking them in the Comtesse Hermine's face. He was trembling with rage and seemed on the point of striking her. She, however, remained impassive.

MAURICE LEBLANC

She made no attempt to deny this latest accusation. It was as though everything had become indifferent to her, this unexpected charge as well as all those already leveled at her. She appeared to have no thought of impending danger or of the need of replying. Her mind was elsewhere. She was listening to something other than those words, seeing something other than what was before her eyes; and, as Bernard had remarked, it was as though she were preoccupied with outside happenings rather than with the terrible position in which she found herself.

But why? What was she hoping for?

A minute elapsed; and another minute.

Then, somewhere in the cellar, in the upper part of it, there was a sound, a sort of click.

The countess drew herself up. And she listened with all her concentrated attention and with an expression of such eagerness that nobody disturbed the tremendous silence. Paul Delroze and M. d'Andeville had instinctively stepped back to the table. And the Comtesse Hermine went on listening. . .

Suddenly, above her head, in the very thickness of the vaulted ceiling, an electric bell rang. . . only for a few seconds. . . Four peals of equal length. . . And that was all.

THE DEATH PENALTY—AND
A CAPITAL PUNISHMENT

The Comtesse Hermine started up triumphantly; and this movement of hers was even more dramatic than the inexplicable vibration of that electric bell. She gave a cry of fierce delight, followed by an outburst of laughter. The whole expression of her face changed. It denoted no more anxiety, no more of that tension indicating a groping and bewildered mind, nothing but insolence, assurance, scorn and intense pride.

"Fools!" she snarled. "Fools! So you really believed—oh, what simpletons you Frenchmen are!—that you had me caught like a rat in a trap? Me! Me! . . ."

The words rushed forth so volubly, so hurriedly, that her utterance was impeded. She became rigid, closing her eyes for a moment. Then, summoning up a great effort of will, she put out her right arm, pushed aside a chair and uncovered a little mahogany slab with a brass switch, for which she felt with her hand while her eyes remained turned on Paul, on the Comte d'Andeville, on his son and on the three officers. And, in a dry, cutting voice, she rapped out:

"What have I to fear from you now? You wish to know if I am the Countess von Hohenzollern? Yes, I am. I don't deny it, I even proclaim the fact. The actions which you, in your stupid way, call murders, yes, I committed them all. It was my duty to the Emperor, to the greater Germany. . . A spy? Not at all. Simply a German woman. And what a German woman does for her country is rightly done. So let us have no more silly phrases, no more babbling about the past. Nothing matters but the present and the future. And I am once more mistress of the present and the future both. Thanks to you, I am resuming the direction of events; and we shall have some amusement. . . Shall I tell you something? All that has happened here during the past few days was prepared by myself. The bridges carried away by the river were sapped at their foundations by my orders. Why? For the trivial purpose of making you fall back? No doubt, that was necessary first: we had to announce a victory. Victory or not, it shall be announced; and it will have its effect, that I promise you. But I wanted something better; and I have succeeded."

She stopped and then, leaning her body towards her hearers, continued, in a lower voice:

"The retreat, the disorder among your troops, the need of opposing our advance and bringing up reinforcements must needs compel your commander-in-chief to come here and take counsel with his generals. For months past, I have been lying in wait for him. It was impossible for me to get within reach of him. So what was I to do? Why, of course, as I couldn't go to him, I must make him come to me and lure him to a place, chosen by myself, where I had made all my arrangements. Well, he has come. My arrangements are made. And I have only to act. . . I have only to act! He is here, in a room at the little villa which he occupies whenever he comes to Soissons. He is there, I know it. I was waiting for the signal which one of my men was to give me. You have heard the signal yourselves. So there is no doubt about it. The man whom I want is at this moment deliberating with his generals in a house which I know and which I have had mined. He has with him a general commanding an army and another general, the commander of an army corps. Both are of the ablest. There are three of them, not to speak of their subordinates. And I have only to make a movement, understand what I say, a single movement, I have only to touch this lever to blow them all up, together with the house in which they are. Am I to make that movement?"

There was a sharp click. Bernard d'Andeville had cocked his revolver:

"We must kill the beast!" he cried.

Paul rushed at him, shouting:

"Hold your tongue! And don't move a finger!"

The countess began laughing again; and her laugh was full of wicked glee:

"You're right, Paul Delroze, my man. You take in the situation, you do. However quickly that young booby may fire his bullet at me, I shall always have time to pull the lever. And that's what you don't want, isn't it? That's what these other gentlemen and you want to avoid at all costs. . . even at the cost of my liberty, eh? For that is how the matter stands, alas! All my fine plan is falling to pieces because I am in your hands. But I alone am worth as much as your three great generals, am I not? And I have every right to spare them in order to save myself. So are we agreed? Their lives against mine! And at once! . . . Paul Delroze,

I give you one minute in which to consult your friends. If in one minute, speaking in their name and your own, you do not give me your word of honor that you consider me free and that I shall receive every facility for crossing the Swiss frontier, then. . . then heigh-ho, up we go, as the children say! . . . Oh, how I've got you, all of you! And the humor of it! Hurry up, friend Delroze, your word! Yes, that's all I ask. Hang it, the word of a French officer! Ha, ha, ha, ha!"

Her nervous, scornful laugh went on ringing through the dead silence. And it happened gradually that its tone rang less surely, like words that fail to produce the intended effect. It rang false, broke and suddenly ceased.

And she stood in dumb amazement: Paul Delroze had not budged, nor had any of the officers nor any of the soldiers in the room.

She shook her fist at them:

"You're to hurry, do you hear? . . . You have one minute, my French friends, one minute and no more! . . ."

Not a man moved.

She counted the seconds in a low voice and announced them aloud by tens.

At the fortieth second, she stopped, with an anxious look on her face. Those present were as motionless as before. Then she yielded to a fit of fury:

"Why, you must be mad!" she cried. "Don't you understand? Oh, perhaps you don't believe me? Yes, that's it, they don't believe me! They can't imagine that it's possible! Possible? Why, it's your own soldiers who worked for me! Yes, by laying telephone-lines between the post-office and the villa used for head-quarters! My assistants had only to tap the wires and the thing was done: the mine-chamber Under the villa was connected with this cellar. Do you believe me now?"

Her hoarse, panting voice ceased. Her misgivings, which had become more and more marked, distorted her features. Why did none of those men move? Why did they pay no attention to her orders? Had they taken the incredible resolution to accept whatever happened rather than show her mercy?

"Look here," she said, "you understand me, surely? Or else you have all gone mad! Come, think of it: your generals, the effect which their death would cause, the tremendous impression of our power which it would give! . . . And the confusion that would follow! The retreat of your troops! The disorganization of the staff! . . . Come, come! . . ."

It seemed as if she was trying to convince them; nay, more, as if she was beseeching them to look at things from her point of view and to admit the consequence which she had attributed to her action. For her plan to succeed, it was essential that they should consent to act logically. Otherwise. . . otherwise. . .

Suddenly she seemed to recoil against the humiliating sort of supplication to which she had been stooping. Resuming her threatening attitude, she cried:

"So much the worse for them! So much the worse for them! It will be you who have condemned them! So you insist upon it? We are quite agreed? . . . And then I suppose you think you've got me! Come, come now! Even if you show yourselves pig-headed, the Comtesse Hermine has not said her last word! You don't know the Comtesse Hermine! The Comtesse Hermine never surrenders! . . ."

She was possessed by a sort of frenzy and was horrible to look at. Twisting and writhing with rage, hideous of face, aged by fully twenty years, she suggested the picture of a devil burning in the flames of hell. She cursed. She blasphemed. She gave vent to a string of oaths. She even laughed, at the thought of the catastrophe which her next movement would produce. And she spluttered:

"All right! It's you, it's you who are the executioners! . . . Oh, what folly! . . . So you will have it so? But they must be mad! Look at them, calmly sacrificing their generals, their commander-in-chief, in their stupid obstinacy. Well, so much the worse for them! You have insisted on it. I hold you responsible. A word from you, a single word. . ."

She had a last moment of hesitation. With a fierce and unyielding face she stared at those stubborn men who seemed to be obeying an implacable command. Not one of them budged.

Then it seemed as if, at the moment of taking the fatal decision, she was overcome with such an outburst of voluptuous wickedness that it made her forget the horror of her own position. She simply said:

"May God's will be done and my Emperor gain the victory!"

Stiffening her body, her eyes staring before her, she touched the switch with her finger.

The effect was almost immediate. Through the outer air, through the vaulted roof, the sound of the explosion reached the cellar. The ground seemed to shake, as though the vibration had spread through the bowels of the earth.

Then came silence. The Comtesse Hermine listened for a few seconds longer. Her face was radiant with joy. She repeated:

"So that my Emperor may gain the victory!"

And suddenly, bringing her arm down to her side, she thrust herself backwards, among the skirts and blouses against which she was leaning, and seemed actually to sink into the wall and disappear from sight.

A heavy door closed with a bang and, almost at the same moment, a shot rang through the cellar. Bernard had fired at the row of clothes. And he was rushing towards the hidden door when Paul collared him and held him where he stood.

Bernard struggled in Paul's grasp:

"But she's escaping us! . . . Why can't you let me go after her? . . . Look here, surely you remember the Èbrecourt tunnel and the system of electric wires? This is the same thing exactly! And here she is getting away! . . ."

He could not understand Paul's conduct. And his sister was as indignant as himself. Here was the foul creature who had killed their mother, who had stolen their mother's name and place; and they were allowing her to escape.

"Paul," she cried, "Paul, you must go after her, you must make an end of her! . . . Paul, you can't forget all that she has done!"

Élisabeth did not forget. She remembered the Château d'Ornequin and Prince Conrad's villa and the evening when she had been compelled to toss down a bumper of champagne and the bargain enforced upon her and all the shame and torture to which she had been put.

But Paul paid no attention to either the brother or the sister, nor did the officers and soldiers. All observed the same rigidly impassive attitude, seemed unaffected by what was happening.

Two or three minutes passed, during which a few words were exchanged in whispers, while not a soul stirred. Broken down and shattered with excitement, Élisabeth wept. Bernard's flesh crept at the sound of his sister's sobs and he felt as if he was suffering from one of those nightmares in which we witness the most horrible sights without having the strength or the power to act.

And then something happened which everybody except Bernard and Élisabeth seemed to think quite natural. There was a grating sound behind the row of clothes. The invisible door moved on its hinges. The clothes parted and made way for a human form which was flung on the ground like a bundle.

Bernard d'Andeville uttered an exclamation of delight. Élisabeth looked and laughed through her tears. It was the Comtesse Hermine, bound and gagged.

Three gendarmes entered after her:

"We've delivered the goods, sir," one of them jested, with a fat, jolly chuckle. "We were beginning to get a bit nervous and to wonder if you'd guessed right and if this was really the way she meant to clear out by. But, by Jove, sir, the baggage gave us some work to do. A proper hellcat! She struggled and bit like a badger. And the way she yelled! Oh, the vixen!" And, to the soldiers, who were in fits of laughter, "Mates, this bit of game was just what we wanted to finish off our day's hunting. It's a grand bag; and Lieutenant Delroze scented the trail finely. There's a picture for you! A whole gang of Boches in one day! . . . Look out, sir, what are you doing? Mind the beast's fangs!"

Paul was stooping over the spy. He loosened her gag, which seemed to be hurting her. She at once tried to call out, but succeeded only in uttering stifled and incoherent syllables. Nevertheless, Paul was able to make out a few words, against which he protested:

"No," he said, "not even that to console you. The game is lost. And that's the worst punishment of all, isn't it? To die without having done the harm you meant to do. And such harm, too!"

He rose and went up to the group of officers. The three, having fulfilled their functions as judges, were talking together; and one of them said to Paul:

"Well played, Delroze. My best congratulations."

"Thank you, sir. I would have prevented this attempt to escape. But I wanted to heap up every possible proof against the woman and not only to accuse her of the crimes which she has committed, but to show her to you in the act of committing crime."

"Ay; and there's nothing half-hearted about the vixen! But for you, Delroze, the villa would have been blown up with all my staff and myself into the bargain! . . . But what was the explosion which we heard?"

"A condemned building, sir, which had already been demolished by the shells and which the commandant of the fortress wanted to get rid of. We only had to divert the electric wire which starts from here."

"So the whole gang is captured?"

"Yes, sir, thanks to a spy whom I had the luck to lay my hands on just now and who told me what I had to do in order to get in here. He had first revealed the Comtesse Hermine's plan in full detail, together with the names of all his accomplices. It was arranged that the man was to let the countess know, at ten o'clock this evening, by means of that electric bell, if you were holding a council in your villa. The notice was given, but by one of our own soldiers, acting under my orders."

"Well done; and, once more, thank you, Delroze."

The general stepped into the circle of light. He was tall and powerfully built. His upper lip was covered with a thick white mustache.

There was a movement of surprise among those present. Bernard d'Andeville and his sister came forward. The soldiers stood to attention. They had recognized the general commanding-in-chief. With him were the two generals of whom the countess had spoken.

The gendarmes had pushed the spy against the wall opposite. They untied her legs, but had to support her, because her knees were giving way beneath her.

And her face expressed unspeakable amazement even more than terror. With wide-open eyes she stared at the man whom she had meant to kill, the man whom she believed to be dead and who was alive and who would shortly pronounce the inevitable sentence of death upon her.

Paul repeated:

"To die without having done the harm you intended to do, that is the really terrible thing, is it not?"

The commander-in-chief was alive! The hideous and tremendous plot had failed! He was alive and so were his officers and so was every one of the spy's enemies. Paul Delroze, Stéphane d'Andeville, Bernard, Élisabeth, those whom she had pursued with her indefatigable hatred: they were all there! She was about to die gazing at the vision, so horrible for her, of her enemies reunited and happy.

And above all she was about to die with the thought that everything was lost. Her great dream was shattered to pieces. Her Emperor's throne was tottering. The very soul of the Hohenzollerns was departing with the Comtesse Hermine. And all this was plainly visible in her haggard eyes, from which gleams of madness flashed at intervals.

The general said to one of those with him:

"Have you given the order? Are they shooting the lot?"

"Yes, this evening, sir."

"Very well, we'll begin with this woman. And at once. Here, where we are."

The spy gave a start. With a distortion of all her features she succeeded in shifting her gag; and they heard her beseeching for mercy in a torrent of words and moans.

"Let us go," said the commander-in-chief.

He felt two burning hands press his own. Élisabeth was leaning towards him and entreating him with tears.

Paul introduced his wife. The general said, gently:

"I see that you feel pity, madame, in spite of all that you have gone through. But you must have no pity, madame. Of course it is the pity which we cannot help feeling for those about to die. But we must have no pity for these people or for members of their race. They have placed themselves beyond the pale of mankind; and we must never forget it. When you are a mother, madame, you will teach your children a feeling to which France was a stranger and which will prove a safeguard in the future: hatred of the Huns."

He took her by the arm in a friendly fashion and led her towards the door:

"Allow me to see you out. Are you coming, Delroze? You must need rest after such a day's work."

They went out.

The spy was shrieking:

"Mercy! Mercy!"

The soldiers were already drawn up in line along the opposite wall.

The count, Paul and Bernard waited for a moment. She had killed the Comte d'Andeville's wife. She had killed Bernard's mother and Paul's father. She had tortured Élisabeth. And, though their minds were troubled, they felt the great calm which the sense of justice gives. No hatred stirred them. No thought of vengeance excited them.

The gendarmes had fastened the spy by the waistband to a nail in the wall, to hold her up. They now stood aside.

Paul said to her:

"One of the soldiers here is a priest. If you need his assistance. . ."

But she did not understand. She did not listen. She merely saw what was happening and what was about to happen; and she stammered without ceasing:

"Mercy! . . . Mercy! . . . Mercy! . . ."

They went out. When they came to the top of the staircase, a word of command reached their ears:

"Present! . . ."

Lest he should hear more, Paul slammed the inner and outer hall-doors behind him.

Outside was the open air, the good pure air with which men love to fill their lungs. Troops were marching along, singing as they went. Paul and Bernard learnt that the battle was over and our positions definitely assured. Here also the Comtesse Hermine had failed. . .

A few days later, at the Château d'Ornequin, Second Lieutenant Bernard d'Andeville, accompanied by twelve men, entered the casemate, well-warmed and well-ventilated, which served as a prison for Prince Conrad.

On the table were some bottles and the remains of an ample repast. The prince lay sleeping on a bed against the wall. Bernard tapped him on the shoulder:

"Courage, sir."

The prisoner sprang up, terrified:

"Eh? What's that?"

"I said, courage, sir. The hour has come."

Pale as death, the prince stammered:

"Courage? . . . Courage? . . . I don't understand. . . Oh Lord, oh Lord, is it possible?"

"Everything is always possible," said Bernard, "and what has to happen always happens, especially calamities." And he suggested, "A glass of rum, sir, to pull you together? A cigarette?"

"Oh Lord, oh Lord!" the prince repeated, trembling like a leaf.

Mechanically he took the cigarette offered him. But it fell from his lips after the first few puffs.

"Oh Lord, oh Lord!" he never ceased stammering.

And his distress increased when he saw the twelve men waiting, with their rifles at rest. He wore the distraught look of the condemned man who beholds the outline of the guillotine in the pale light of the dawn. They had to carry him to the terrace, in front of a strip of broken wall.

"Sit down, sir," said Bernard.

Even without this invitation, the wretched man would have been incapable of standing on his feet. He sank upon a stone.

The twelve soldiers took up their position facing him. He bent his head so as not to see; and his whole body jerked like that of a dancing doll when you pull its strings.

A moment passed; and Bernard asked, in a kind and friendly tone:

"Would you rather have it front or back?"

The prince, utterly overwhelmed, did not reply; and Bernard exclaimed:

"I'm afraid you're not very well, sir. Come, your royal highness must pull yourself together. You have lots of time. Lieutenant Delroze won't be here for another ten minutes. He was very keen on being present at this—how shall I put it?—at this little ceremony. And really he will be disappointed in your appearance. You're green in the face, sir."

Still displaying the greatest interest and as though seeking to divert the prince's thoughts, he said:

"What can I tell you, sir, by way of news? You know that your friend the Comtesse Hermine is dead, I suppose? Ha, ha, that makes you prick up your ears, I see! It's quite true: that good and great woman was executed the other day at Soissons. And, upon my word, she cut just as poor a figure as you are doing now, sir. They had to hold her up. And the way she yelled and screamed for mercy! There was no pose about her, no dignity. But I can see that your thoughts are straying. Bother! What can I do to cheer you up? Ah, I have an idea! . . ."

He took a little paper-bound book from his pocket:

"Look here, sir, I'll read to you. Of course, a Bible would be more appropriate; only I haven't one on me. And the great thing, after all, is to help you to forget; and I know nothing better for a German who prides himself on his country and his army than this little book. We'll dip into it together, shall we? It's called *German Crimes as Related by German Eye-witnesses*. It consists of extracts from the diaries of your fellow-countrymen. It is therefore one of those irrefutable documents which earn the respect of German science. I'll open it at random. Here goes. 'The inhabitants fled from the village. It was a horrible sight. All the houses were plastered with blood; and the faces of the dead were hideous to see. We buried them all at once; there were sixty of them, including a number of old women, some old men, a woman about to become a mother, and three children who had pressed themselves against one another and who died like that. All the survivors were turned out; and I saw four little boys carrying on two sticks a cradle with a child of five or six months in it. The whole village was sacked. And I also saw a mother with two babies and one of them had a great wound in the head and had lost an eye.'"

Bernard stopped to address the prince:

"Interesting reading, is it not, sir?"

And he went on:

"*26 August.* The charming village of Gué d'Hossus, in the Ardennes, has been burnt to the ground, though quite innocent, as it seems to me. They tell me that a cyclist fell from his machine and that the fall made his rifle go off of its own accord, so they fired in his direction. After that, they simply threw the male inhabitants into the flames.' Here's another bit: '*25 August.*' This was in Belgium. 'We have shot three hundred of the inhabitants of the town. Those who survived the volleys were told off to bury the rest. You should have seen the women's faces!'"

And the reading continued, interrupted by judicious reflections which Bernard emitted in a placid voice, as though he were commenting on an historical work. Prince Conrad, meanwhile, seemed on the verge of fainting.

When Paul arrived at the Château d'Ornequin and, alighting from his car, went to the terrace, the sight of the prince and the careful stage-setting with the twelve soldiers told him of the rather uncanny little comedy which Bernard was playing. He uttered a reproachful protest:

"I say! Bernard!"

The young man exclaimed, in an innocent voice:

"Ah, Paul, so you've come? Quick! His royal highness and I were waiting for you. We shall be able to finish off this job at last!"

He went and stood in front of his men at ten paces from the prince:

"Are you ready, sir? Ah, I see you prefer it front way!... Very well, though I can't say that you're very attractive seen from the front. However... Oh, but look here, this will never do! Don't bend your legs like that, I beg of you. Hold yourself up, do! And please look pleasant. Now then; keep your eyes on my cap... I'm counting: one... two... Look pleasant, can't you?"

He had lowered his head and was holding a pocket camera against his chest. Presently he squeezed the bulb, the camera clicked and Bernard exclaimed:

"There! I've got you! Sir, I don't know how to thank you. You have been *so* kind, *so* patient. The smile was a little forced perhaps, like the smile of a man on his way to the gallows, and the eyes were like the eyes of a corpse. Otherwise the expression was quite charming. A thousand thanks."

Paul could not help laughing. Prince Conrad had not fully grasped the joke. However, he felt that the danger was past and he was now trying to put a good face on things, like a gentleman accustomed to bear any sort of misfortune with dignified contempt.

Paul said:

"You are free, sir. I have an appointment with one of the Emperor's aides-de-camp on the frontier at three o'clock to-day. He is bringing twenty French prisoners and I am to hand your royal highness over to him in exchange. Pray, step into the car."

Prince Conrad obviously did not grasp a word of what Paul was saying. The appointment on the frontier, the twenty prisoners and the rest were just so many phrases which failed to make any impression on his bewildered brain. But, when he had taken his seat and when the motor-car drove slowly round the lawn, he saw something that completed his discomfiture. Élisabeth stood on the grass and made him a smiling curtsey.

It was an obvious hallucination. He rubbed his eyes with a flabbergasted air which so clearly indicated what was in his mind that Bernard said:

"Make no mistake, sir. It's my sister all right. Yes, Paul Delroze and I thought we had better go and fetch her in Germany. So we turned up our Baedeker, asked for an interview with the Emperor and it was His Majesty himself who, with his usual good grace. . . Oh, by the way, sir, you must expect to receive a wigging from the governor! His Majesty is simply furious with you. Such a scandal, you know! Behaving like a rotter, you know! You're in for a bad time, sir!"

The exchange took place at the hour named. The twenty prisoners were handed over. Paul Delroze took the aide-de-camp aside:

"Sir," he said, "you will please tell the Emperor that the Comtesse Hermine von Hohenzollern made an attempt to assassinate the commander-in-chief. She was arrested by me, tried by court-martial and sentenced and has been shot by the commander-in-chief's orders. I am in possession of a certain number of her papers, especially private letters to which I have no doubt that the Emperor himself attaches the greatest importance. They will be returned to His Majesty on the day when the Château d'Ornequin recovers all its furniture, pictures and other valuables. I wish you good-day, sir."

It was over. Paul had won all along the line. He had delivered Élisabeth and revenged his father's death. He had destroyed the head of the German secret service and, by insisting on the release of the twenty French prisoners, kept all the promises which he had made to the general commanding-in-chief. He had every right to be proud of his work.

On the way back, Bernard asked:

"So I shocked you just now?"

"You more than shocked me," said Paul, laughing. "You made me feel indignant."

"Indignant! Really? Indignant, quotha! Here's a young bounder who tries to take your wife from you and who is let off with a few days' solitary confinement! Here's one of the leaders of those highwaymen who go about committing murder and pillage; and he goes home free to start pillaging and murdering again! Why, it's absurd! Just think: all those scoundrels who wanted war—emperors and princes and emperors' and princes' wives—know nothing of war but its pomp and its tragic beauty and absolutely nothing of the agony that falls upon humbler people! They suffer morally in the dread of the punishment that awaits them, but not physically, in their flesh and in the flesh of their flesh. The others die. They go on living. And, when I have this unparalleled opportunity of getting hold of one of them, when I might take revenge on him and his confederates and shoot him in cold blood, as they shoot our sisters and our wives, you think it out of the way that I should put the fear of death into him for just ten minutes! Why, if I had listened to sound human and logical justice, I ought to have visited him with some trifling torture which he would never have forgotten, such as cutting off one of the ears or the tip of his nose!"

"You're perfectly right," said Paul.

"There, you see, you agree with me! I should have cut off the tip of his nose! What a fool I was not to do it, instead of resting content with giving him a wretched lesson which he will have forgotten by to-morrow! What an ass I am! However, my one consolation is that I have taken a photograph which will constitute a priceless document: the face of a Hohenzollern in the presence of death. Oh, I ask you, did you see his face? . . ."

The car was passing through Ornequin village. It was deserted. The Huns had burnt down every house and taken away all the inhabitants, driving them before them like troops of slaves.

But they saw, seated amid the ruins, a man in rags. He was an old man. He stared at them foolishly, with a madman's eyes. Beside him a child was holding forth its arms, poor little arms from which the hands were gone. . .

THE END

A Note About the Author

Maurice Leblanc (1864–1941) was a French novelist and short story writer. Born and raised in Rouen, Normandy, Leblanc attended law school before dropping out to pursue a writing career in Paris. There, he made a name for himself as a leading author of crime fiction, publishing critically acclaimed stories and novels with moderate commercial success. On July 15th, 1905, Leblanc published a story in Je sais tout, a popular French magazine, featuring Arsène Lupin, gentleman thief. The character, inspired by Sir Arthur Conan Doyle's Sherlock Holmes stories, brought Leblanc both fame and fortune, featuring in 21 novels and short story collections and defining his career as one of the bestselling authors of the twentieth century. Appointed to the *Légion d'Honneur*, France's highest order of merit, Leblanc and his works remain cultural touchstones for generations of devoted readers. His stories have inspired numerous adaptations, including *Lupin*, a smash-hit 2021 television series.

A Note from the Publisher

Spanning many genres, from non-fiction essays to literature classics to children's books and lyric poetry, Mint Edition books showcase the master works of our time in a modern new package. The text is freshly typeset, is clean and easy to read, and features a new note about the author in each volume. Many books also include exclusive new introductory material. Every book boasts a striking new cover, which makes it as appropriate for collecting as it is for gift giving. Mint Edition books are only printed when a reader orders them, so natural resources are not wasted. We're proud that our books are never manufactured in excess and exist only in the exact quantity they need to be read and enjoyed.

bookfinity™

Discover more of your favorite classics with Bookfinity™.

- Track your reading with custom book lists.
- Get great book recommendations for your personalized Reader Type.
- Add reviews for your favorite books.
- AND MUCH MORE!

Visit **bookfinity.com** and take the fun Reader Type quiz to get started.

Enjoy our classic and modern companion pairings!

Classic & Modern

Printed in the USA
CPSIA information can be obtained
at www.ICGtesting.com
JSHW022332140824
68134JS00019B/1440

9 781513 292441